THE MANDALA MANEUVER

CHRISTINE POPE

DARK VALENTINE PRESS

THE MANDALA MANEUVER

978-0615970752

Published by Dark Valentine Press

Cover design and interior layout by Indie Author Services

Visit www.christinepope.com for more information
or to contact the author.

For Ayanna, who wanted more stories about the Zhore

THE MANDALA MANEUVER

PROLOGUE

Ambassador Lirzhan, who had been given his assignment to the Zhoraani delegation on the Galactic Council's space station in the Targus system just days earlier, intended to go directly to that remote star system upon receiving the orders for his new post. However, just prior to leaving his home world of Zhoraan, he was instead given secret communiqués for the Zhoraani ambassador on the neutral world of Eridani, missives so secret that they had been printed out in hard copy and hidden amongst Lirzhan's heavy, concealing robes, the robes his people wore at all times, save when they were with the most immediate members of their families.

"You must destroy the papers, if anyone should approach you," Zhelaar, his superior in the diplomatic corps on Zhoraan, told him. "A risk, but a small one. It is far safer to carry them in this manner than to have them in electronic format, what with the way the Gaians and

Eridanis gleefully hack into anything that seems as if it might be remotely important."

Although he wanted to ask more questions, that would not have been been proper. So he only inclined his head, accepted the papers, and then carefully hid them amongst the folds of his robes. Outwardly, the galaxy was a civilized enough place. None of the Zhore had ever been attacked or interfered with as they went about their travels—not that his people generally left their home world, judging it to possess a far more appealing environment than anything they might encounter out in the greater galaxy. Indeed, his own desire to learn more of alien cultures and planets had come across as strange to most of those he met, even as his government gladly took him into Zhoraan's perpetually understaffed diplomatic service.

Honor required that he not peek at those documents, and so of course he did not look, but he thought he had an idea as to the information they contained. It was no secret among his own people that their world had been in decline for some time, with birth rates dropping at a precipitous pace, although they had managed to conceal any information regarding the tragedy from outsiders.

But then a miracle had happened—on a forlorn colony world called Lathvin IV, one of the Zhore had managed to reproduce with a Gaian female. The child was healthy.

The child was hope.

And so Lirzhan traveled to Eridani, a long-civilized world inhabited by the clever and generous humanoid race who had first given interstellar flight to his own people. He brought the papers to the Zhoraani embassy there, where he stood by as the ambassador read them and nodded. Why exactly the word had been sent here, Lirzhan did not know for sure, although he surmised that his superiors back on Zhoraan most likely guessed that if their race could interbreed with humans, then they could do the same with the Eridani, who had been intermingling with the Gaians for more than a century.

Such a leap would require a tremendous shift in mindset, for as a rule the Zhore kept to themselves out of necessity. Low-level empaths, they were often negatively affected by the emotions of those around them, despite the muffling robes they wore out of necessity. It had always been easier to keep all non-Zhore at arm's length, except when strictly necessary.

For it was not enough to have biological compatibility—a Zhore could not reproduce until he or she found the one who resonated on all levels, emotionally, intellectually, spiritually. This resonance was called *sayara*, and up until he had heard of the miraculous birth on Lathvin IV, Lirzhan had not thought such a connection was possible with anyone not a Zhore. Certainly he had been in contact with far more females of other races than most of his kind, and he had never felt such an attachment to any of them. He had seen much to admire in their intelligence, their ability, and their efficiency, but admiration was not *sayara*.

This particular state of affairs did not particularly please him, but he had become resigned to it. Better that than to rail against a universe which seemed determined to keep him alone for the rest of his days....

ONE

AMBASSADOR ALEXA CRAIG shifted in her seat and stared out the window at the roiling colors of subspace as the small ship defied conventional physics to make the journey from Eridani to the Targus system in hours instead of centuries. Her sole companion on the cramped shuttle, Ambassador Lirzhan of Zhoraan, sat still and quiet in the seat cater-corner from her. She hadn't been overly thrilled with his presence here, since she'd thought she would have the shuttle to herself, but she'd made herself exchange a quiet greeting with him when he boarded. Anything else would have been rude.

He seemed to sense her mood, or at least appeared to have had no more wish for conversation than she did, because he'd taken out his tablet computer and begun working away on it almost as soon as the shuttle lifted from Eridani's surface. She'd caught a glimpse of the screen once as he shifted the tablet, but as it was covered in odd, elegant symbols, obviously Zhoraani script, she had no idea what had kept him occupied this whole time.

For herself, she'd shifted in her seat, stared out the window, tried to work, but she couldn't focus for some reason. Now, six hours into the voyage, her right foot was beginning to fall asleep. She adjusted her position, and cursed the stinginess of the Consortium's engineers, who couldn't even make a simple shuttle comfortable for a voyage of more than a few hours. And if she was uncomfortable, she didn't even want to think of how Ambassador Lirzhan must be feeling. He topped her by almost a foot, and was proportionately broad-shouldered. Or perhaps that was all his robes and not actually him, as she had no clear idea of a Zhore's body conformation. Even so, these cramped seats must be taking their toll.

Her chronometer told her they were barely halfway to their destination. Time to try getting some work done, since she knew she couldn't possibly sit here and stare out the window for another six hours. The seat next to her was empty, and she'd set her satchel down there. As she reached inside it, fingertips drifting over the smooth titanium surface of the tablet inside, she felt the little ship shudder. At once she sat up, frowning. Ships traveling through subspace were not supposed to do that. It was only in realspace that one might encounter the kinds of physical hazards that would impact a vessel's flight.

But then she felt the ship shake again. Although she couldn't imagine how such a thing might happen, it almost seemed as if it had hit a physical barrier. Outside the windows, the shivering colors of subspace disappeared, to be replaced by utter black, broken by a few twinkling points of light, distant and scattered stars. At the same time, the ship jolted, and Alexa felt her head snap forward. It was only reflex that made her fling out her hands to keep her forehead from impacting on the seatback in front of her.

The pilot's voice blared from the speakers. "We are under attack! Passengers to escape capsules! This is not a drill! I repeat—"

His voice broke off just as another blow struck the ship. Whether he'd been hit directly in the cockpit or had simply been knocked out, she didn't know and didn't have time to guess. This time she saw harsh orange light flare outside the window, even as Lirzhan rose from his seat and stumbled back toward her.

"Door to your left!" she gasped. "Mine's directly opposite."

He nodded, but then the vessel shuddered again. Whoever was out there wasn't taking any chances. They wanted to make sure this ship didn't get where it was going.

How they could have tracked its course, or pulled it from subspace, when such a thing was supposed to be impossible, she couldn't say. No time to think about that—no time to think about anything except grabbing her satchel and lurching toward the capsule's hatch, all the while praying she could get there before the fragile shuttle was stuck by a killing blow. All diplomatic vessels had shields, but they weren't military grade. Another hit or two, and the thing would fold up like crumpled aluminum foil.

A blur of black out of the corner of her eyes told her Lirzhan had gone to work the controls of his capsule. The ship was a four-seater, which meant there were four of the little escape pods. Her own fingers scrabbled at the buttons to open the door and allow her entry, but even when she stabbed her thumb into the button a second and a third time, nothing happened.

"It's jammed!" she cried out, unable to keep a note of panic from her voice.

"Leave it," Lirzhan said, his voice calm and deep, despite the situation. "Come with me."

She wanted to protest, to say the capsules weren't designed for more than one person, but his was only two paces away, while the remaining escape pods were located aft, a good three meters away. Besides, there was no guarantee that those capsules or their respective hatches hadn't also been damaged. Better to take a chance on doubling up in Lirzhan's pod.

So she nodded dumbly and followed him into the cramped little capsule, letting him take the seat first so she could collapse onto his lap. With one hand he wrestled the harness around them as he reached out with the other to punch the control that would shut the hatch.

The door shut, enclosing them in a tiny bubble of air and warmth. At once the capsule's rockets flared, pushing them away from the beleaguered shuttle. From this angle she couldn't see through the tiny window to get an idea of who was attacking the ship.

Not that it mattered. A second later, a flash of brilliant white light glared, driving back the blackness of space for a few seconds. The shuttle was gone, and they were alone in the darkness, falling toward the blue-green crescent of a planet which revealed itself through that same window as the capsule's automated systems honed in on the closest possibility of refuge.

If they even made it that far. For the first time she was aware of Lirzhan's arms around her, clutching her tightly against him, as if he feared the safety harness was not sufficient to keep her in place during reentry and landing. Maybe it wasn't. She'd never heard of an escape capsule holding two people at once, so who knows what its designers had engineered as the outer limits of its capability.

What she did know was that the Zhore's body felt human enough beneath her, two arms holding her, two strong legs beneath her own. Had the xenobiologists gathered even that much information about this alien race? His breath was warm against her neck as he murmured, "It will be all right."

She wanted to laugh but didn't quite dare. No, she didn't think it was going to be right at all, not as they plummeted toward a strange planet with only the fragile shell of the capsule between them and oblivion.

"If you say so," she managed, even as she shook her head. Funny; she'd always thought somehow she would die alone.

Well, she might be about to die, but she certainly wouldn't be alone. Not that she'd ever imagined it would be an alien Zhore who ended up being her companion on her journey to the afterlife. Then again, she really didn't believe in such things. Her time here might be almost over, but she didn't think anything would follow, save a long black sleep.

They hit the upper atmosphere of the strange world, a red-hot glow building up along the capsule's hull as the metal super-heated with the friction of re-entry. At the same time the window blacked out, an intentional safety feature designed to protect the occupants of the escape pod from the blinding light outside.

Lirzhan's arms tightened around her, but Alexa found she didn't mind as much as she'd thought she would. His presence assured her that she was not alone, that at least someone was here with her in the dark.

He breathed something in her ear, but she couldn't make out the words. His own language, she supposed. She had never heard it spoken before, but there was something sibilant and flowing and lovely about it.

"What was that?" she asked, her voice sounding tiny and scared, almost drowned out by the screech of the super-heated winds outside the capsule.

"A prayer," he replied. "A wish for the hand of Irzhaan to guide us safely to our destination."

She didn't bother to ask who or what this Irzhaan was. The Zhore equivalent of God, she supposed. She didn't believe in God and never had, but if uttering such an invocation made Lirzhan feel better, she certainly wasn't going to deny him such comfort now.

The rattling grew louder, and she shrank against him, even as his arms tightened further. "Almost there," he said quietly. "Hang on."

Oh, how her colleagues would laugh if they could see her now, burrowing into this alien male for comfort instead of bravely facing her fate. But she didn't care. She just wanted some reminder that she was not alone, here at the end.

"Almost there," she repeated, although she wasn't sure she believed the words.

Pale gray-white light blazed into the capsule as the blackout film on the window retracted. Outside she couldn't see much except the pale streaks of clouds passing by. They dropped lower, and the capsule jolted as its retro-rockets began to fire.

Relief coursed through her. If the rockets had been activated, it meant they were safely through to the planet's atmosphere, and that the automated systems on the capsule were honing in on a more or less safe place to land.

It seemed she wasn't going to die after all. At least, not here and now.

A thump, and then the pod came to rest. She and Lirzhan both sat quietly for a few seconds, not speaking, as if neither one of them was quite sure what to do next.

Then he murmured in her ear, "Are you all right?"

"A little jarred, but that's all," she told him. "I'm fine."

How long she—they—would be fine remained to be seen. She guessed they did not have a great deal of time. Although she hadn't seen who had attacked the shuttle, and had no way of knowing whether their assailants had spied the lone escape capsule falling away from the main ship, she and Lirzhan couldn't take the risk of remaining in one place for very long, just in case those unknown attackers had managed to track the pod's escape trajectory.

As to who those assailant were, and why they'd gone after an unarmed shuttle carrying a couple of low-level diplomats, she had no idea. Certainly Alexa Craig, junior ambassador to the Galactic Council, was not important enough to warrant this kind of deadly attention. In Lirzhan's case, she didn't know enough about him to decide if he were a likely assassination target, but she somehow doubted not. She'd seen his name on the personnel roster for Targus Station, and, like her, he was only an assistant ambassador, not someone who held a key enough position to be attacked in such a way.

For now, though, she needed to stop speculating and get moving. Alexa shifted, pulling against the alien's strong grasp. It seemed for a second that he would not release her, as if he almost wanted to remain seated there with her in his arms. Foolish, of course—he was probably just attempting to determine that she really had survived the landing more or less unscathed, even though she'd just told him she was fine.

"I need to check where we are," she said, and at once his arms fell away, even as he replied,

"Of course."

She wriggled off his lap, her legs more than a little weak beneath her. That was to be expected, of course. Luckily she didn't have to do much more than stand, as the capsule's control panel was less than an arm's length away. As she did so, she paused, getting a feel for this world's gravity. Good. Close to Gaian normal, maybe a little lower.

Her fingers shook slightly as she accessed the onboard computer and pulled up their coordinates. Out in the middle of nowhere, off the main space lanes, in a backwater system that only had a numerical designation—GSC 2897. The world itself, however, had been named by its discoverers.

Mandala.

"So where are we?" the Zhore asked, undoing the safety harness and sitting up in his seat, although she noted he did not attempt to rise. Good idea, as there really wasn't room for him anywhere except in that chair.

"A world called Mandala, a few thousand light-years from where we were headed. Good news is that it's been catalogued." She squinted down at the information scrolling past on the computer screen. "Looks like there's an automated science station about a hundred kilometers from where we are now. I think that's our best bet—even if it's unmanned, it'll still have communications equipment."

"And this capsule does not?"

"Not subspace comms. It would've sent out an automatic distress signal, but I don't know how helpful that is, since the closest people to receive it would have been the ones trying to shoot us down."

A pause, and then Lirzhan replied, "I see your point. Then I would suggest that we salvage what we can here and remove ourselves from the vicinity as soon as possible."

"I agree." She bent down and retrieved her satchel from the floor of the capsule, pulling out her tablet as she did so. A second or two to hook it up to the onboard computer, and then a few seconds more to dump the data onto the small handheld processor. "Okay, I've got everything useful off the computer," she said. "There should be an emergency kit in that panel directly behind you."

The Zhore nodded and used his gloved fingers to pry open the small metal panel, then retrieved the waterproof bag containing a week's worth of water and rations, as well as survival gear such as a thermal blanket and emergency lighting. Never mind that the kit had been designed to keep one person alive for a week, not two full-grown adults.

Maybe she should've pushed to get to that other escape pod. Then they would have had double their current supplies. On the other hand, there was a very good chance the two pods would have landed kilometers apart, and that would've been even worse. She had no idea who or what was after them, or why they'd been shot down. It was better to be with the Zhore than alone. She'd just have to hope they could find some potable water on this world. The survival gear would have a testing kit for that. As for the rest....

Well, it shouldn't take them a week to hike a hundred kilometers, even if the terrain proved to be difficult. Her brief scan of Mandala's data had told her that the world was classified as "unimprovable, with no exploitable resources," which meant that it had too much native flora and fauna to be worth colonizing without a massive sterilization and replanting. The Consortium tended to leave such worlds alone, as the costs of making them over in Gaia's image were actually higher than terraforming a planet from scratch. The atmosphere was breathable, though, and she'd already determined that the gravity would not be a problem. As for that flora and fauna—

Horror stories of the early days of galactic exploration, of man-eating plants and predators who sprayed their victims with acid before devouring them so they would be easier to digest, flitted across her mind's eye. No, she couldn't worry about that now. The kit had a knife and a pulse pistol. They wouldn't be completely defenseless.

She hoped.

"Ready?" she asked, reaching out for the controls to blow the hatch.

"Ready," Lirzhan said quietly.

Alexa pushed the button, and the light and air of Mandala flowed in around them.

TWO

LIRZHAN WATCHED ALEXA CRAIG step outside, the gray-white light of Mandala's sun turning her hair almost to silver around the edges before she disappeared through the hatch. Something in him had wanted to stop her so he could go first, but with the way the tiny capsule was set up, that would have been nearly impossible. Even so, he hurried after her as quickly as he could, the heavy emergency kit slung over one shoulder. He did not want to let her out of sight, not now, when he had finally met the one he had been seeking for so many years.

When he'd entered the cabin of the shuttle that scant seven standard hours ago, knowing that he would be sharing it with Ambassador Craig, he had not expected anything save the brief greetings custom required. He had not expected to see her lift her head and murmur a softly voiced hello in Galactic Standard, and to feel that one simple word like a shock to the very center of his being.

She was beautiful, yes, the alien beauty of a Gaian, with her pale smooth skin and dark gold hair. That hair had been pulled severely back into a knot at the base of her neck, revealing the fine lines of her jaw and throat, the curve of her high cheekbones. He'd wanted to pull the pins out of that hair and see it cascade over her shoulders and caress her neck. He'd wanted—

All of her. In that moment he'd felt a brief pulse of annoyance, and then almost a mental shrug, as she turned away from him to look out the window. But beneath that annoyance he sensed sadness, and he'd wished he could go to her and comfort her, take her in his arms.

Madness. And yet, it was more than that. The resonance was there. His mother had tried to explain it to him, and his father had made the attempt as well, but although Lirzhan understood the concept on an intellectual level, he could not fathom how it would feel in real life.

"Ah, well, you'll know one day," his mother told him, and smiled, sending a loving glance in her husband's direction.

Lirzhan had hoped that day would come, the day when he would meet the woman of his heart. He'd just never expected it would come in the form of a Gaian female.

And now...

The air that met his nose smelled damp and fresh, overlaid with hundreds of complicated scents—unfamiliar flowers and grassy plants, dark earth beneath his feet, an atmosphere thick with moisture, although it was not raining at the moment. He sensed nothing inimical nearby, although a dusky odor beneath all the others told him that this world was not free of predators.

Alexa Craig stood a few paces off, head tilted upward as she surveyed the trees that towered around them. Some sort of deciduous variety, he decided, looking at the delicate, lacy leaves and the wide, spreading branches. Above, the sky was a greenish-blue, streaked with clouds in shades of pale gray. Flowers of a subtle blue dotted the vegetation below his booted feet.

All in all, he thought, Mandala seemed to be rather a lovely world. He wondered why the Gaians had not yet settled here.

"The science station is that way," Alexa said, after a brief glance downward at her tablet, and pointed ahead of her and slightly to her right. "Not that I see any real paths, but the ground doesn't look too rough here."

He took in her tailored jacket and skirt, and wondering how she was going to hike through miles of jungle in such attire. "Do you think you'll be able to manage the terrain?" True, her boots had low, sensible heels, unlike some of the footwear he'd seen women teetering around in during his time on Eridani, but the rest of the outfit was definitely not suited for arduous outdoor travel.

Her sky-blue eyes narrowed, and one hand planted on the curve of her hip. He tried not to stare. She was... distracting.

"Why shouldn't I?" she replied. "I train for at least an hour in the gym every day. I passed my last physical with flying colors. I'm sure I can handle it just fine."

"Of course," he said quickly, wishing he hadn't asked. "If you're sure," he added, realizing that any comments he made as to the viability of her outfit in such conditions would most likely be met with hostility.

Alexa Craig might be *sayara*, but she did seem rather...prickly.

"Of course I'm sure," she responded at once. "It's not as if we have much of a choice. We certainly can't stay here. That capsule can't have been that hard to track." A lift of one delicate eyebrow, and she added, almost as if she'd somehow read his thoughts, "And yes, if I'd known how my day was going to end up, maybe I wouldn't have dressed to impress, but I can't really change that now, can I?"

Under the hood, Lirzhan's lips quirked. Good thing she couldn't see his smile; he had a feeling she would not have appreciated it. "This is true. Please lead on, Ambassador Craig."

By her expression, she did not appear particularly mollified, but she only nodded and struck out for the least overgrown section of ground that presented itself. He knew better than to offer to take the tablet from her and step out in front, even though he guessed he had far more experience with this kind of terrain than she did. Zhoraan had been kept in its natural state as much as possible, and all of its people knew how to make their way through the wilderness while impacting the natural world as little as possible.

Lirzhan could not say the same for the Gaians.

However, Alexa seemed to move confidently enough, and at the moment the route she had chosen did not seem all that difficult. So he followed her in silence, letting her set the pace. She did seem quite fit, as she had asserted before. If the terrain took a turn for the worse, then he would volunteer to lead. Until then....

Until then, he was experiencing a quite un-Zhore-like pleasure in watching the movement of her hips and rear end in the slim-fitting skirt she wore. The women of his race swathed themselves in heavy robes, the same as the men did, and so he had not had much opportunity to admire the female form. True, the women of Eridani and Gaia and Minari did not hide their bodies, but he had experienced no attraction to any of them. After all, they were not *sayara*.

But this woman....

He set his jaw and tore his gaze away from her slender but well-curved form and instead looked around him. This deciduous forest appeared to extend in all directions. Far above them he heard odd chittering sounds, most likely from some sort of arboreal creatures, although even his keen eyes could not detect them among the thick foliage. Whatever they were, they seemed to be keeping their distance, most likely frightened by the two interlopers making such a racket as they moved through the woods.

He was glad of the thick foliage overhead, and the multiple life signs around them would possibly make it more difficult for them to be tracked. Every minute or so he would glance up, halfway expecting to see a gleaming ship descending from the clouds, hot on their trail, but so far the skies were empty of anything except those clouds, and a few avian creatures circling high overhead.

At least the temperature was pleasant here beneath the trees, although his heavy robes had been designed to accommodate extremes of climate, whether hot or cold. And since there were no signs of immediate pursuit, he began to wonder if this trek might not be so terrible after all. A few days of hiking through the woods…a few days to be alone with Alexa Craig. And at the end of it, a science station with the communication equipment that would bring their desired rescue. Perhaps by that point she would have opened up to him somehow. She did not seem the type for confidences, but spending a good deal of time in another person's company often changed such predispositions.

A hiss, along with a wave of that dusky predator scent he had noticed earlier, were his only warnings. A blur of pale grayish fur dropped from one of the trees above them, landed a few feet in front of Alexa, and launched itself at her so quickly that Lirzhan had no time to think.

He leapt forward, pushing Alexa to the side while at the same time pulling the pulse pistol from where she had it tucked into her belt. While his people did not condone taking another living being's life, even they acknowledged that sometimes such things were necessary in self-defense.

So he raised the pistol and shot the beast between its glaring violet eyes just as it snarled and turned toward him, accurately gauging that he and not Alexa was the true threat here. At once the animal slumped to the forest floor, dark blue blood trickling from the hole in its forehead. Lirzhan murmured a few words, asking the beast to forgive him for protecting himself and Alexa. Even in death it was beautiful, some sort of feline with intricate patterns in shades of gray along its back, no doubt to help it blend in with the gray-green foliage of the trees around them. But, beautiful or no, it would have killed him or Alexa…or both…if not for the pistol Lirzhan held in his left hand.

He turned to Alexa, who had gone sprawling into the dead leaves and underbrush, and who only now was pushing herself up to a sitting position, face pale and eyes wide as she took in the still form of the dead predator lying a meter away. Dirt now streaked her immaculate suit, but she seemed to pay it no mind.

When she spoke, though, her voice sounded remarkably calm. "I didn't know Zhore could be that fast."

For some reason, her words surprised him. He'd halfway expected her to offer some remonstrance for so brusquely taking the gun from her and knocking her out of the way. "When the occasion calls for it," he replied.

An unexpected, almost wry smile touched her full mouth. "Obviously you're better suited to this whole survival thing than I am. While I'm not thrilled about being knocked on my ass, I can see why you did what you did." That said, she pushed herself up to her feet and brushed the last of the stray leaves and dirt from her crumpled skirt. A small shake of the head as she looked down at the damage to her attire, and then she shot him a sideways look. "You know, it's probably a good idea if you take the lead from here."

As she fell in behind Lirzhan's black-robed form, Alexa couldn't seem to keep her hands from shaking. Stupid, really. She was fine, except for some bruises and maybe a damaged sense of dignity. Getting tossed ass over teakettle was something a bit outside her experience. But it was obvious she'd taken this world for granted—it was beautiful, and they had survived the landing here with no real problems, and maybe she'd started to feel a confidence that had clearly proved to be misplaced, lulled into a false sense of safety because no one seemed to be pursuing them. Not all predators went on two legs.

What else might be lurking in the trees, she didn't know, but she made sure to stay only a pace or two behind the Zhore, who obviously knew a thing or ten about surviving in the wilderness. The Consortium had never managed to get any spies on Zhoraan, despite its best efforts, and so all intelligence of the planet was based on scans taken from several hundred thousand kilometers away. Even so, it was clear enough that much of the planet remained wild…"unimproved," as the politicians liked to say. This was of course a matter of opinion, as she surmised that the Zhore were probably just fine with their planet the way it was.

But she'd never been anywhere wilder than a city park. Stubborn pride had prompted her to take the lead at first, since it was her tablet whose tracking hardware would lead them to the automated science station. Pride wouldn't help much in keeping them alive on this planet, so she'd swallowed hers and let Lirzhan take the position he should have had all along.

However, chugging along in his wake and trying to pretend her boots were more comfortable than they actually were didn't appeal to her all that much, either. No matter what else happened, they would be spending the next few days in one another's company, so she figured she should attempt to learn more about the enigmatic alien who had become her unexpected travel companion.

She picked up her pace so she was more or less even with his shoulder. "I suppose you have a lot of experience with this sort of terrain?"

The hood angled slightly in her direction, but even staring up into it revealed nothing of the features hidden within its shadowed confines. "Not precisely like this, but similar. The forests near the home where I grew up were not quite as dense, and there were more hills."

"Really?" she asked. Even this small tidbit tantalized her, although she had a difficult time imagining any of

the Zhore as children. Did they run around in minia-
ture versions of their parents' bulky robes? She wanted
to ask, but knew such a question would be futile. The
Zhore revealed as little of themselves as possible. "Are
there a lot of forests on Zhoraan?"

He looked away from her then, and something in
his posture seemed to stiffen, although his pace did not
falter. "I think you are trying to get some information
out of me."

Damn, there was something so disconcerting about
having to talk to a blank, faceless figure like that. Of
course she'd been trained to work with alien races,
but Stacians and Eridanis, and humanity's own exotic
off-shoots, the Bathshevans and the Minari, had facial
expressions you could analyze, even if they weren't all
precise analogues of those of Gaian-based humans. A
Zhore was an entirely different story. She might as well
have been talking to a wall for all the readings she could
get off his hidden expressions.

"And what if I am?" she returned evenly. *Never let
them see you sweat...*

"I admire your persistence, even under our present
conditions. However, the affairs of Zhoraan are its own.
Besides, I have no doubt that my planet's topography,
vegetation, and fauna have been extensively scanned
from far orbit."

No point in denying that. "Yes," she admitted, "but
you've still never allowed off-worlders on your planet.

Not even one still camera. Nothing. Can you blame me for being curious?"

Surprisingly, he chuckled. His laugh had a warm, rich sound, quite human in tone, even if she had no idea what exactly he was hiding under those robes.

Scratch that. She had a small idea—she'd felt his arms, and his legs, and the broad, strong expanse of his chest against her back in the capsule, which was probably more than any other human being knew of his race.

That recollection was more than a little discomfiting, for reasons she really didn't want to go into at the moment.

"No, I suppose I cannot blame you," he replied. "You Gaians are an inquisitive lot. I believe it would be difficult for you to deny your nature. But it is not my place to speak of such things, no matter how much you would like to know more of them."

Well, damn. She'd expected as much, but some part of her had been hoping she wouldn't get shot down quite so quickly. Distracted, she stumbled over a tree root, and at once Lirzhan's strong gloved hand was on her arm, steadying her so she could regain her footing. Damn it. She'd face anyone in the galaxy across a negotiating table, even a fierce-browed Stacian, and yet here she was, tripping and blundering her way through the wilderness like the most pathetic of romance-vid heroines, needing a big strong male to protect her.

Alexa almost jerked her arm away, but she knew that would be rude. He was only trying to help, after all. Instead she mumbled, "thanks," and waited a proper interval of a few seconds before gently easing her arm from his grasp.

He let go at once. "And what of you?" he inquired. "Were there woods nearby where you grew up?"

She let out a brief, bitter laugh before she collected herself. "Most of Gaia is pretty built up."

That was all she could trust herself to say. She wasn't about to let herself start spilling the intimate details of her barren childhood—the mother who had abandoned her to the Consortium's tender mercies almost as soon as she was born, the sterile foster homes where she'd grown up. Adoption was an expensive luxury, whereas the state paid people well to foster unwanted children. Add in the fact that children raised in such homes were supposed to repay their debt to the Consortium by enlisting in the Gaian Defense Fleet, or the Exploration Commission, or the Diplomatic Corps…well, she'd chosen the latter because it had seemed the most appealing to her, but she never forgot that her life wasn't entirely her own, that she was expected to give at least another ten years after graduating from college to the service before she could even think of doing anything else. And at that point, what else could she do? She had no other skills, no other education. It was quite a clever trap.

Of course she could not tell this alien any of that. It was none of his concern, after all.

"There are still some preserves where the natural landscape has been maintained," she continued, hoping he hadn't detected any hesitation in her reply. "But the population pressure was just too great to not develop as much of the land masses as possible."

"Yes, I have read of that," Lirzhan said. "And seen vids and stills, but it does not seem quite real to me, that a world could be so paved over."

Maybe she was just feeling on edge, but she thought she noted a tinge of condemnation in his voice. "We did what we had to do. It is what it is."

"Of course," he said immediately, and this time she could definitely hear the apology in his tone. "We must all walk our own paths. Speaking of which"—he lifted her tablet and eyed the coordinates and topo map displayed on it—"we must veer to the north a few degrees. That way."

He pointed with his free hand, and Alexa felt a prickle of unease work its way down her spine. So far they'd been following a more or less undemanding route through the trees, generally using the "path of least resistance" method as long as it kept them basically on track. But the direction Lirzhan had just indicated had a steep incline, and the trees seemed to crowd more thickly there, as if there were more competition for sunlight in that part of the wood.

Yes, she'd always made sure that she worked out on a regular basis, as the best defense against traveling from planet to planet and dealing with differences in gravity and climate was to be in shape. However, there was a world of difference between exercising under carefully controlled conditions in a gym and spending what looked like the next several hours climbing up a steep hill. In dress boots. And a pencil skirt. However, she'd always aced her physicals. This would be difficult, but she'd never been one to avoid a challenge.

She wouldn't allow herself to sigh. At least she was alive—thanks to the Zhore who stood next to her now. And perhaps the rougher terrain and thicker cover would help to hide them. She'd seen no signs of pursuit yet, but that didn't mean they shouldn't remain wary.

Tone unruffled, she said, "No problem."

He could tell the climb was a strain for her, but he did not offer her a hand as they struggled their way over the increasingly rocky terrain which lay before them. He sensed that she did not want his help, that she needed to do this for herself, and so, barring an actual fall or a stumble that would result in physical injury, he allowed her to carry on without any assistance.

Not that he was doing all that much better himself. He could continue for some time, but soon they would need to take a break, as they had not eaten or drunk anything since leaving the capsule. Too keyed up from their narrow escape to be thinking of practicalities, perhaps. He wondered at the lack of pursuit. Had the trees hidden them from unfriendly eyes overhead? He had to hope so, as there was little they could do to protect themselves except keep moving.

The data on this world showed that it had a day of some twenty-one hours, shorter than Zhoraan, but close enough to standard that he thought he could judge the time of day more or less accurately. The sun was now a little past its zenith, and they had been walking for nearly four hours. At least they seemed to have left the predators behind in the thick woods; out here he had spied nothing more than a few avian creatures circling high overhead, but they had not come any closer. He was glad of that. One such confrontation was quite enough. Of course, he had no idea what might happen once the sun went down.

"We should stop there, under that tree," he said, pointing toward a massive specimen with jagged blue-green leaves. He was glad of its presence, for the vegetation had become sparser as they climbed, and the sun had begun to beat down with little mercy. His robes protected him, but he could tell the heat was taking its toll on Alexa; her cheeks were flushed, and her hair had begun to stick to her forehead and neck.

She nodded, offering no protest as they covered the last few meters between themselves and the tree. Once they arrived at their destination, she gave the space before her a cursory examination before lowering herself to the ground and leaning back against the tree's trunk.

He pulled a bag of water from the emergency kit and handed it to her. They had enough to last another day or so, but they needed to find another source, a river or stream or lake. Odd that they had not yet crossed any bodies of water yet, but he hoped that was just bad luck.

Alexa took the water and drank, but he noted she was careful about how much she swallowed, allowing herself three or four measured sips before sealing the opening once more and giving the bag to him.

"How far have we come?" she asked, and then ran a hand over her damp forehead and looked down at her moist palm with some distaste.

"Approximately twelve kilometers." He lifted the water container to his lips and allowed himself a healthy swallow. It almost seemed as if he could taste some ghost of her essence on the thin plastic, but that, he told himself, was mere fancy.

"That's all?"

"It was mostly uphill."

She gave a little shrug and then looked away from him, her gaze moving over the rocky hillside around them. The tree where they had taken their rest stood on the crown of the bluff, and so the next leg appeared to be mostly downhill.

Lirzhan also wished they had covered more ground, but they had no control over the terrain, or the route they must take. It was unfortunate that the capsule had not landed closer to the science station. One would have thought it might have locked on the automated facility's beacon. Since he did not know how precisely the capsule was programmed—it might have been set up to take the safest trajectory to a planet's surface, rather than to the closest beacon—he decided it was useless to speculate on what might have been. He did hope that the rest of the day would be easier, so they might make up some lost time. At this rate, they would be hard-pressed to get to the science station before their food began to run out.

Tomorrow's troubles for tomorrow, he told himself, and pulled out a small packet of the specially dried food that seemed to inhabit emergency kits the galaxy over. He tossed it to Alexa, who caught it neatly and pulled the tab on the wrapper. Inside was a small hard bar of some brownish substance. She broke it in half and held out one piece to him.

"What is in it?" he asked, hoping it was something he could actually consume. Gaian and Zhore diets didn't always match up.

She squinted down at the wrapper, apparently reading the contents. "Processed protein—"

"Protein from what?" The words came out more sharply than he had intended.

Her brows drew together. "Probably some kind of animal protein. It provides the most bang for the buck, and a lot of people on Gaia have developed soy allergies, so they try to avoid using soy-based products in the kits."

His stomach clenched. "I cannot eat animal protein."

She stared up at him expectantly, although something in her expression told him she already knew what he was about to say.

"My people do not consume animals, or products made from animals."

"So the Zhore are vegetarians?"

"Yes." He wished he did not have to reveal even that much, but she would have found out sooner or later. Not that he was ashamed of his people's dietary rules, of course not. It was only that she had seemed so eager to learn more of his race, to discover things that had been kept secret for decades. No Zhore had ever sat down at table with the Gaians—or the Eridanis, for that matter. Those in the diplomatic service might attend social functions, but they would not eat the alien food, nor drink anything save water.

She shrugged. "So are a lot of Gaians. Check the other labels. I'm sure there's something in there you can eat."

Her nonchalance reassured him. So his diet was not considered all that odd on Gaia? This was something he had not known. "Are you...vegetarian?" he asked, feeling his way around the unfamiliar word.

"No. That is, I'm not big on red meat—too expensive to have when I was growing up, and when I finally did try it, I didn't like it much." A frown pulled at her well-arched brows, and she shook her head, as if attempting to dismiss some unpleasant memory. "Anyway, I don't go out of my way to avoid animal protein, but I've had plenty of meals I've enjoyed that didn't have meat, either."

He nodded, glad to know she at least didn't have the appetites of a Stacian, and would not require him to hunt down the local fauna and roast it on a spit for her. She had mentioned nothing about using the animal he had killed for food, and he guessed the thought hadn't even crossed her mind, sheltered and civilized as she was.

With one hand he scrabbled inside the kit, found another bar, and drew it out. An examination of the tiny print in Galactic Standard on the label confirmed it had been made from a combination of beans and grains, and had nothing in it that would offend his stomach.

Relieved, he set down the kit and opened the package, taking care not to tear it so he could wrap the thin foil around the half of the bar he planned to save for later. As he did so, he glanced up at the sky again, marking the position of the sun.

"What is it?" Alexa asked, and Lirzhan could hear the fear sharpening her tone. "Do you see something?"

"Nothing, save the sun," he told her, hoping she could sense some of the reassurance he was attempting to convey to her. "There were some avians earlier, but we must be larger than their normal prey. No, I was only attempting to determine how much more daylight we have."

She was silent for a moment, squinting up at the sky and the faint clouds that streaked across it. "Not very much."

"I agree. I think we only have four hours at best. Less, really, as we should locate a suitable spot to rest before the sun is fully down."

"True." He thought he saw her shiver, but she only broke off another bite of her protein bar and chewed it before saying, "Then I suppose we shouldn't stay here too long," and pushing herself to her feet.

"We can afford a few more minutes' rest—"

"I'm good," she broke in. "Maybe a little more of that water first?"

So he handed her the pouch and watched as she allowed herself the same measured sips that she had drunk before. Then she gave it back to him and waited as he secured it in the kit, while at the same time finishing off the last few bits of his bean-and-grain bar. The taste was unfamiliar, bland and slightly sweet, but he could tell it would give him the energy he needed.

And then, since he could sense that arguing for more rest time was useless, he stowed the half-empty water container in the bag containing their emergency supplies, and struck out northward again. With any luck, they would find some sort of hospitable spot to camp for the night.

Then again, their luck so far had been questionable at best.

THREE

As they began to walk again, at first Alexa was cheered by the fact that their route seemed to be following a downhill course. Her over-stressed leg muscles had already begun to ache, and she didn't want to think about the sore spot being rubbed into the back of one heel. Funny, if asked before this, she would have said her boots were very comfortable, and something she could have worn for hours with no problem. However, she probably would have been thinking about wearing them all day while in the comfort of the Gaian consulate on Eridani, or at worst while wandering through one of Teliir's fashionable entertainment districts. Not quite the same thing as hiking over miles of rough terrain, with nary a path in sight.

Lirzhan walked on tirelessly, apparently immune to the damp heat and the rocky ground underfoot. As the afternoon sun beat down on her, she'd thought about removing her jacket, but all she wore underneath was a thin camisole of stretch fabric, and she wasn't sure she wanted to be flashing that much flesh in front of the Zhore, alien or no. Oh, she knew there had never been even a whisper of a rumor that the Zhore had any interest in Gaians. Even so, the thought of exposing herself around Lirzhan made her uncomfortable. Besides, the sun was beginning to set off to their left, disappearing behind a range of mountains so rugged that it was obvious Mandala was a young world, in geological terms. In another hour or so, she'd be damn glad of the jacket that she currently was cursing as too warm.

Neither of them had said much since their hasty not-quite meal in the shade of that alien tree. Probably better that way; they needed to conserve their energy, and if they didn't speak, then there was no chance of letting slip revelations better left unsaid. What had possessed her to make that comment about red meat being too expensive for her to eat growing up? Oh, it was true enough—only the rich could afford the luxury these days, and such a thing certainly wouldn't be wasted on a foster child—but there was no need for her to blather on about it to the Zhore ambassador.

Back at the university on Gaia, a group of hard-partying students had started referring to her as "the Ice Queen," an epithet that unfortunately followed her into the diplomatic corps, but she'd ignored them, just as she ignored everything that wasn't a direct threat or a barrier to advancement. So what had happened to that frosty wall she'd built around herself? She shouldn't have spoken so freely to Lirzhan.

Actually, being known as "the Ice Queen" had made it easier for her in one way. No one approached her or attempted any sort of advances. No one, that was, except Trin Elsen, an Eridani who'd either never heard of her nickname or didn't care what her reputation might be. He'd done a fairly good job of melting her icy exterior... at least when they were alone.

Annoyed with herself, Alexa tried to focus on her surroundings. If it weren't for being dropped here with inadequate gear and uncertain company, she might have been tempted to say Mandala was beautiful. She hadn't had much experience with open spaces on Gaia, and of course any posting at an embassy would keep her at the heart of a city, but there was something oddly attractive about these wild, open spaces, about the stark beauty of the gray rocks thrusting upward and the strangely delicate trees that dotted the landscape. The air, too, tasted clean, untouched by technology. Up until now she hadn't seen much of the allure in settling on empty, uninhabited planets, with none of the comforts of civilization. It was clear, though, that civilization had its own drawbacks.

Speaking of which...

Just who the hell *had* shot down their shuttle? As with all diplomatic flights, the details of her trip had been classified. No one outside the embassy's immediate support staff knew when she was leaving, or which ship was transporting her. Obviously some strings had been pulled in certain channels, or Lirzhan would not have traveled with her, but he was also a diplomat, someone with high clearances. It wasn't as if anyone outside their respective embassies would have known of their itinerary. She hadn't even told Trin exactly where she was going, or when she planned to leave Eridani. All she'd told him was that she was being transferred, and that was that. No time for tears.

Well, not much, anyway.

She hadn't bothered to keep the relationship a secret, because it would have been discovered anyway. Luckily, Trin worked in a non-sensitive area—he was a professor of sociology at the local university—and Gaians and Eridanis had been consorting almost as long as the two races had known one another. Perhaps her liaison with Trin had raised a few eyebrows among the more conservative members of the embassy's staff, but since she was as transparent as possible about the whole thing, no one had commented, or attempted to advise her to break if off.

Unless, of course, her transfer to the Targus system had been an oblique way of telling her that she should be maintaining all her focus on her duties.

She frowned then, and narrowly missed stumbling over a rock just large enough to be troublesome. Amazing how Lirzhan appeared to glide over the rough landscape, his heavy robes never catching on anything, the dirt somehow seeming to slide right off the thick dark fabric's surface. Nice trick, that.

"Ambassador," she said.

He paused, the hood turning as he regarded her over his black-clad shoulder. "Surely there is no need for such formalities when it is only the two of us here."

Fine. Feeling a little strange, she said, "Okay... Lirzhan."

"Are you all right? Do you need to rest a bit?"

So solicitous. Frankly, she wasn't used to anyone being all that concerned about her welfare. She shook her head. "No, I'm fine. It's not as if we're climbing or anything. It's just...."

"Just what?"

His voice...it sounded so very human. No trace of an accent at all, unlike the Eridanis and Stacians she'd known. His tones were smooth and rounded as those of a vid-caster, his command of Gaian idiom quite masterful. Then again, he was a diplomat. He must have studied such things in order to work effectively with humans.

Taking a breath, she replied, "I was thinking about the crash...how we ended up here. Yes, both our embassies knew of our flight, but it's certainly not information that was widely disseminated."

"Yes." The briefest of pauses, and he added, "And drawing a ship from subspace...I had not thought such a thing was possible."

"It isn't," she said flatly. "That is, I've never heard of it happening before this."

"But your scientists are always working on such projects, are they not?"

Was she imagining things, or was that a note of accusation in the velvety timbre of his voice? "I wouldn't know. That's not my field." And she sounded stiff even to herself. But what did he expect, that she would start blabbing about rumors of the technology she'd heard was coming out of the Consortium's skunkworks?

"Of course." The hood tilted up at the sky. "We should keep going."

"What about your scientists?" she inquired as she scrambled after him, for he had assumed a brisk pace almost before his last words to her were out of his mouth.

He didn't turn to look back at her. "What about them?"

"Surely you don't think I'm naïve enough to believe that they don't have their own projects going all the time?"

"No, I don't think you are naïve at all. However, you know nothing of the Zhore if you suspect us of creating the sort of damaging technology that would drag a ship in flight out of subspace."

"Well, whose fault is it that we know so little of the Zhore?"

This time he did pause, and stood staring down at her. Damn. He was so very tall, looming over her as the afternoon shadows began to lengthen around them. She didn't lack for height herself—part of the reason she tended to choose low-heeled shoes—but she didn't think she would even reach the Zhore's chin.

If he had a chin, of course.

"We Zhore value our privacy, if that is what you mean," he said smoothly. "It is true that we do not quite comprehend the Gaian tendency to broadcast every smallest detail about ourselves, whether it is of interest to anyone else or not."

"So you don't find us interesting?"

Something in his attitude shifted then, and although she could not see his face, somehow Alexa got the impression he was amused. "*Some* of you are…quite interesting."

Her cheeks heated with an unexpected flush. "Well, that's a relief."

His head lifted, and he turned away from her. "Do you hear that?"

"Hear what?"

He raised a hand, and so she closed her mouth around the next question she'd been about to ask, to inquire if it sounded dangerous. As she strained to hear what had caught his attention, she thought she detected a hint of something. An odd rushing noise.

"Water," he said, the relief clear in his tone. "And in the direction we were heading. Come."

He began to walk again, this time with a stride so brisk she felt almost as if she had to trot to keep up. Maybe she could have asked him to slow down, but doing so seemed to hint of weakness. Instead, she hurried after him, cursing the growing blister on her heel and wondering how far they had to go before they came upon the source of the mysterious sound.

Not quite a half-kilometer away, they descended into a shallow valley with a brisk stream cutting across its center. Here the ground was covered with a bluish grass-like vegetation, and trees clustered around the water, their thirsty roots soaking up the precious liquid. More chittering came from those trees, similar to what they had heard in the woods where they first landed, but it seemed to her that those avian creatures, whatever they might be, were not dangerous. Otherwise, they certainly would have attacked by now.

"We should make camp here for the night," Lirzhan said. "Look, there is a sheltered spot amongst those boulders, and if the water is safe...."

"Let's test it," Alexa said at once. She was too tired to protest that they had at least another hour of daylight. Certainly they hadn't come across any spots as hospitable as this one. The quiet little valley seemed like an ideal place to rest.

The Zhore nodded and took the water-testing kit from the emergency pack, then went over to the stream and dipped the clear plastic rod into it. Immediately the liquid inside turned blue, indicating that the water being tested contained safe levels of any heavy elements and no detectible pathogens or toxins. Of course, the risk on an alien world was that there might a microbe or unknown trace metal the test couldn't identify. Even so, the kits did tend to be correct about ninety percent of the time.

Alexa wouldn't let herself worry about that other ten percent. As it stood, the water they carried wouldn't have been enough to sustain the two of them all the way to the science station, so between certain death via dehydration or a ten-percent chance of getting the Mandala equivalent of Montezuma's Revenge, she would go for the latter option.

"Looks good," she said.

He nodded and set the testing kit aside. "It would appear so. But let me drink first."

She let out an uneasy laugh. "Really? How…chivalrous of you."

A lift of the shoulders beneath the heavy robes. "I do not see it that way. I have a larger body mass than you. If there is something toxic in the water, I would most likely be able to process it better than you."

There didn't seem to be much an argument to counter that reasoning, so she only said, "All right," and watched him dip his gloved hands into the water and bring few mouthfuls to the face hidden within his robes. A long, tense moment as he apparently swallowed and then evaluated the effects—if any—of the water he had just drunk, before he said,

"I am not noticing any adverse reactions. It appears to be safe. In fact, it tastes very good."

That was all Alexa needed to hear. She came up beside him and knelt in the soft grayish sand at the stream's edge, and scooped up some water for herself. It was cool against her skin, and nothing, not even the expensive Eridani wines Trin had shared with her, had ever tasted so good.

Once she had drunk enough to drive away the dry tickly sensation she'd been feeling in the back of her throat for the past few hours, she gathered up a few more handfuls and splashed them against her face. Any cosmetics she had been wearing would have been long gone by that point anyway, so she figured she might as well feel more or less clean.

"Better?" Lirzhan asked, once she was done with her ablutions.

"Much," she replied. "There are little expandable bags somewhere in the emergency kit that we can use for water storage, but I suppose we might as well worry about that in the morning when we set out."

"That is a good idea." He got to his feet.

As much as Alexa felt like sticking her whole head in the water, to get rid of as much trail dust as possible, she knew that heading into the cooler nighttime hours with a headful of damp hair wasn't a very good idea. So she pushed herself back to her feet and began to head toward the sheltered spot Lirzhan had suggested as their evening's campsite. Her heel twinged, and she stumbled.

At once the Zhore was at her side, gloved fingers on her elbow. "What is wrong?"

She made an offhand wave. "Oh, nothing. I think I have a small blister. It will be fine once I sit down."

"Let me look at it."

"No, that's really not necessary—"

"But it is." His voice was firm. "If you have a wound, it may become infected. It should be treated as soon as possible. There is a medical kit in the emergency bag, is there not?"

She nodded.

"Well, then."

With an air of resignation, she limped over to the little cubbyhole between the two rocks. She eased herself down onto the ground, and watched as the Zhore dropped to his knees, then got out the first aid supplies. Nothing too elaborate, but there were bandages in various sizes, and antiseptic wipes, cold compresses, and a variety of analgesics and antibiotics, all of which were designed for Gaian constitutions. She had no idea whether Lirzhan would even be able to take any of them, should the need arise. The shuttle had been a Gaian craft, outfitted for Gaians, or, in a pinch, Eridanis, whose biology was very similar. Lirzhan had come on the ship at the last minute, with little accommodation for his being there. Then again, it was supposed to be a routine flight. None of this should have been an issue.

He reached for her boot, and she lifted a hand. "I'll get it." No way she was going to let the Zhore play a reverse Prince Charming and yank her shoes off her feet.

Good thing the sun had already begun to go down behind the hills and they were in shadow, or there was no way Lirzhan could have missed the flush that went over her face in that moment. She bent her head and unzipped the offending boot, then rolled down the thigh-high stocking she wore.

To her relief, he did not appear particularly enthralled by these actions, and in fact had busied himself with getting out the LED lanterns from the emergency kit while she was baring her foot and leg. Now that he had sufficient lighting to work with, he turned back to her.

"May I?" he asked, gesturing toward her heel.

Well, no point in stopping now, she thought, but she only nodded.

His gloved fingers touched her foot. For some reason she had thought they would be cold, but she could feel the warmth of the flesh beneath the black—well, it couldn't be real leather, not if the Zhore were vegetarians, but the material was remarkably similar. He turned her ankle slightly so as to cast more light on it, and she could see then that the blister in question had in fact popped, and was now an angry red, the moisture beneath the broken skin gleaming in the blue-white light of the LED lamp.

"Ah," was all he said before he reached for the antiseptic wipes.

She let out a hiss as the sharp disinfectant touched the raw wound.

"Am I hurting you?"

"Well, it hurts, but it's not your fault. It's fine."

He nodded, and swiped a second antiseptic patch over the blister before taking out a bandage and applying it to her skin. While he worked, Alexa tried not to think too hard about the strangeness of the situation—of having a Zhore handle her bare foot, gloved fingers of one hand supporting her ankle as he finished treating her heel with the other. Had any other human ever had contact this intimate with one of the aliens?

Somehow she doubted it.

But at least he went about the process quickly and efficiently, and showed no desire to continue fondling her foot or leg after he was done. He set her foot down gently, and asked, "How does that feel?"

She bent to touch the bandage; it was padded, and should afford some protection against further chafing when she put her boots back on the next day. "Better. Much better. Thank you."

Another nod, and then he reached into the emergency bag and pulled out her half-eaten protein bar. She had a feeling she was going to be heartily sick of those things by the time they got off this rock.

If they got off it.

No, she wouldn't let herself think that. They'd survived their first day, and so far Mandala had seemed serene enough…besides the attack by that feline predator back near their landing site. But they'd seen no animals larger than that since then, so perhaps most of Mandala's fauna was relatively harmless.

Lirzhan retrieved his own bean-and-rice bar, and settled himself against one of the rocks while he ate quietly. He didn't seem particularly inclined toward conversation, for which Alexa was grateful. She was already tired, and she found it hard sometimes to know what to say, to attempt to guess what he would respond to, or what would make him shut down. Not that that was necessarily a bad thing. She had a feeling she'd probably already told him too much.

Oh, well, she thought, as she settled herself down for the night. *It's only four more days....*

He'd taken the first watch, saying she needed her rest more, and after a few attempts at demurral, Alexa had given up and wrapped herself in one of the odd reflective blankets that had come with the emergency kit, huddling against one of the boulders as if trying to access some of the sun-warmth that had been stored in it during the daylight hours. Now she slept, and something hard and wary in her features seemed to smooth itself away in slumber. How he wished he could go to her, wrap her in his robes, hold her close and keep out the night's chill, but he knew that time was not yet here. Perhaps it never would be.

Still, he had to permit himself a tiny flicker of hope. She had let him help her, let him touch her and treat the wound on her foot. Surely if she were disgusted by him, she would not have allowed him to do even that much, would have insisted on handling the matter herself, even if it required a good deal of contortion.

Or perhaps she is merely practical, and realized that letting you take care of it made the most sense. From what he had seen so far of Alexa Craig, that appeared to be the most logical explanation.

Across the canyon, some creature let out a long, mournful cry, and he stiffened, scanning the darkness for any imminent threat even as his hand strayed to the pistol, which he'd kept in a pocket of his robes. But the sound moved off and he relaxed, even as Alexa stirred within her blanket, then pulled it more tightly about herself as she seemed to fall into heavy sleep once again.

He allowed himself a few seconds of admiration, not just for the symmetry of the features revealed by the light of the LED lantern, but also the steely determination that had forced her to keep up with him across the rough miles. She was a city dweller, certainly unused to such exertions, and yet he had not heard one word of complaint from her. Of course, they had days to go yet, but he guessed she would not complain. Not aloud, anyway.

It might only be her diplomatic training that had kept her from grumbling about their situation. Perhaps if she were around one of her own people, she would be acting quite differently. Somehow, though, he did not think that was the case. He sensed that she presented the same face to everyone.

Whether it was her true face...well, that was the question. He had a feeling she kept much hidden. That same sadness he had first sensed on the shuttle seemed to pulse from her, but he did not think it had very much to do with their current situation. Certainly it was nothing one could see in her public aspect. But she was *sayara*, and her soul resonated with his, even if she did not know it yet.

He shifted, finding a slightly more comfortable position, and lifted his face to the heavens. The stars here were numerous and bright, but there was no moon. According to the data on Alexa's tablet, the planet did have two satellites, but they had not yet risen yet. All was utter blackness around them, save the small pool of pale light from the lanterns, pushing back the darkness.

A small gasp, and her eyes fluttered open, blinking at the unfamiliar surroundings for a second or two before she focused on him. Comprehension lit their deep blue depths, and she relaxed slightly, although her mouth was still grim.

"I heard something," she said.

"There was a night bird, or the Mandala equivalent, a minute ago. But that is all," he added, trying to reassure her. "Other than that, I have only heard the wind in the grasses, and the sounds of the stream moving over the rocks. It is safe here, I think."

"You think." Her voice held a note of dry humor.

"Well, I cannot be positive, since we do not have the necessary scanning equipment to tell us if the surrounding area is completely clear. But it feels safe."

"Oh, then, it's fine, isn't it?" But she took the sting from her words by chuckling, and he saw an amused glint in her eyes. Then her expression sobered. "Is it time for me to take over yet?"

"Not yet," he replied at once. "You still have some hours left." He didn't add that he intended to let her sleep longer than she planned. His body did not require the same amount of rest hers did, and she needed to maintain her strength. But trying to explain that would most likely result in another argument.

"Good," she said. "Despite everything, I was having a nice dream."

"About?"

She only shook her head, and smiled, then rolled up in the blanket again and turned away from him.

FOUR

THE CHRONOMETER STRAPPED TO HER WRIST had not been calibrated to Mandala time. Even so, Alexa had a feeling she'd slept for more than the four agreed-upon hours when Lirzhan finally woke her with a gentle hand on her shoulder. Oddly, she had not startled at his touch, but only nodded and said, "I'm awake."

He withdrew then, huddling in his robes and burrowing into a depression in one of the boulders that sheltered them, and seemed to go to sleep. In the darkness he almost appeared to be part of the rock itself, in his bulky, shapeless robes. Apparently they were warm enough on their own, as he hadn't taken the second of the two blankets in the emergency kit.

Now, in the bitter hours just before dawn, she thought she could use that blanket herself, so she rummaged through the bag and pulled out the little folded square, then shook it over her legs before wrapping the first blanket more tightly around her shoulders. She wasn't precisely warm, but at least now she thought she could survive the chill until the sun came up. Funny how uncomfortably warm it had been here during the day—and how quickly that warmth had disappeared once night fell.

She pulled her knees up to her chest and settled her chin on them, eyes straining against the dark beyond the small circles of light provided by the lanterns. Just above the horizon to the east hung two moons, one a fingernail crescent so thin she could barely see it, the other just past the quarter. Neither of them provided much in the way of illumination.

Figures, she thought. As Lirzhan had told her earlier when she'd briefly wakened, all was still here. The stream chattered softly over the stones a few meters off to her left, and beyond that she heard a soft, eerie rustle that had to be the wind in the grass, although she'd never heard such a thing before. But there were no animal sounds that she could detect. Just as well, because Lirzhan still had the pulse pistol hidden somewhere about his person. Now, maybe he would wake up fast if they were attacked—he'd certainly been speedy enough when that feline came out of nowhere and almost made her its lunch—and maybe he wouldn't. She didn't have the heart to rouse him now just so she could retrieve the pistol, so she'd have to hope for the best.

It's not as if you could hit what you were shooting at, anyway, she thought, and let out a sigh. Sure, she'd had some rudimentary arms training, enough that she knew how to shoot a pulse pistol, but that didn't mean she was a very good shot. She'd never seen the need, frankly. It wasn't as if she were a member of the Defense Fleet or even the Exploration Commission, where having such skills would come in handy. Up until today, all the predators she'd ever met had walked on two legs and faced her across a negotiating table.

Without really meaning to, she glanced over at Lirzhan where he slept huddled against the boulder. That is, she assumed he was asleep. Impossible to say for certain with the way his hood dropped so low, hiding his face. How he was able to see past it, she had no idea, but obviously it hadn't slowed him down any on the way here.

Something in her was sorely tempted to creep over there, to push back the hood to see what it concealed. Of course such an action would be a horrible breach of protocol, and she would never *actually* do such a thing, but....

It was difficult spending so much time with someone whose face she couldn't see, whose expressions she couldn't gauge. He might as well have been wearing a mask.

That notion jogged a memory in her mind, of an old book she'd read years ago as a girl, when she had devoured numerous public domain works that didn't require an outright purchase. God, what was that story? Something about a singer and a deformed genius....

The Phantom of the Opera. That was it. Somehow she doubted that creeping up on Lirzhan and pushing back the hood would have a better outcome for her than it did for the hapless Christine Daaé when she sneaked up behind the Phantom and removed his mask. Better to quell her curiosity than risk an interplanetary incident.

Still, she couldn't help but wonder exactly what he was hiding under there. Speculation had been ongoing for the greater part of a hundred years, ever since the Gaians and the Zhore first crossed paths. If anyone had ever seen one of the secretive aliens, though, the information must have been immediately suppressed.

She heard a screeching cry then and stiffened, eyes straining against the dark—well, actually, it wasn't full dark anymore. The first gray light of dawn had come upon her while she was ruminating, and she hadn't even noticed. Some lookout she was.

But she could see well enough to make out a largish avian creature, a bit larger than a Gaian crow, dive for the stream and then fly off with something dangling from its beak or proboscis or whatever passed for such things in these parts.

*Even on Mandala the early bird gets the worm, she thought, a*nd grinned a little. *Or fish, as the case may be.* Maybe those fish were edible, but they didn't have the equipment to test them, even if they could somehow manage to catch one.

"Another avian?" came Lirzhan's deep voice from behind her.

"Yes. It's already gone. And the sun is starting to come up."

"Good." He pushed away from the boulder and stood, brushing at his robes. Alexa thought she heard a few cracks of his joints, and almost shook her head at the incongruity of the sound. Sure, she'd heard a few of those coming from Trin as he got up in the morning to make a pot of tea, but somehow she hadn't expected that a Zhore would be subject to the same early morning pops and creaks.

A wash of pale light came over the hills to the east, and suddenly it was day again. She pushed away the blanket covering her legs but kept the one wrapped around her shoulders, then stood up to survey their surroundings. The wind had shifted direction slightly, seeming to come from the north now instead of the northwest. Alexa decided to take that as a good sign, since their destination lay due north from where they were currently encamped.

"Wish I could offer you some coffee or tea, but the emergency kit wasn't quite that civilized," she remarked. "Can I interest you in half a veggie protein bar and some water?"

Something that sounded suspiciously like a chuckle emerged from the hood. "That will have to do, I suppose." He came over to her and took the bar she had just dug out of the emergency bag. As he did so, his gloved fingers brushed over hers, and she forced herself not to flinch. Stupid reaction, really, when she'd let him handle her bare foot just the night before.

"So what's the plan for today?" she inquired, her tone sounding too cheerful even to herself. Overcompensation, probably.

He scanned the valley around them before answering. "The stream appears to cut more or less north and south through this canyon, so I believe we should follow it for as long as possible. It seems more sheltered down here, and the ground is smoother. We should be able to move more quickly, at least in the beginning."

That sounded like a good enough plan to her. But first....

There really wasn't a good way to take care of certain necessary functions while wandering through the wilderness, although the emergency kit did at least provide a packet of toilet paper and some disposable towels, along with disinfecting mouth wipes. Alexa excused herself, found a concealing rock, and did what was necessary. Afterward she went to the stream and splashed some water on her face, then performed an abbreviated version of what her university roommate had referred to as a "birdbath"—a quick cleaning of certain essential body parts—before putting her jacket back on and heading back to their makeshift campsite, where Lirzhan was already putting away her discarded blankets and stowing the empty protein bar packaging in a pocket of the emergency kit. Whether he'd attended to his own needs while she was otherwise occupied, she didn't know and certainly wasn't going to ask.

She could only hope she wasn't flushing too furiously when she asked, "Ready to go?"

"Yes," he said simply, and threw the emergency bag over his shoulder.

That science station had better have a decent bathroom when we get there, she thought as she followed him up along the stream. *Because after this I'm going to want to take a shower for at least a day or two.*

As he had hoped, the stream wound its way northward for a good ways, sheltering them in a canyon that did not seem to be inhabited by anything larger than the blue-winged avians who dove into the water at irregular intervals, clearly intent on the aquatic life that appeared to dwell in its depths. There seemed to be every chance that they would cover more kilometers today. Perhaps as many as twenty-five, if they were lucky.

Alexa strode along behind him; if her foot still bothered her, she didn't show it. She'd abandoned the tight knot of hair at the base of her neck and instead had it bound loosely with a piece of brown elastic. The golden-brown edges of her ponytail blew in the breeze, and between that and her lack of makeup, she looked curiously young and vulnerable.

Appearances, he knew, were just that…appearances. Irzhaan help anyone who thought of Alexa Craig as vulnerable.

After a while, he looked over his shoulder at her and inquired, "How is your foot?"

She appeared surprised that he had inquired about it. "Fine. I hardly notice it. But thank you for asking."

Her tone was cool and casual. If only he could think of something to say that would break down her wall of reserve, but nothing came to mind. For an instant he almost wished they hadn't made such good time so far today. At the rate they were going, they'd reach the science station without making any kind of a connection.

Frankly, the entire situation rather flummoxed him. If the woman with whom he'd felt the *sayara* bond had been another Zhore, this would have been easy, for she would be experiencing the same sensations he was. But with a human? If he had not seen the reports of what had transpired on Lathvin IV, had not felt his own connection with Alexa, despite her apparent lack of interest, he would have believed such a thing was impossible.

Still, he had to try. "I am glad to hear that your foot is doing well. But please tell me if it begins to give you any discomfort—we may need to change the wound dressing."

One of her well-arched brows lifted. "I will. I think I'm okay for now, though."

Her words had a tone of finality to them, as if she wanted to close down the conversation before it even got started. Very well. They still did have at least two more days to go after this, and that was only if all went well. He must not be impatient. He must—

An odd whirring filled his ears, one that sounded too mechanical, too precise to have come from an as-yet-unknown avian creature. He glanced up, just as pale green pulse bolts rained down from overhead. His unbelieving eyes registered some sort of small atmospheric craft, although he did not recognize the type.

"Run!" he cried, grabbing Alexa by the hand even as he tightened his grip on the emergency pack, then dashed away from the stream, down a narrow defile that branched off from the main canyon.

At least she did not protest, but pounded alongside him, her face grim and her eyes filled with questions she didn't have the breath to ask. In here the trees were not as thick as they had been along the stream, but they did provide some cover. Besides, the walls of the narrow ravine were not wide enough to accommodate the unknown machine, although that didn't seem to prevent its pilot from raining down pulse bolts at the two of them.

They crashed through the stunted, sun-deprived trees, Lirzhan attempting to zig and zag back and forth as much as possible and present a moving target that would be difficult to hit. He couldn't stop to wonder who might be shooting at them, and why…although he guessed they must be connected in some way with whoever had been behind the attack on the shuttle.

The ravine branched, and he took the northerly defile, hoping to keep them more or less on track. Here the trees and brush began to grow more thickly, and he felt Alexa stumble over a tree root and grip his hand tightly to keep from falling. He increased his own grasp on her fingers and propelled her forward, all the while praying that neither of them would suffer a real fall. That emergency kit did not contain anything that would help with setting bones.

As quickly as it had attacked, the machine peeled off and headed back in the direction it had come, clearly unable to prosecute its assault with any real efficiency. Lirzhan would not take that as a signal to ease up, however, and kept moving forward, thinking it couldn't hurt to put as much distance between them and their attackers as possible. True, their assailants could always fly ahead and wait for them to emerge from the other end of this ravine—wherever that might be—but going back certainly wasn't an option.

"Look!" Alexa called out, and pointed with her free hand. Ahead of them and partway up the cliff wall were a series of dark openings in the gray rock.

A cave sounded like an excellent idea at the moment. He wouldn't let himself stop to think what sort of inimical creatures might live in such an environment. Then again, most of the fauna they had encountered on Mandala so far had been relatively benign. Better to take their chances with a series of unknown creatures than face the ones who had already proved themselves to be more than hostile.

"This way," he said, after analyzing the rock formations ahead. There did seem to be a narrow natural path that zigzagged up the hill.

She nodded grimly and followed him, this time seemingly content to let him take the lead and determine the best route over the treacherous ground. Once or twice her slick-soled boots slipped on the rock, and again she hung on to his hand for dear life, cursing under her breath. He tightened his fingers around hers and more or less dragged her up the last few feet before they slipped into the cool darkness of the cave, leaving the sunlight behind.

Immediately she let go of his hand and cast a baleful glance over her shoulder at the now-empty skies above the canyon. "Just what the *hell* was that?"

She should have known they'd be tracked. She'd let the relative ease of their journey so far lull her into thinking that all they had to do was sidestep a few alien birds and suffer a few uncomfortable bivouacs, and then they'd be at the science station and calling in the cavalry.

Too bad the galaxy really didn't work that way.

Lirzhan stood silently watching her, as if he were afraid that if he said the wrong thing, she'd explode even worse than she already had. She took a deep breath, calming herself. He'd probably saved her life back there; his reflexes were a lot better than hers.

Even that realization irritated her. Nothing in her training had prepared her for this, so logically she knew it really wasn't her fault that she didn't have the skills to wrest the pulse pistol from the Zhore and magically shoot their assailants out of the sky. She wasn't a warrior. She was a diplomat. But she knew she'd better start thinking like a warrior if she wanted to survive this.

On top of everything, her heel had begun to throb again. Probably the bandage had worked itself loose during their headlong flight down the gully. She couldn't worry about that right now, though.

Lirzhan had pulled out one of the lanterns from the emergency kit and had turned it down the passageway beyond them. That is, it looked like a corridor of some sort, although she knew it had to be a natural formation. It was very quiet. She could hear the angry beating of her own heart, and the slow drip of moisture somewhere down the passage.

"Does it go through?" she asked.

"I don't know," he admitted. "I am no Stacian, bred to know the underground ways. But the air smells fresh enough, and I can see no end to the opening. I am willing to risk it if you are—but there is always the chance that it does not go through, and we will end up trapped somewhere far under the surface."

"Well, the surface wasn't too friendly, either," she said, and let out a shaky laugh. "Maybe it goes through, and maybe it doesn't, but if we disappear long enough, maybe our friends in the skimmer will give up and go home."

"Perhaps," Lirzhan replied, although he did not sound particularly hopeful. He flashed the lantern down the passageway once more and added, "Stay close."

Like I need to be reminded. If someone had asked a few minutes ago, she would have said walking so close to the Zhore that she could practically feel his body heat was not high on her list of preferred activities, but now his presence was more than a little reassuring. That was twice he'd saved her life in the last forty-eight hours. Damn straight she was going to stick to him like iron filings to a magnet.

"No worries," she told him, and hoped he wouldn't hear the edge of a tremor in her voice. "Just let me know if I step on your robes."

He actually chuckled. "I will."

Then he held the lantern at about shoulder level, and began walking forward, Alexa not half a step behind. She could even feel the brush of the heavy fabric of his garments against her sleeve or leg from time to time, but she found she didn't mind so much. It meant he was there with her in the darkness, and she wasn't alone.

The passageway sloped slightly downward, and she wondered how deep they would have to go before it began to climb again. Thank God for the LED lanterns and their practically unlimited battery life. At least she wouldn't have to worry about the light going out and leaving them here in the utter black of these caves, hundreds of feet underground. She sniffed the damp air, vaguely recalling horror stories of pockets of bad air or poisonous gas in the mines on Gaia back in the bad old days, but all she smelled was damp rock, and a faint woodsy scent she guessed must be coming from Lirzhan's robes.

Probably smells better than I do, she thought wryly, although the antiperspirant treatment she used was supposed to last up to a week. Then again, its manufacturers probably hadn't counted on having to prevent the sort of flop sweat pure fear could produce.

"It must have been when we came out into the open," the Zhore said in quiet, musing tones. "For the first leg of our journey, we were in thick woods with abundant life, and perhaps our assailants did not have good enough trackers to locate our biological signatures. But once we camped, and then headed farther up the stream—well, then they had a chance to do more sweeps and find us."

This sounded plausible enough, and Alexa nodded. "That sounds about right. I recognized the ship—it's a modded version of the skimmers the GEC uses for planetfall on its big exploration ships, since those stay in orbit. Good little craft, which is why a lot of mercs and other free agents buy up decommissioned versions and modify them for their own uses."

"Mercenaries," Lirzhan repeated. "What would mercenaries want with us?"

"I have no idea." And truthfully, she didn't. Her posting to the Council's station in the Targus system was a big deal for her—and her career—but she wasn't self-centered enough to think that she couldn't be replaced easily enough if she were taken out of commission. Maybe some individuals in the diplomatic service's chain of command had been less than thrilled by her relationship with Trin, but shooting her out of the sky while on her way to a new post wasn't the way they would have handled it. No, she would've been shuffled off to some backwater armpit like Iradia, and that would've been the end of her career. Message sent.

Lirzhan was silent as they continued to walk through the corridor, ducking once or twice when the roof of the tunnel dipped low enough to interfere with his passage. His lack of further response unnerved Alexa, and she began to wonder if she wasn't seeing the whole picture here, if he were concealing something he didn't want her to know.

"Or maybe," she said, an edge to her words, "maybe they really didn't care about Ambassador Alexa Craig, but I just happened to be in the way of their real target. You."

At that he stopped and stared down at her. "That is not the case."

"It isn't? How can I know that for sure?"

"Because I just told you it wasn't."

"Oh, and the Zhore never lie."

"As a matter of fact, we don't."

Since she couldn't think of any real way to answer that, she began walking again. This time it was Lirzhan who made sure to come closer to her, to make certain too large a gap didn't open up between the two of them.

"Well, they had to be after something," she said, after an uncomfortable interval of silence.

"Obviously, but I do not know what it could be. Unless…"

"Unless what?"

"Unless we were merely expendable pawns in a larger game."

She knew they needed to keep walking, so she didn't stop, but rather slowed her steps so she could look up into the blackness of the Zhore's hood. "I don't follow."

"Neither of us had ever heard of a device that could pull a ship from subspace, and yet we both experienced it. So perhaps someone was testing such a device, thinking they would be tampering with a slow ore freighter or a small personal transport, and when they realized their catch was a diplomatic shuttle, they took the necessary steps to ensure there were no witnesses to their crime."

That actually did make some sense. How someone as apparently guileless as a Zhore could come up with such a theory, she wasn't sure, but she didn't have a better explanation. She let out a bitter laugh and asked, "Have you been watching imported Gaian detective vids or something?"

"No. Why do you ask?"

"Because it sounds like the sort of thing the scriptwriters might come up with."

"Ah," he replied, which could have meant anything.

Yes, Lirzhan's explanation seemed plausible enough…on the surface. However, just because it was plausible didn't mean it was true. The Zhore could still be hiding something, even if he did claim that his people were unable to lie.

She wondered what that something might be. Maybe he was carrying information that someone really, really didn't want to get to Targus. Unlike her, he'd left the shuttle empty-handed, although she'd seen him carrying a satchel similar to hers when he boarded the ship. Which meant if he'd been transporting any sensitive information, it would have been blown up along with the shuttle…unless he was carrying it on his person.

And what are you going to do, tackle him and frisk him?

The image of her jumping Lirzhan and attempting to pat him down was so ludicrous that she almost laughed out loud. Somehow she held it in, though; the last thing she wanted at the moment was to have to explain a burst of hysterical laughter.

She pushed back her left sleeve slightly to check the chronometer on her wrist. True, it was still set to Gaian mean time, the standard for onboard chronological calculations throughout the Consortium, but at least it could help her calculate how long they'd been walking. As far as she could tell, they'd been underground for almost two hours now, which meant it was way past time to stop and take a meal break. Besides, her foot was starting to kill her.

"Lunch?" she suggested. "And I think I'm going to need a new bandage."

"Your foot is paining you?" he asked quickly.

"Starting to," she lied. No point in telling him that it had been hurting for quite a while now. "And it couldn't hurt to take a breather, although I have to say it's actually easier to walk in here without worrying about tripping over tree roots or getting sunburned."

She wondered about that, actually; the passage was so very smooth and regular, one would have thought it had been excavated by the Consortium's Engineering Corps. But she'd read of lava flows creating tunnels like this, so she thought that might have been the case here. If it were, she hoped that whatever volcano had created these formations had been dormant for a long, long time.

He raised the lantern higher, as if surveying the tunnel ahead of them. "It looks as if there is a wider area a few hundred feet ahead. Let us rest there."

So she followed him to the spot he'd indicated, then sank down on the floor of cold rock, feeling it radiate upward through the fabric of her skirt. Damn. She should have thought to put down one of the blankets first.

Lirzhan set the lantern on a low rock before pulling the second lamp out of the emergency kit so he could more fully illuminate the area. Just as he flipped the switch, Alexa let out a little "ahh!" and stared around her in amazement.

Embedded in the dark rock were tiny sparkling crystals that glittered in shades of pale blue, making it seem as if they were in some sort of fairy cave rather than a bleak underground hole.

"What is it?" she breathed.

The Zhore put a gloved hand up against the rock, as if he were somehow sensing its vibrations through the thin leather-like fabric. "Some kind of quartz, I think, although I've never seen a specimen quite like this."

"It's beautiful."

"Yes, it is," he said, turning his hooded head to gaze at her for a few seconds.

She had the feeling he wasn't talking about the rock formations. Not sure what to say, she instead turned her attention to removing her boot and pulling off the stocking underneath. Sure enough, the bandage had shifted from its original position, and most of the wound was now uncovered and had been rubbing against the inside of her boot. No wonder it hurt like a bitch.

Lirzhan let out a breath. "That is not good. I shall have to clean it again."

And so they went through the whole process a second time, Alexa once again trying to keep herself from muttering a curse as the Zhore dabbed at the affected area with one of the disinfectant wipes. He pressed down firmly on the bandage once he had it in place, as if hoping that the extra pressure would discourage it from shifting any further.

"That should hold," he said at length, and sat back on his heels.

"Well, unless I have to run away from a skimmer again," she replied.

She'd almost thought he would chuckle at that remark, but he didn't, instead going in silence to the emergency pack and once more extracting two of the survival bars that she'd already begun to loathe. He handed one to her, and she took it.

"How far do you think these tunnels go?" she asked, unwrapping the bar in distaste. She tried not to think of her last dinner with Trin, of the elegantly sauced waterfowl and the twenty-year-old bottle of wine they'd drunk with it.

He glanced past their glittering resting place, down the darkening passageway. "Difficult to say. This range of hills seemed to extend some miles northward, but I cannot hazard a guess as to how far. However, I would like to hope that they go almost all the way to the science station."

"That would be a little too convenient, don't you think?"

"Probably."

They chewed their makeshift meal and drank some water. At least they'd been able to replenish their water stores before breaking camp that morning, and so wouldn't have to worry about running out before they reached the science station.

And what then? she thought. *What if the mercs are waiting for us there?*

She really didn't have an answer for that. All she could do was hope that they'd abandon the search once they realized they'd lost all trace of their quarry, and would leave the scene of the crime before anyone else came along.

Not very likely, but hope was about all she had right now.

FIVE

AFTER LUNCH THEY MADE GOOD TIME, walking along the preternaturally smooth tunnels in a more or less northerly direction. Still the passageway sloped downward. Lirzhan kept his fear to himself, that it would keep going down until it abandoned them in some dead end kilometers below the surface of the planet. No, he refused to believe that. Surely they could not have survived so much already, only to be lost in the bowels of Mandala.

Alexa did not appear inclined to talk, and he allowed her that silence. Truly, he did not know what he should say to her. She had hit a little too close to the mark there with her probing questions about precisely why they had been the targets of the attack. He had told her the truth when he said those of his race could not lie, but that did not mean they wouldn't dance around an issue when necessary. Yes, he had been carrying no sensitive papers with him when they were attacked, as those had already been delivered to the head ambassador on Eridani. Even so, he possessed knowledge that many unscrupulous souls in the galaxy might kill to get.

Right now, it did really not matter why they had been attacked, whether such a thing had been deliberate, or whether they had simply been caught in the aftermath of an experiment that had nothing to do with them, as he had postulated to Alexa. The only thing that mattered at the moment was surviving. They could decides on the whys and wherefores once they reached the station.

He looked down at her, saw how her steps had begun to slow, how her slender shoulders were drooping with weariness. Unlike her, he wore no chronometer, but he guessed a good five hours or more had passed since they had last eaten. There had been no signs of pursuit, no sounds of footsteps coming after them, and so he thought they were safe here underground. So far they had seen no creatures of any sort, and only a few clumps of oddly glowing fungus that shriveled as soon as the light from the lantern struck them. The likelihood of an attack was small.

For the last few minutes they had been walking through a largish cave where the tunnel had opened up, and it seemed as good a place to stop as any. "Time to call a halt, I think," he said.

Alexa stopped at once and glanced around her. "Not a very defensible place, is it?"

Well, that was true enough. The cavern was wider than it was long, floor and ceiling smooth, with no signs of the stalactites and stalagmites common in such sorts of caves. "At the far wall, then," he said, pointing to the place where it narrowed down once more into the same sort of tunnel they'd traveled through to get here.

"Sounds good."

He watched her carefully as she made her way over to the spot they'd chosen, but he could see no signs of a limp. Apparently the bandage was holding this time, probably because she'd done nothing more strenuous than walk in a straight line for the past few hours.

"Blanket?" she asked, extending a hand toward the emergency kit. "This rock is damn cold."

"Of course," he replied at once, and extricated it from the kit.

She took it from him and settled it on the ground, then said, "Actually, better give me the other one, too."

He did as she requested, and looked on as she layered the second blanket over the first. It was chilly down here—or at least it would be chilly for her, in her knee-length skirt and plain jacket. The cold could not penetrate his heavy robes, and he wished he could offer to wrap her in them, hold her close so the temperature of the rocks underneath them wouldn't affect her, but he doubted she would accept such an offer, even if he were brave enough to make it.

Once again they shared the ritual of eating half a protein bar and drinking a careful amount of water. After they were done, he folded the wrappers and placed them back in the emergency kit, along with the water containers. He'd just begun to settle himself on the ground a few feet away from her when an odd glow at the far end of the cavern caught his eye. Pausing, he narrowed his eyes at the strange phenomenon, wondering if it were perhaps a particularly large clump of the phosphorescent fungus they'd seen earlier.

But then he realized it was moving toward them.

Alexa had obviously seen it, too, for she rose to her feet, saying, "Lirzhan—"

"I see it," he told her.

"What is it?"

He began to respond by saying he had no idea, but the glow—whatever it was—had picked up speed, almost as if it had sensed them in some way. It came just close enough for him to see a ghastly green-white gleam, baleful black eyes on stalks, a long slug-like body trailing away from them.

"Go!" he shouted, and Alexa scrambled toward the opening in the cavern that led to another tunnel. He hoisted the emergency kit over his shoulder and grasped the lantern, then fled after her, hearing horrible squelching noises as the beast lumbered after them, bringing with it a noisome scent of decay.

She had just entered the tunnel when he caught up with her, stumbling over the rough ground. For whatever reason, this opening was far more rugged than the ones they had traveled through previously. No time to worry about that, or anything else, as he heard a hissing noise and felt the thud as the monster careened into the opening of the passage, far too large to actually fit through it.

Chancing a quick glance over his shoulder, he saw that somehow the creature was melting the opening, as if its very touch was acidic. But it was slow going, and it soon dropped out of sight as they staggered their way through this new tunnel. After a minute or so, he heard a mournful bellow, followed by the squelching of the beast moving off. Apparently it had decided they weren't worth the effort.

"What—was—that—thing?" gasped Alexa.

"One of Mandala's less hospitable denizens, I presume. That would explain the smoothness and the size of those other tunnels we used, though. The creature is highly acidic, and seems to have made its own pathways through the rock."

She stopped then and looked around the tunnel where they now stood. "But not here."

"I don't think so." Lirzhan lifted the lantern and shone it all around them. The roof of the opening was only a few inches above his head, and was rough with what were clearly outcroppings of solidified metamorphic rock. "This appears to have been a lava tube. That creature has clearly never come down here."

"Thank God," she said, and pushed a few stray strands of hair back off her forehead. In the blue-white light from the LED lantern, she looked almost ghostly pale, the usual color in her cheeks gone. "So what now?"

"We push on. We certainly can't go back, and it doesn't seem as if any of those creatures could fit down here."

"Unless they have babies," she said darkly.

That thought hadn't occurred to him, and he didn't like it any more than she clearly did. Still, they really had no choice but to go on...and hope that the pulse pistol he carried would be good enough to protect them, if the creature actually did have any offspring.

"Let us hope it is not mating season," he replied, and a second or two later she gave an unwilling laugh and began picking her way over the jagged ground.

Holding the lantern high, Lirzhan followed her.

It was better if she didn't think about it. If she just concentrated on keeping her footing in this new tunnel, then she couldn't think about the horror they'd left behind them, couldn't think about what other nightmares might be lurking down here in the dark. True, she could see well enough with the way Lirzhan kept the lantern aloft, could tell that there wasn't anything around them except bare dark rock, glistening here and there with more of those pale blue crystals. Even so, shivers continued to run down her spine, shivers that had nothing to do with the chill air around them.

How could the Zhore be so calm, marching along a pace behind her, lantern held at a constant height to keep back the darkness? Or was it just easier to hide what he was feeling because of those damn robes obscuring every inch of his body?

She didn't know, and she didn't dare ask him. For herself, she knew she'd never been this scared, not when their shuttle came under attack, and not when they had plummeted through Mandala's skies, not knowing whether the retro thrusters were really going to fire or not.

Before Mandala, she'd never really known fear. Anxiety, sure—worry that she'd be shuffled into yet another foster home when her current foster parents didn't want to be bothered with her anymore, concern that her scores and grades wouldn't be good enough, and she wouldn't qualify for the full scholarship she needed to get through college, since no one else was going to pay for it. Fear that somehow someone would guess that behind the cool, placid face she presented to everyone she was a welter of doubt and unease, that someone would see through her, see that somehow they'd guess she wasn't as qualified as everyone thought she was, that she was just some kid from the eastern projects in Chicagoland, a girl no one had wanted.

But none of that was the same as staring death in the face, seeing it looking back at you, just waiting for you to make the wrong move. This planet would kill them if they weren't careful, and maybe even if they were. No telling if this passageway would bring them to safety, or abandon them somewhere far from this alien sun, leaving them to die and become a feast for those glowing slug-creatures…or worse.

Directly ahead the tunnel branched right and left. She stopped, and looked back at Lirzhan. "Any suggestions?"

He stepped forward so they stood abreast, and gazed down first the left, and then the right tunnel. "I believe we will stay more on course if we take the right branch."

Did all Zhore have what one of her foster mothers had once referred to as a "bump of direction," or was he just particularly talented? Alexa would have to go with his recommendation, since they didn't have an old-fashioned compass, and of course GPS required actual satellites to work. Whether signals from those satellites could even reach this deep was moot, since Mandala had no such network in place. If it had been scheduled for development and terraforming, then the satellites would have been some of the first technology deployed here, but the Consortium had no such plans for this world. Not yet, anyway.

Not ever, she thought, recalling the slug and shuddering.

"The right branch it is," she said.

Lirzhan nodded, and they both headed in that direction. Normally she would have had some choice words about the rough going, but in this case the irregular ground beneath her feet actually reassured her. A smooth tunnel meant more of those creatures. She'd gladly suffer a whole hell of a lot of bumps and scrapes rather than face one of those things again.

The adrenaline rush subsided, though, and she realized that they had now pushed on long past when they should have stopped to rest for the night. Exactly where they were going to settle this time, she didn't know; the terrain around them wasn't exactly conducive to a good night's sleep. Well, she supposed they'd keep going until a location presented itself. And if it didn't….

She was saved from having to face that contingency, because just as the thought crossed her mind, the tunnel opened out into a cave—a small one, though, definitely not large enough to accommodate one of those creatures, should it somehow even make its way down here. The roof was still only a few inches above Lirzhan's head, but the cave itself seemed to be about three meters in diameter, with a relatively flat floor.

"And here we are," he said, somewhat unnecessarily.

She caught an edge to his normally smooth voice, and guessed he must be very tired as well. How many hours straight had they been going this time? She didn't know, because she hadn't even bothered to look at her chronometer since they'd evaded the slug-creature.

"Thank goodness," she replied, and then paused in consternation. Damn it—they'd left the blankets on the ground when they fled that monster, and now she had nothing to put between her and the cold, hard rock.

Somehow seeming to understand the source of her hesitation, Lirzhan said quietly, "My robes are very warm."

Oh, she guessed they probably were. She almost retorted that she was just fine without the blankets and without his help, but stopped herself. It would be foolish to decline his offer simply because she didn't exactly fancy spending the night snuggled up against him. Actually, now that she thought of it....

"Thank you," she told him, then watched as he settled himself on the ground. She paused for a second or two, gathering her nerve, before she, too, sank to the rocky floor of the cavern and then scooted over next to him. He'd thoughtfully spread out a fold of his long, heavy cloak so she could sit on it, and she situated herself with care, making sure none of the rock was actually touching her.

Quietly, he lifted his arm, and she moved closer, leaning herself against him, feeling him pull his robes around both of them so they were wrapped in a cocoon of warmth. All right, this wasn't so bad. He held her close, allowing her to rest her head on his chest. His heartbeat was slow and strong, reassuring in its regularity, drawing her down toward sleep.

Crazy how comfortable she was like this, how relaxed and easy. It felt right to be here, her head pillowed on his broad chest, which rose and fell beneath her cheek. His soft, steady breaths and the rhythm of his heart blended to make quite an effective white-noise generator, and she let herself fall into darkness, secure in the knowledge that he was there to keep her from harm.

She slept, her hair coming loose from its elastic and gleaming across the dark fabric that covered his chest. It seemed to glow in the light from the lantern, pale and lovely, so unlike the hair of a Zhore. He wished he could bend down and kiss the crown of her head, but he knew better than to take such a liberty. Enough that she should have agreed to share the warmth of his robes, had actually dared so much physical contact.

His need for her was an actual physical ache. He forced himself to breathe in and out, to focus on their surroundings, although all seemed quiet and still. There had been no talk of taking watches this time, probably because she was so weary that the thought hadn't even crossed her mind. No matter; he sensed they were safe enough here. Even so, he would remain awake for at least another hour, just in case.

He took a deep breath, tasting the flavor of the rock, noticing an increased level of humidity in the air. What that meant, he wasn't sure. He heard no sounds of an underground stream, or even dripping from the rocky roof overhead. Perhaps it was just the density of the air down here. At least he smelled nothing beyond the gritty aroma of stone and a faint sweet scent from Alexa's hair. No predators, none of the noisome odor of the slug-creature.

It was better that he occupied himself with such things, rather than the feel of Alexa's head against his chest, or the curve of her body as it snugged so perfectly up to his. Desire was not an emotion he had much experience with; among the Zhore, one only felt desire for one who was *sayara*, in which case it was reciprocated. His people had no long courting periods, because they knew from the beginning if they were compatible. Before Alexa, he'd had no conception of how this wanting could be a physical torment, a gnawing, cramping hollowness somewhere in his breast.

He would have to ignore it. He certainly could not act on it, not before he knew whether or not she would be receptive to such advances. Certainly she'd given no hint up until now that she felt any attraction toward him. Rather the opposite, unfortunately.

Frowning, he took in another breath, and then shut his eyes. If anything untoward should occur, he knew he could be awake in a millisecond. But he needed his sleep as well, or he would not be effective the next day, with whatever it might bring. So he held himself still and let oblivion wash over him. If he were very lucky, he might dream of Alexa, although he couldn't imagine any dream being better than this, with her asleep in his arms.

If he dreamed, he didn't recall any of those dreams when he awoke some five hours later, the woman he loved still a warm sleeping weight against his shoulder and chest. Very gently he touched her hand and whispered, "Alexa."

Her eyes fluttered open at once, wide and worried. "What is it?"

"Nothing. But we have slept a good while, and I think it's time we ate and pushed on."

She nodded and blinked, obviously attempting to rid herself of the last dregs of sleep. "Got it." And then she pushed herself away from him, unwrapping his cloak and standing. One hand went up to her loose hair, and she frowned. "Have you seen my hair band?"

He hadn't, but he felt around on the ground next to him and located it a few seconds later. "Here."

Taking it from him, she pulled her hair back into a sloppy tail. A little pang went through him at that, for he thought her lovelier than ever with her long hair cascading over her shoulders. But he supposed it would get in the way. He definitely knew better than to mention that he liked her hair better loose.

They ate and drank, and used a little of their water to splash their faces and hands. And then it was time to go, heading toward the far end of the cavern where it narrowed down into a tunnel once more, the lantern showing more of the same rough floor and walls and roof as the passageways they'd traversed the day before.

The way continued to slope downward, and Lirzhan frowned within his hood. Surely at some point it must begin to rise again? But that was only hope, not knowledge. And they could not go back; whatever happened, they must press on.

Now the air began to feel damp as well as taste that way. It smelled moist here, too, and in the reflected bluish glow of the lantern he could see the stone walls around them gleaming with wet.

Alexa sensed it as well. Her head cocked, and she sniffed the air before reaching out to touch the wall of the tunnel, bringing away fingertips covered in the moisture. She rubbed her fingers together. "Seems like regular water."

"Smells like it as well," he replied. "Perhaps there is an underground stream, or fissures in the rock that go all the way to the surface and let in rainwater."

She nodded, saying, "Let's hope it isn't anything bigger than a str— " And her words broke off as the tunnel opened up before them, revealing a cavern vastly larger than the one where they'd encountered the slug-creature.

They'd found the source of the moisture. It wasn't an underground stream, or even a river.

It was a lake. It stretched out in all directions, appearing to touch the cave walls to either side. There did not seem to be any way to walk around it. They would have to swim.

"I guess I shouldn't have opened my mouth," Alexa managed after a strained pause.

"I believe the lake would have been there regardless of what you said." He made sure to keep his tone light, but he could feel his heart rate accelerate. If they were to swim for it, he could not do so garbed as he was. He would have to take off his robes, for once they were waterlogged they would weigh him down far too much.

And that meant she would see him.

A Zhore only revealed himself to his mate. She of course would have no idea how significant such a gesture was among his people, but he would.

"Can you swim?" she asked, and her voice sounded a little shaky.

"Yes," he said. "There was a lake near the house where I was born. My mother used to call me her little *treska*—similar to what you refer to as a 'tadpole' on Gaia."

"*Treska*," Alexa repeated. "I like it." The faint smile she'd been wearing faded, and she said, not looking at him, "Lirzhan, I'm afraid I don't know how to swim."

The Zhore did not normally curse, but Lirzhan suddenly found himself understanding why the practice was so popular among the other humanoid races of the galaxy. "You don't? But so much of Gaia is covered in water."

"Not where I grew up. Oh, there were rivers and small lakes, and municipal swimming pools, but my—that is, the people who raised me didn't think it was worth spending the money on lessons. So I never learned." During this little speech she continued to stare down at the dark rock beneath her feet, as if by looking up she'd somehow sense the condemnation in his posture, even though she couldn't see past the hood.

"It is no matter," he told her, keeping his tone as reassuring as possible. "I can support you. Once you're in the water you will be buoyant, and the extra weight should not slow me down terribly much."

She did not look all that convinced. "You're going to swim across that lake carrying me and wearing those?" And she pointed to the heavy robes he wore.

"No," he replied, trying to keep his tone light, as if what he was about to propose did not go against everything he had been taught. "They will only weigh me down. I will fold them up and put them in the emergency kit. Luckily, the bag is waterproof."

"You'll—" The words broke off, and she stared at him with unbelieving eyes. "But a Zhore never goes out in public without his robes."

Oh, yes, I know that. "True, but this is not so public after all. It is only you and I here."

Because he knew he would have to do it now, before he lost his nerve, he set down the lantern, and reached up and undid the clasp at his throat. Then he grasped the edges of the heavy fabric and pulled it away.

SIX

ALEXA THOUGHT FOR SURE he must be making some kind of macabre joke. She couldn't believe for a second that Lirzhan would actually remove those robes. They were like armor or something for the Zhore.

But his gloved hands gripped the heavy fabric and pulled it away, hood falling back even as he drew off the bulky garment, sliding free of the arms. He lifted his head, and gazed calmly at her.

And she—well, she could only stand there and stare. Incongruously, she almost wanted to laugh. So many rumors and stories about the Zhore's ugliness. Because really, what other reason could they have for covering themselves from head to toe, never allowing any off-worlders to get even a single glance at them?

He wasn't ugly. Far from it. Humanoid, not human, skin black but with a faint iridescence that she real-ized came from thousands of tiny scales, far finer than those of the reptiles on her own world. Fine, strong nose and beautiful planes of cheekbone, forehead, and chin. Beneath straight, expressive black brows, eyes of a startling green stared back at her. His hair was long and black, possibly even longer than her own, caught away from his face in some sort of clasp.

The silence was deafening. She couldn't think of what to say, except maybe something along the lines of, *You're doing the women of the galaxy a grave disservice by depriving them of the opportunity to see that.* But that was too casual, too flip. She somehow sensed that what he had just done was very, very difficult for him.

Instead, she said quietly, "Thank you," and smiled.

He remained still for a few more seconds, gazing down at her, and then he smiled as well, a beautiful smile, with white human-looking teeth…although she thought that perhaps he had a few more than she. Then he sobered. "You will need to take off your boots, and your jacket. I will take off my boots as well."

For the first time she focused on what he had been wearing under the robes—a high-necked black tunic and close-fitting black trousers tucked into high black boots. The ensemble revealed what could only be guessed at before—that he was slender but well-built, with broad shoulders and a nice, wide chest.

That chest had felt awfully good when she rested her head on it the night before.

But that realization began to lead her thoughts in directions she wasn't sure she wanted them to go.

Anyway, they had more important things to worry about right now. Like getting across that lake.

"Got it," she replied, and eased off one boot, then the other, followed by her stockings, which she rolled up and put in the boots. The rock under her bare feet was icy cold, and she wondered what the temperature of that black water before her must be. Definitely not spa temperature, she guessed. How long did it take to be affected by hypothermia? If she'd ever known, she couldn't recall now.

She hesitated a second or two before reaching up to undo the buttons on her jacket. Silly to be acting prudish right now, especially when Lirzhan had just done the Zhore equivalent of getting naked in front of her. Yes, the camisole she wore under that jacket was pretty skimpy, but she thought he probably had more important things on his mind than looking at her chest.

However, she understood his reasoning for wanting her to take off the jacket. By stowing it in the emergency bag, it would remain dry, and so she'd have something warm to put on once they got to the other side.

If they got to the other side.

"How far can you swim?" she asked, not precisely meeting his eyes as she folded up her jacket, then handed it to him.

"Far," he told her, taking the garment from her and stowing it in the emergency bag before gathering up her boots and stuffing them in as well. "Once I swam almost ten kilometers, although I do not think we have nearly that far to go." He paused, elegant head tilted to one side as he appeared to listen to the lap of the water on the rocky shore. "It is very faint, but I believe I can hear the echo of the water splashing on the other side. Perhaps it is no more than half a kilometer."

That was good news. Surely if he'd once managed ten kilometers, then less than a tenth that shouldn't be any problem at all.

If it was even safe. "Maybe we should try the water testing kit before we dip our toes in, so to speak."

"Excellent idea." He rummaged around in the emergency bag, presumably having to push past their discarded clothing and boots to locate the little plastic tube.

As she took it from him, Alexa forced herself not to stare up into his face. It was more difficult than she thought, because some part of her wanted to keep looking and looking, to finally put features to the voice she had been hearing for the past few days. Since she didn't imagine he would be particularly pleased with such an inspection, she somehow refrained and pushed her attention back to the black water. It seemed quiet and calm enough, with no sign of any fish or other creature she could see. Of course, that didn't mean the slug-creature's aquatic cousin couldn't be lurking somewhere in the depths....

She gave a shake of her head and told herself not to manufacture problems. Making sure to hold the tube by her fingertips at its very end, she dipped it into the water and watched as it turned a cool, serene blue, almost the color of Gaia's skies. "Looks all right." Well, chemically, anyway. She was still worried about the temperature, so she stuck one finger into the water. It was cool, but not the shocking cold she had expected...more like a bath that had gone tepid. "That's strange—shouldn't it be a lot colder than this?"

In reply, Lirzhan also knelt at the water's edge and drew off one of his gloves before plunging his entire hand into the lake. He moved his fingers back and forth several times, then withdrew his hand and wiped it off on his trousers. "It does seem rather mild. Perhaps it is fed by warm springs coming up through the rock."

She supposed that was a plausible explanation, especially when taking the volcanic nature of this mountain range into account. All she could hope was that it wouldn't decide to blow while they were still down here. "Maybe. I'm just glad I won't be doing a *Titanic* survivor impersonation in freezing water."

"*Titanic?*" he repeated, brows lifting.

Probably it was a bit much to think he would be familiar with that particular footnote to Gaian history. "A ship that sank in the North Atlantic in the early part of Gaia's twentieth century. People died because the water was below zero Celsius."

"Oh. That would be tragic, but it is not likely here." He straightened, then asked, "Are you ready?"

Not really, but.... "Yes."

"I will go in first, to test the depth, and then you can follow me. Do you think you can hold on to the lantern with one hand while I swim?"

Oh, hell yeah. Going out into that dark lake would be nearly unbearable without being able to shed some light on the subject. And she hadn't even thought of the depth, that maybe the ground would drop away immediately once they left the shore. If that were the case, Lirzhan would have to begin treading water right away. "Okay."

He stepped into the water, paused, and then took a few more steps and stopped again, the water now up to a little above his knees. "It seems gradual enough. Come in."

Sucking in a breath, Alexa put one foot into the water, then the other. The surface under her bare feet felt rocky, just like the shore she'd just left. But it was only cool, not cold, and better that it be rocky than slimy mud. Another step, and she was only a few inches behind him.

"Reach over my shoulders," he instructed. "Hold there, but don't obstruct the movement of my arms. Understand?"

She nodded, then realized he probably couldn't see the gesture, since she was standing directly behind him. "I understand," she replied, and reached up and wrapped her arms over his shoulders, standing on her tiptoes to do so.

"All right. I'm going to go all the way in now. Are you ready?"

His tone was gentle, as if he recognized her fear and didn't want to push too hard. Irritation with herself boiled up from within, at lacking such a basic skill as knowing how to swim, even though this was the first time in her life it had really mattered to her one way or another. Somehow this planet had reduced her to the sort of helpless female she normally despised, and she found she really didn't care for it too much.

"I'm ready," she said, her voice surprisingly steady.

He moved forward then, sinking into the dark water, bringing her with him. Even though it really wasn't that cold, she still barely refrained from gasping as the lake came up around her, soaking her camisole and skirt and the underwear she wore beneath.

Well, that's one way of getting it washed....

Lirzhan struck out in earnest then, cutting through the water as if he had been born to it. Alexa hung on, seeing how their forward motion had her trailing behind him, almost bobbing on the surface as his powerful legs churned away below.

Better not to think too hard about those meters of black water below her, of how anything could be living down there, might come thrashing to the top at any moment to see what was creating so much noise. No, that was definitely not the best thing to be thinking about right now. She forced herself to stare forward, to maintain her death grip on the lantern as its light flickered and danced on the dark, almost oily-looking surface ahead of them.

The only sound was the splashing of the water as they moved through it. Of course Lirzhan would have to save his breath, since he was supporting her as well as himself. And she couldn't think of anything she wanted to say…except maybe, "Please, God, don't let me die down here."

Funny how even a hard-core agnostic like herself could suddenly find religion when faced with the prospect of a horrible death.

How long this went on, she couldn't begin to guess, since she had no way of looking at the chronometer on her wrist. It seemed to take forever, but she knew time could be subjective in these instances, could appear to stretch on interminably when only a few minutes had passed. Then she thought she saw an answering gleam up ahead and squinted at it, wondering what was flashing at them in the darkness.

"The wall," Lirzhan murmured, not quite gasping. "The minerals."

Of course. They were now drawing closer to the other side, and that flickering light she'd seen was more of those little bluish crystals, catching the beam from her lantern and sending it back at them, guiding them to safety.

A minute or so later, he stumbled, then told her, "I can feel the bottom. It's safe for you to let go now."

Yes, but did she really want to? Perversely, she almost wished she could continue to hold on to him, to have the reassuring solidity of his body against hers. But that was just crazy. The poor man had just swum the equivalent of a quarter-mile; the last thing he needed was her clinging to his neck like an anchor.

So she dropped away, and felt the familiar rocky surface beneath her feet. They both made their way on shore and then dropped to the ground, Lirzhan's breathing sounding labored. She guessed hauling her all that way hadn't been quite as easy as he'd anticipated.

"Are you all right?" she asked.

He lifted a hand. "Yes. I just need a minute to recover." Reaching back, he pulled the clasp out of his hair and ran the fingers of one hand through it, to brush the strands that had come loose away from his face.

Again she wanted to stare, but she forced herself to look away. "I think I'll get my jacket and boots."

She lifted the emergency bag from where he'd dropped it on the shore, and placed his own boots on the ground next to him, along with his robes. Her jacket followed, with her own boots coming out last. Putting on the jacket over her wet camisole and bra didn't seem like such a great idea, so she turned away from him and pulled the sodden garments over her head, then quickly drew on the jacket. So she'd just flashed the Zhore her naked back. All she could do was hope she hadn't violated some sort of taboo in his culture.

After wringing out the camisole and bra, she folded them up and put them in the bag. What she really wanted to do was hang them to dry, but she didn't see that happening anytime soon.

When she turned back around, she saw that Lirzhan had slipped on his boots, but that the robes remained in a pile next to his feet. He appeared to follow her questioning gaze, and remarked, "It is no use to put those on when my other garments are still wet. I will wait, I think." And he picked them up and handed them back to her.

"That's probably best," she managed, and stuffed them into the emergency kit—after making sure several layers of plastic separated them from her own wet clothing.

"If you are ready to go on?" he said, lifting the lantern from its resting place on the ground. "I see another tunnel over there."

She glanced in the direction he'd indicated, and sure enough, she saw an opening in the rock, very similar to the one they'd traversed on the other side of the lake, although not quite as high. Lirzhan might have to bend his neck a little to fit.

That didn't sound very comfortable, but there wasn't much they could do about it. All she could do was hope that this tunnel would finally lead them to the surface... preferably not through the lair of one of those slug-creatures this time.

She wouldn't mind another lake, though.

He had to stoop at times, for this tunnel was not as large as the others they'd traveled through. But it was rocky and clean and carried no smell of the slugs or any other predators, and so a stiff neck or shoulders seemed a small enough price to pay.

Alexa trudged along beside him, for although the tunnel was not all that tall, at least it was wide enough for the two of them to walk abreast. Poor choice of words there; he'd seen the smooth, pale expanse of her back and the barest flash of the side of a creamy bosom before she shrugged herself into her jacket. As weary as he was, desire licked through him as he recalled that glimpse of her body. Somehow it didn't matter to him that she was alien, that her skin was so very different from that of his own people. Her shape was delectably female, and he wanted her now more than ever.

He could tell, too, that she was fascinated by him, that she had to force herself not to stare at the features he had kept hidden up until now. Surely that must be a good sign, for if she were repulsed by his appearance, she wouldn't seem to be so intrigued. Or perhaps not; perhaps it was only simple curiosity, for being the only one of her race to have ever looked upon the face of a Zhore. Well, the only one that she knew of; that unknown girl on Lathvin IV was truly the first to have ever seen one of his people face to face.

There was no way to ask what Alexa was thinking without being horribly intrusive, so he said nothing, only continued their passage through the tunnel—which, he was beyond relieved to note, had begun finally to slope upward. If there were any mercy in the universe, they would finally regain the surface, taste the wind and see the sky, but he did not want to speak of his hope, not yet when so many things could still go wrong.

His clothing gradually dried as they walked, and he began to be cold. Several hours had passed since they emerged from the lake when he paused.

Alexa stared up at him, blue eyes wide with concern. "What is it?"

"Nothing, except that I think I am now dried off enough to put my robes back on."

Was that a flicker of disappointment he saw cross her lovely features? But she only nodded and said, "Sure, just a minute," before pulling them out of the emergency bag and handing them to him.

He took them gratefully, shrugging into the heavy garments with the ease of long practice. Warmth surrounded him, dispelling some of the chill he had felt ever since leaving the water. Out of habit, he reached up to pull the hood back over his head once more.

Her voice stopped him, surprisingly hesitant for someone so forthright. "Do you—that is, do you think you might leave the hood down for now? There's no one else here to see, after all."

Joy surged through him then, for he was sure she would not have made such a request if she weren't in some way pleased by looking at him. He sensed confusion from her, an odd diffidence, as if she were struggling with feelings she couldn't quite comprehend.

"Of course, if you wish it," he said, and let his hands fall back to his sides.

She flashed him a quick, uncertain smile before turning back to the empty tunnel ahead of them and beginning to walk again.

Lirzhan knew it would be better if he said nothing else. Things had perhaps begun to change between them, but no use in pushing when their connection was still so fragile. For now he was content to walk beside her, and know she was glad that he hadn't decided to retreat to the safety of the hood once more.

When light flooded the tunnel, he blinked, because he'd been halfway expecting that they would continue to trudge through these barren, rocky caverns forever until their food and water was gone. Next to him, Alexa went stock still. In unbelieving tones she asked,

"Are we out?"

It appeared they were. Or almost, anyway. The tunnel opened out into a shallow cave, and the cave in turn opened on a hillside far more lush than the one they had left behind two days earlier. Trees in shades of olive and dark teal crowded the view outside, and above them the sky was a serene gray-blue, clouds streaking it that were beginning to turn shades of pink and coral. There were no skimmers in sight.

"Sunset or sunrise?" he asked, as he could not see the sun itself, not with it low in the sky and tall hills crowding on every side. Oddly, his sense of direction seemed to have deserted him for the moment.

She pushed back the sleeve of her jacket and looked down at her chronometer. "It's not an exact match, but as far as I can tell, it's sunset."

That wasn't optimal, for striking out just as the sun was beginning to go down seemed to him to be a very bad idea. Still, the cave where they stood now appeared to be empty and clean enough, with no trace that any living thing had stood here before, no bones or scat left behind by predators. "Then I think we should stay here for the night and set out in the morning. That will give us time to rest, and I can't imagine that we would find a more secure place by heading out into that forest."

Something about her posture seemed to change, as if she had relaxed slightly, knowing that they would push on no further this day. "Let's see my tablet. Maybe now that we're back on the surface we'll be able to pick up a signal."

He drew it out for her, although he wasn't certain she would have much success. Lacking satellites, the beacon on the science station worked more or less on line of sight, although the signal must be very strong out of necessity.

But she tapped away, and then let a little relieved gust of breath out between her lips. "Looks like our luck might be changing. I'm getting something, even though it's a little faint. Must be the mountains in the way. You can still see the route, though. Look."

She angled the screen so he could see what she was talking about. Sure enough, the signal for the station pulsed away, a reassuring green, showing that they did not have as far to go as he had feared. Another thirty kilometers, maybe a little more. That was even something they might be able to accomplish in a day, although he glanced at the mountainsides directly across from them, now turning darker and darker with the setting of the sun, and wondered if they were as impassable as they looked. Well, that was something to be tackled tomorrow. At least they had made good progress while they toiled away underground.

"We are getting close," he told her. "All the more reason to rest now, so we can leave early in the morning. With any luck, we may reach the station before night comes again."

"I'm not much acquainted with luck," she told him, "but one can always hope, I suppose." She turned away from the cave opening and inspected the bare floor, which was much smoother than the caverns they'd left behind. She smiled at him then, and this time he noted no hesitancy in either her expression or her tone. "Mind if I borrow some of that robe to sit on again?"

SEVEN

ALL RIGHT, SHE REALLY DIDN'T WANT TO ADMIT to herself how good it felt to sit here, the fabric of Lirzhan's robe protecting her from the dirty ground, her back up against the cave wall, her head resting against his shoulder, the meager meal she'd just consumed keeping the worst of the hunger pangs at bay. Maybe it was just the chance to sit down after so much walking—seriously, she hoped she'd never have to walk any farther than down a hallway at work or from a cab to her apartment again—but somehow she knew it was a little more than that. Something had changed.

You are so goddamn shallow, she told herself. *You barely wanted to talk to him, but now you've seen his face and know he isn't Quasimodo or something under there, suddenly you want to get all cozy with him?*

Put that way....

All right, maybe that was a little bit true. But after years of hearing rumors about the Zhore's unprepossessing appearance, it was a little disconcerting to find that instead he looked like some dark elf out of those old Norse tales she'd read as a child, hiding under the covers with a tablet loaded with free public domain stories so she could try to avoid the ugliness of her life. Hard to accept that she found his face oddly beautiful. If she were any kind of an artist, she'd want to paint those elegant planes and angles, try to capture something of the light in those deep jade-green eyes. But she wasn't, so the only thing she could do was try to watch him without staring, to commit as much of his features to memory against the time when the outside universe intruded again, and he retreated to the safety of that damned hood.

For now, though, they were alone, and it was all right to lean against him, to feel the warmth of his body against hers, although the night air on her face was downright chilly. No one was here to judge, or wonder how she could allow herself to be wrapped in those heavy, concealing garments, snuggled up to one of the galaxy's most secretive aliens.

Not that she imagined anything was really going to happen between them. No, they'd share these few odd hours of intimacy, and then they'd be rescued and— well, all right, they wouldn't really be going their separate ways, not with the two of them both assigned to the Council's headquarters in the Targus system, but she couldn't imagine anything much happening after that.

It wouldn't be like being with Trin. Yes, he was an alien, too, but humans and Eridanis had been mingling for more than a hundred years now. No one batted much of an eye to see members of those races having relationships, or even marrying and starting families together. There were a few people at the embassy who had been less than pleased, but that was probably more a territorial thing than because they were racist. The Consortium couldn't exactly tell its diplomats to stay single…much as its representatives probably would have liked to. Even so, having a member of the embassy staff involved with one of the locals was not exactly encouraged.

But since Trin was a university professor with a spotless reputation, and because his work had absolutely nothing to do with Alexa's own duties, the whole thing was let slide. She imagined that suddenly going out for drinks with Lirzhan at the Targus station's commissary wouldn't exactly meet with the same placid reception.

Getting a little ahead of yourself, aren't you? Next thing you know, you'll be settling down with him on a colony somewhere and popping out a bunch of half-alien babies.

That was definitely ridiculous. She'd never given any thought to marriage at all. She had nothing to model on—no happy home life to make her want anything more than a life of service. There had been a few men, but not many. She wasn't very good at the whole trust thing. The only reason she'd started seeing Trin was that he'd been so importunate in his pursuit of her, so clearly enchanted. If he'd heard any rumors about the "Ice Queen," he definitely didn't show it. He told her she was beautiful, that she was intelligent and exotic. What woman wouldn't want to hear such things, even an ice queen?

She'd known even as the relationship began that it wouldn't last, and had tried to let him know they really didn't have a future together. He hadn't wanted to listen; it was pretty obvious that he thought he could change her mind. No such luck for him.

She shifted slightly, and felt Lirzhan move as well to accommodate her new position. What he thought of her, she had no idea. Probably that she was some sheltered female who couldn't even be bothered to learn how to swim, who was woefully unprepared for the ordeal they were now enduring. Well, she couldn't argue with that. Then again, she'd never signed up for this sort of duty. If she'd wanted bivouacs and slogging through the wilderness and dodging wild animals, she would've enlisted in the GEC rather than the diplomatic corps.

Anyway, all she could do was hope, as she drifted off to sleep, that he didn't think her too much of an idiot.

This might be the last night he could be with her like this, her head pillowed on his shoulder, the warmth of her body seeming to fill the space within the robes wrapped around them both. If they made it to the station tomorrow, they would have proper beds to sleep in, and she'd have no more need to huddle against him as protection from the chill of the night.

He wished he could ignore the pang that went through him as he contemplated this prospect. Something in her seemed to be softening, but whether it would soften enough in time...well, that was the real question. There was every chance that rescue would come before he had the chance to say anything to her, explain the *sayara* bond...try to tell her why, through some happy accident of mind and spirit and body, she was the one most suited to being with him.

Yes, somehow he had a feeling that sort of announcement would not go over very well.

A sigh reached his lips, but he did not let it out. He did not want to do anything that might wake her, not when she slept so peacefully, eyes shut, lashes dark against her pale cheeks. One of Mandala's moons was tracking through the sky, casting a pale bluish light over the landscape and pouring through the cave opening. In its radiance she looked oddly fragile and even more beautiful. He wished he could touch her, could reach over to push back that loose strand of hair which looked as if it might fall across her closed eyelids at any moment.

No, that wouldn't do. She might sense the lightest brush of his hand near her face, and misinterpret the gesture. So guarded, so many walls within her. She'd been hurt deeply, that much he could sense, and he wondered if she would ever feel free to discuss such things with him. He thought that perhaps she did whatever she could in order to avoid talking about herself. In a way, being in the diplomatic service made sense for such a personality, for she could put her own ego aside as needed to work through the issues of the opposing sides.

But such self-abnegation must come at a cost. He'd begun to see the smallest change in her, the tiniest hint that the edges of her flinty exterior were beginning to chip away. With all that, though, he feared that the second they were back in civilization, had returned to their duties and routines, all the walls would be back up again, and their chance together would be forever lost.

It was not normally his way to accept defeat before it had even occurred, but he had never met a woman like Alexa Craig before. There were no stunted childhoods, no bleak emotional landscapes, among his people, for such things were nigh impossible when every intimate relationship was based on such deep compatibility, such harmony on every level of body and mind and soul. Once he had ventured out into the galaxy, he saw that his people were an anomaly, and that there was much conflict he could not even begin to understand. He could only hope that whatever might lie in Alexa Craig's past, it hadn't scarred her irrevocably.

Another morning, another stiff neck. She pushed herself away from Lirzhan with care, feeling several vertebrae crack as she did so.

Hope there's a good chiropractor on Targus Station, she thought, and looked over to see Lirzhan gazing out at the bright morning beyond the cave opening.

"All well with the world this morning?" she asked.

"As far as I can tell," he replied quietly. "I have been listening to the birds, or whatever they are, and I believe I hear the buzzing of insects in the trees, but other than that, things seem peaceful enough."

"Good." Yes, a nice quiet walk through the woods would be a welcome change of pace. True, those mountains didn't look all that promising, but maybe there was some sort of pass they weren't seeing because of all the trees clustering on the mountainsides.

They both lapsed into silence then, sharing the ritual of eating their protein bars and drinking enough water to wash them down sufficiently. One good thing about that dunk in the underground lake yesterday—Alexa felt a lot cleaner, although she still longed for the bathrooms at the science station. Most of the time they were equipped with solar water heaters, so there might even be a hot shower in the offing if she were really lucky.

Afterward, they packed up their empty wrappers and set out again. The walk down the hillside below the cave mouth was steep but not impossibly so. And of course going down was easier than going up.

All around them clustered trees in various shades of gray-green and green-blue, actually quite lovely with their lacy, almost feather-like foliage. The forest floor was coated with more leaves in various states of decay, muffling the sound of their footsteps. From time to time she could hear odd little rustling sounds in the undergrowth, as if small creatures were fleeing from the clumsy two-legged creatures blundering through the woods, but she saw no sign of them.

"This is quite a beautiful world," Lirzhan said after some time had passed. "I am surprised the Consortium has not begun colonizing here."

"They probably will, if they get desperate enough," Alexa replied. "The GEC actually prefers barren worlds that it can terraform. Trying to coexist with native flora and fauna has proved deadly too many times, so even if they eventually decide to come back here, they'll just scorch-earth the place and start over."

He turned and sent her a disbelieving look. "You mean to tell me that your people would actually rather destroy all this rather than attempt to live peacefully with the plants and animals that have evolved on this world?"

She found she didn't much like being on the receiving end of his narrow, green-eyed stare. It wasn't a policy she particularly liked, or approved of, but she wasn't in the GEC and had no control over that organization's actions. "Well, the Gaian Exploration Commission will. There are actually people who've been protesting such policies for years, but it hasn't done much good."

"Why not?"

"Because, well—" She floundered for a second. "It's complicated."

"I believe that is what your people would refer to as an excuse."

He had her there. "Look, Lirzhan, you're a diplomat, so I know you must've done some serious study of Gaian culture and politics. The corporations have a stranglehold on the government, so even if there are well-meaning people who don't agree with some of the Consortium's more destructive policies, they don't have enough of a voice to effect any real change." She paused, noting the disapproval that seemed to fairly pulse from him. "Don't try to tell me that any of this is a real surprise to you."

"It isn't. I suppose I had hoped—" He broke off, and appeared to be deciding exactly what he wanted to say next. "That is, I suppose I find it surprising that one of the Consortium's representatives would be so frank on the topic."

She met his gaze, trying to focus on the condemnation on his face, and not the beauty of its particular features. "You know a lot more about us than we do about you," she said, not bothering to hide the weariness in her tone. "I'm pretty sure I'm not telling you anything you didn't already know."

He did not blink. "True enough. But what do you think about it?"

"I hate it," she told him shortly, then turned away and kept trudging ahead, her boots making soft rustling sounds on the bed of dead leaves beneath her feet. "But it doesn't really matter what I think."

"I think it matters very much. You have a powerful position in your government. Surely if someone at that level were to speak up, to decry such policies—"

A wry bark of a laugh escaped her throat before she could hold it back. "I take back what I said. Obviously you don't know as much about Gaian politics as I thought you must."

Reaching out, he caught her by the arm, pulling her to a stop. She glared at him, and stared pointedly down at the black-scaled hand wrapped around her sleeve. The nails were cut short, not talons at all…although they did have an odd iridescent gleam similar to the one she'd seen on his fine-scaled skin.

"Alexa," he said, a note of quiet intensity to his voice that for some reason made her hold her tongue, wait to hear what he had to say next. Or perhaps it was simply because he hadn't called her by her first name before. "If not you, who? If not now, when? The worst thing well-meaning people can do is simply let things remain as they are."

"And when they try to change them, they find them-selves without jobs, without friends, with their entire support structure taken away. Idealism is wonderful in theory, Lirzhan, but in practice? Not so much."

She pulled her arm away, and he let her go, his eyes sorrowful. Without looking at him, she began strid-ing forward. No wonder the Zhore were so difficult to deal with—they had no frame of reference for how the galaxy actually worked. Oh, she knew that the Gaians' mercenary ways generally met with varying levels of scorn from the other humanoid races, but their censure had never really bothered her before this. There was something about seeing it in those clear jade-green eyes, seeing the downward droop to Lirzhan's finely sculpted mouth, that made her begin to question the things she'd been taught her entire life.

And she certainly didn't want to do that, because if she challenged those ideas, then the shaky framework she'd built her entire existence upon would begin to fall apart, and she'd be left with even less than she had now.

"I am sorry," he said quietly. "I did not mean to upset you."

"I'm not upset." *Keep walking, keep looking forward.*

"Yes, you are."

At that she found herself stopping, despite her earlier admonition to herself to keep going no matter what. "You want to know what *really* upsets me, Lirzhan?"

"What?" he inquired, in tones of real interest.

"People telling me I'm upset when I'm not."

And she stomped off, blindly winding her way through the trees, not paying much attention to where she was going. This was ridiculous. Bad enough that they should be stranded here, bad enough that she hadn't had a shower in three days or a decent meal or a chance to brush her teeth…but to have this alien trying to psychoanalyze her, or turn her into some sort of proselytizer for the "no footprint" tree-huggers? No, thank you.

"Alexa—"

"What?" she snapped.

"I would suggest that you stop exactly where you are."

Something in his voice, some warning note, told her that she should listen to him. She came to an abrupt halt, then really focused on the path in front of her and almost screamed. Stretched between two trees was an enormous—well, spiders were Gaian creatures, so she didn't know for sure what had spun the pale-green web-like structure. What she did know was that she really, really didn't want to go blundering into it.

"Okay," she said shakily, and began to back toward him.

Almost at once a dark blur shot down from the canopy above, skittering over the web and heading straight for her. This time she did let out a little shriek, propelling herself backward so quickly she almost tripped over a tree root. Even as she fought for her balance, a pair of bright green pulse bolts went flying past her head and connected with the blur, which resolved itself into a dark bluish shell with ten legs and huge blobby black eyes and mandibles dripping some sort of dark fluid she guessed must be a poison of some kind.

She glanced back at Lirzhan, saw him standing there with the pulse pistol in his left hand and a grim expression on his face. For a second or two, neither of them said anything. Then he glanced upward.

"I believe from now on we should walk with care."

Swallowing the acid taste of bile, Alexa could only nod.

After that they continued, warily watching the openings between the trees for more of those webs, and often glancing upward to make sure no dark insectoid forms were scuttling down to finish what their compatriot had attempted earlier. Lirzhan saw nothing except the wind in the trees, and the high, circling shapes of more avian creatures, but he could not blame Alexa for being a little jumpy. She was still quite pale.

He had not meant to make her angry earlier, but he knew anything else he might say on that former topic would only raise her ire once again. Odd that she could find it within her to serve a government whose policies she clearly disagreed with, but he had read multiple texts on human psychology in preparation for his post in the diplomatic service, and so he did understand that the human mind could be a very complex thing.

…and the human female mind even more so.

So he held his tongue for the most part, only offering brief comments when they needed to shift their route slightly, or to warn her about depressions he'd noticed in the ground, so she would not be taken by surprise and possibly twist an ankle, or worse. At least she seemed to accept these mild overtures without any outward signs of hostility, and even thanked him when he pointed out a particularly nasty-looking clump of thorny bushes.

Some hours later they stopped to eat their midday meal and check their location. Again they had covered a good deal of ground, more than Lirzhan had expected. Perhaps there was something to be said for marching along in silence and concentrating only on the path in front of you, even with the steady upward climb they'd been experiencing for the past hour or so.

"Only twenty kilometers more to go," he said, after analyzing the map on her tablet. They obviously had a much better connection to the beacon at the station from here, as it pulsed a clear, bright green.

"That's not too bad," Alexa replied, the note of relief clear in her voice. She drank some water, then asked, "Do you think we'll be able to make it by nightfall?"

"At our current pace...perhaps." He looked past her to the trees crowding the skyline, then back down the way they had come. Truly, they had ascended more than he had first thought. Perhaps another kilometer or so more before they reached the top of this pass, which had turned out to be a gentler summit than he had expected. And then they would be walking downhill, and the way should be much easier.

She appeared to follow his gaze. "Looks like we don't have that much more climbing to do, so ten kilometers shouldn't be too difficult."

The hope in her voice was so clear that he didn't have the heart to quash it completely. "I don't think so, but we will have to see how it goes."

A nod as she once again followed the ritual of folding up the wrapper for the protein bar she'd eaten and stowing it in the emergency bag. Indeed, the thing fairly crackled with all the spent wrappings they'd stored in there. It did prove one thing, however—as much as she might want to appear nonchalant about her race's impact on other worlds, she had never once suggested that they leave their trash behind.

By an unspoken signal, they turned northward once again, following the lure of the elusive beacon, that glowing green dot on the map display of her tablet. Lirzhan could only hope that the station would be more or less intact by the time they got there. After all, he didn't know how long it had been since the science team had done its survey and departed Mandala, and the place could have been overtaken by the native flora, or plundered by smugglers, or any of a number of different scenarios that would have rendered the data incorrect.

From time to time he allowed himself a surreptitious glance at Alexa, to make sure she was still faring well enough, that she hadn't begun to limp again because of the blister on her heel. But she appeared to be soldiering on, chin up, eyes fixed forward, scanning the landscape for any possible threats.

They crested the mountain pass—or rather, the hillside pass, for he was not sure whether these ranges really would qualify as mountains, rather than very tall foothills—and began their descent. Here the trees were also thick, but even as the landscape became gentler, he began to see open patches with some sort of wildflowers growing in shades of palest aquamarine and lavender, the ground underfoot rolling rather than studded with sudden outcroppings of rocks.

"You were right," Alexa said after a prolonged silence.

"I was?" Lirzhan responded, not sure what she meant, although all he sensed from her was, oddly enough, a feeling of contentment, of relaxation.

"It is beautiful here. I hope—I guess I hope the Consortium decides this world really isn't worth terraforming. Maybe it has really poor mineral wealth. I don't know."

He looked down at her then, shocked at her words, but at the same time trying not to show his surprise at her comment. Quietly, he said, "Well, perhaps it is far enough from the most-traveled space lanes that it's of little use."

"One can hope," she replied. They walked a little further in silence, through air thick with the scent of sweet pollen and filled with the low humming of some insect he couldn't identify. Then, her tone diffident, "Sorry I almost bit your head off back there. Automated defense systems kicking in and all that."

"It's fine." He didn't dare trust himself to say more.

"No, it's not fine." She paused then and gazed up at him, and that was a miracle in itself, that she should look up into his face without flinching, without subjecting him to the sort of needle-sharp stare that was a medical examination unto itself. "You hit on some truths there, and I really didn't want to acknowledge them."

"I suppose it is natural that we should all want to defend our home worlds."

"Yes…if they're worth defending in the first place."

He felt his eyebrows shoot up, and she grinned. It was the first wholly unguarded expression he had yet seen from her.

"Does that shock you?" She shook her head. "I guess being thrown into this kind of situation gives a person a chance for some reflection."

"And what have you been reflecting on?"

"Gaia. Me. Why I was here in the first place." She stopped. "All right, not *here* here, but why I was going to the Targus system at all."

"And why were you?" He purposely kept his tone soft, sensing that she was on the brink of some sort of revelation and not wanting to do anything that might prevent her from proceeding.

"Because it's what I was trained to think I wanted. Greater good of Gaia and all that." A low chuckle, and those beautiful sky-colored eyes turned up toward him.

"And you don't believe in the greater good of Gaia?" He knew the question was disingenuous, but he wanted to hear what she had to say.

"I would, if it were for the Gaian people, or the reha-bilitation of sectors of the planet itself. But the more time I spend out here, the less I actually believe that."

Although he knew they should keep pressing on, that their longed-for destination was still some kilometers ahead, he found his footsteps slowing. "And it's not?"

Her mouth tightened. "Not really. You know—everyone knows—that the corporations have had a stranglehold on our planetary government for centuries."

"I will allow that that is somewhat common knowledge."

"So the problem is, nothing we can do is purely altruistic because behind it is always that old chestnut: 'What's in it for me?' Or, more to the point, what's in it for corporations like MonAg or Hallbrecht or BlackSky?" She made a sound of disgust. "We got started down that path hundreds of years ago, and somehow we never managed to reverse our course."

There seemed to be little he could say, except, "I am sorry you have been put in such a position."

She scowled, and began walking forward again, hastening her stride as if to indicate that she thought she had already wasted enough time. "You don't know the half of it."

"Tell me."

A quick glance upward. "I'm not sure I should be telling you *all* my deep dark secrets, Lirzhan."

"I doubt they could really be that deep or dark."

"You might be surprised."

Perhaps he would, but as long as she was talking to him now, he wanted to encourage her, to learn as much as he possibly could. "Tell me."

A small sigh escaped her lips, even as she stepped over a patch of scree and continued their downward progress. "I'll probably regret this in the morning."

"Is telling the truth ever something we should regret?"

"You might be surprised."

He did not reply, but waited for her to go on. Speaking again would only interrupt her, and he didn't want to do anything to prevent her from continuing.

She seemed to sense that, and said, "I'll let you in on a dirty little secret. Everyone knows that the Consortium expects colonists to put in 'X' number of years to work off their passage and earn their homesteads. What they don't know is that they charge you for every member of your family, no matter how young they might be."

Lirzhan's eyebrows lifted, and she essayed a bitter little smile.

"Oh, yes, that's how I got thrown on the foster care system. My mother wanted off Gaia—I really don't know why she even had me. Probably one of those 'oops' things, even though our methods of contraception are extremely effective...when used properly. Anyway, she met someone new when I was a little over a year old, and ended up marrying him. Neither she nor her husband had any substantial prospects, and they fell for the GEC's propaganda hook, line, and sinker. Problem was, declaring me as their child would add another five years to their homestead mortgage."

Someone else might have thought she kept her gaze downcast merely because she was focusing on the downward slope of the ground beneath her feet, on navigating around the outcroppings of native blue-gray rock or the low shrubby bushes that had begun to supplant the trees in these lower elevations. Lirzhan knew better, however.

Still not looking at him, still picking her way between the various obstacles in her path, she went on, "Anyway, neither of them was from a family with any money or any position. The most they could look forward to was living in a dingy high-rise and working in a factory or low-level service job. The robot labor force that generations past expected would create utopia still hasn't materialized, and it's people like my mother and her husband who do most of the dirty work."

Lirzhan hadn't really thought about that aspect of Gaia's technological development. His own world had always focused on sustainable technologies, and never had much in the way of heavy industry. No greater status was assigned to, say, a university professor than someone who helped in the manufacture of starship parts. All these tasks were useful and necessary, and so no one's status was elevated over another's. But he decided to keep these facts to himself for now, partly from fear of interrupting her, and partly because he certainly did not want her to think he believed his people were superior simply because their ways were so different.

She glanced up at him, as if expecting some sort of comment, so he nodded in what he hoped was an encouraging way. Apparently it worked, for she went on, "When my mother realized she'd have to give the majority of the earnings from the homestead to the Consortium for fifteen years instead of ten, she and her husband decided it would be best if they left me behind. After all, they could always have another child—a child that was both of theirs—once they were settled on the homestead." A pause. Lirzhan could see the muscles working in her fine jaw. "So they went, and I was placed in foster care, because by that point I was almost two, and most people who are looking to adopt want infants. The government pays the foster parents, so while I'm sure some of them do it out of the kindness of their hearts, not all do. The ones I had certainly didn't."

"And you had no relatives who could step in?"

"None that I was aware of. My mother had left her family when she was young. They probably didn't even know I existed. I must have some relatives, but I never bothered to find them. Why should I? If they knew anything of what had happened to me, they certainly didn't do anything to change it." She gave a shrug, and in that one small gesture Lirzhan read all the years of anger, of doubt, of wondering why she should be thrown out like a piece of rubbish.

He said softly, "But you've done very well for yourself, despite them."

Another lift of her shoulders. "I suppose so. 'Compensating by overachieving,' as one psychologist put it. It's done. I survived. I just told you that story so you'd understand why sometimes it's hard for me to be too gung-ho about the Consortium's policies when it's those very policies that ruined my childhood. Anyway, that's enough story hour for now."

She picked up her pace and he followed, watching her with sorrowful eyes. How different from his own world, where every child was a blessing, especially these days, when a birth was an increasingly rare event. But he sensed that what she wanted now was silence, and he would honor her wishes in that.

He knew he could do no less for her.

EIGHT

WHAT THE HELL HAD POSSESSED HER to go and dump the sob story about her childhood on Lirzhan like that? All right, she'd begun by simply trying to explain herself, but that didn't mean she had to go into all the gory details. She'd told the Zhore things she hadn't even revealed to Trin, and he'd gotten closer to her than anyone else. Yes, all the dry facts of the matter were contained in her personnel file, along with her psych evaluations and aptitude tests and all the other mumbo jumbo the Gaian bureaucracy just loved to accumulate on all its citizens, so she knew her superiors had access to all those details. But otherwise her history was supposed to be confidential, and it would've stayed that way…if she'd only kept her mouth shut.

She couldn't begin to figure out what it was about Lirzhan that made her want to confide in him. All right, so something in his eyes was downright sympathetic, and he was a good and quiet listener, not the type to interrupt every sentence with his own input and opinions, but still....

Well, she couldn't do anything about it now. She thought she trusted him not to say anything to anyone else about what she'd told him, but that didn't change the fact that now he knew one of the Consortium's dirty little secrets, something she doubted its officials would really like to have spread around the galaxy. All colonists were required to sign confidentiality agreements, and the penalties for revealing the details of a homestead contract were painfully high. They had every reason in the world to keep their mouths shut.

But she didn't. She hadn't signed any damn agreement, that was for sure. Maybe one could argue that as an official of the Consortium government, she had a fiduciary responsibility to maintain its secrets as well, but the hell with that. It wasn't as if she'd granted an interview to a news agency or written a tell-all book. No, she'd only told one person, someone who wouldn't betray her confidence. At least, she was fairly certain he wouldn't.

He remained silent as they finished the last leg of their descent from the mountain pass. The ground began to level out, and even the low shrubby bushes began to disappear, giving way to a wide plain of billowing pale blue grass, broken only occasionally by a lone, wide-limbed tree here and there. She didn't want to acknowledge the way the sun kept dipping lower and lower to her left, how the light was beginning to fail. No, they *would* make it to that science station tonight, damn it.

Lirzhan came up beside her. For the last few kilometers he had kept back a pace or two, as if realizing that she needed her space, but now he held her tablet, clearly indicating that she needed to stop and look at it. So she took it from him and gave a quick glance at the display. "Seven kilometers to go. That's not much."

"True, but night is falling."

She knew that already. Somehow, though, hearing the words spoken out loud made her even more irritated by the fact. "Yes, but there isn't much out here in terms of decent places to camp. It's flat ground, easy to navigate. I think it would be better to keep going after dark. We have the lanterns, after all."

For a second or two he didn't reply, but lifted his head and appeared to survey the plain on which they stood. No analogue of the old American West here— they hadn't seen anything bigger than some small furry creatures that dashed away through the high grass as soon as they approached. This savannah might look like an alien version of the great plains, but there definitely weren't any Mandala versions of the bison here.

"All right," Lirzhan said at last, and reached into the emergency kit and pulled out one of the lanterns. "Shall I hold this while you navigate?"

"That should work," she replied. They didn't need the light quite yet, but she'd noticed that dusk didn't seem to linger for very long on this world. She was also noticing the way the brisk wind was playing with the ends of his long black hair, the way a few loose strands blew around his face. The fine profile was outlined against the dimming light, looking like one of those old reverse cameos, with the silhouette cut out of ebony or jet.

Then she told herself that she really shouldn't be paying attention to those sorts of things. All right, the unthinkable had happened, and she'd realized a Zhore could be attractive...handsome, even. Time to worry about what that meant later, after they were safely to the science station.

Then again, being stuck in confined quarters with him, waiting for help to come....

She shook her head and started walking, not bothering to look to see if he was following. Of course he would be. He'd stuck to her side this long, so she knew he wasn't about to let her get more than a few paces away.

The thought did cross her mind that they were awfully exposed out here, and waving a lantern around in the gathering darkness might be the best way to attract attention, but they were so close.... Besides, there'd been no sign of pursuit since they emerged from the cave. Whoever was gunning for them seemed to have decamped after losing their trail for the greater part of two days. And seven kilometers was nothing after all the ground they'd already covered.

With that thought in mind, she increased her pace, knowing that Lirzhan would match his strides to hers. She glanced down at the tablet, looked at the numbers on the screen gradually counting down as they walked, and watched the glowing green symbol for the science station grow brighter and brighter.

At some point she realized the sun had truly gone down, but with the Zhore holding the lantern before him, the way was illuminated almost as brightly as it would have been during the day. She jogged slightly to avoid one of those large spreading trees, then course-corrected once they were on the other side. Five kilometers to go…four kilometers…three….

A dark mass appeared before them, and she slowed down. Lirzhan lifted his lantern higher and stared forward. "Another forest, it seems," he said. "The station must be within its borders."

"I'll back off a little, then," she said, although with some reluctance. "I'm not really in the mood to blunder into one of those webs."

"If they're even in this wood at all. But yes, it's probably better to exercise caution."

The grass gave way to low shrubs, and then small trees clustered together. They increased in size as Alexa and Lirzhan moved forward, and within another half hour they were truly within the borders of the forest. It closed around them, dark and still, even the insects apparently going silent at the sound of the two off-world intruders moving through the trees.

And then she saw the building, a dark shape in a clearing, one that glowed pale once Lirzhan turned the lantern fully on it. It looked like the sort of standard prefab structure the GEC preferred—walls of extruded composite, flat roof with solar panels that glittered suddenly as the light struck them. The door was closed, the metal shutters on the windows locked down. In short, it looked exactly the way it should have: closed down and waiting for the next team who had need of it.

Something like a little sob of relief left her throat, and Alexa surged forward, only to have Lirzhan say,

"Wait."

"What?" she demanded. All she wanted was to be inside, to take off these damn boots and get a real shower and some food in her that wasn't a ration bar.

"We should look around first. Just because it appears undisturbed doesn't mean someone hasn't been here looking for us—or isn't still in the area, waiting for us to show up."

Of course he was right. She swallowed her disappointment and said, "Okay…which way?"

"Around to the left and behind, and then we'll circle back to the front." As he spoke he handed her the lantern, and reached to pull the pulse pistol from his belt.

She shifted the tablet to her left hand so she could hold the lantern with her right. Not much need for the tablet at the moment, anyway; it had gotten them where they needed to be.

They'd only taken a few steps before Lirzhan pointed at the ground. "Look."

There in the mud and trampled bluish grass were the outlines of several pairs of large booted feet. She wanted to say that maybe they'd been left behind by the GEC team before they cleared out, but she knew that wasn't very likely. The time stamp on the last report filed by the team was more than two standard years ago. No way a set of footprints could last that long, even in a more or less sheltered spot like this one.

She nodded, and followed him as he crept around the back of the station, pausing every few seconds to listen or smell or whatever it was that he was doing. It had become clear to her several days ago that his senses were sharper than hers, and that he had a lot more experience dealing with the great outdoors, so she was going to let him handle this, even if it meant yet another instance where she was relegated to sidekick status. But better a sidekick than dead.

He didn't seem to find anything, or hear anything, and so continued his progress around the building until they were back at the entrance.

"They were here approximately thirty hours ago, I think," he told her. "It was logical for this to be our destination. Luckily for us, they came here while we were still in the caves and their instruments were unable to detect us. I suppose there is always the chance they might come back, but it seems safe enough for now."

"Thank God," she replied, and reached out to open the door. From what she'd heard, it would be latched but not locked. Oftentimes these stations were abandoned completely, but if not, they were intended to be easily accessible.

The door swung open, the lights going on automatically overhead. On the laminate floor she saw at once evidence of more footprints, although nothing seemed to have been disturbed. "They searched the whole place, looks like."

"I wouldn't have expected anything less." He came in after her and gazed around the room with obvious interest.

Not that there was all that much to look at. As with most of these stations, the main room was a square, with a short hallway at one end that led to a bathroom and one or two bedrooms, depending on how big the team stationed here had been. The counters and tables were bare, since any valuable equipment would have been packed up and removed by the GEC team when they left. At one end was a small kitchen with a heating element, refrigeration unit, and sink.

She went to the cupboards above the heating element and wanted to cry with relief when she saw stacks of SRPs in there. "There's a good supply of standard ration packs, so we can say goodbye to the protein bars." Before he could ask the question, she added, "And there are some marked as vegan, so you don't need to worry about that."

"Excellent." He set the emergency kit down on one of the tables. "I'll admit that after that trek across the plains, I am a bit hungry."

"Just a bit?" she teased, and was rewarded with a flash of white teeth. Damn, he did have a nice smile.

"Actually, I am very hungry." He came to her and took the SRP she handed him. "How does it work?"

"Just pull the tab, and it'll self-heat."

A puzzled expression crossed his face. "Then why the heating unit?"

"For boiling water, that sort of thing." She selected a package that advertised itself as chicken marsala, then pulled out a couple of plates from the cupboard and heavy-duty plastic flatware from the drawer immediately beneath. After she'd set those items down on the table, she pulled the tab on her SRP. As she waited for the requisite thirty seconds to pass, she said, "Check to see if the water supply is still working."

He went to the tap and turned it. Water came out immediately, and she let out an audible sigh of relief.

"Should I test it?" he inquired.

"You can if you want, but it should be quadruple filtered. These GEC teams don't take chances." *Not like we did down in the caves, or before that, drinking from the streams…but beggars can't be choosers.*

Appearing to accept this explanation, he returned to the cupboard and found some plastic tumblers, then filled them almost to the top. He handed one to her, and she drank deeply. It did taste better than what they'd taken from the streams, probably because of the multiple filtration processes it had undergone.

The tab on her SRP turned red, indicating that it was ready. She tore open the pouch and dumped it on her plate, inhaling the rich scent. All right, it probably smelled better than it tasted, but after four days of protein bars, it was going to be ambrosia.

On the other side of the table, Lirzhan had performed a similar procedure with his own meal, which looked to be some sort of roasted vegetables on rice. He sniffed appreciatively before picking up his fork and taking a few bites. After chewing for a few seconds, he swallowed, then nodded. "It is not bad."

"Gourmet it's not, but it'll keep us going until help arrives." She helped herself to some of her own dish, judging it a little too salty but otherwise just what the doctor ordered. "Speaking of which, we'll need to find the beacon."

Lirzhan scanned the room briefly, then turned back to her, his expression troubled. "I don't see anything that looks like any sort of computer or automated device."

"They wouldn't leave it lying out, just in case." A few years ago she'd read a series of write-ups on GEC procedures, mainly because she was helping to write a brief for one of her superiors on the subject. "It might be in one of the cupboards here, or back in one of the bedrooms. We can check after we're done eating."

"Very good."

After that conversation ceased for a while, since both of them were too busy filling stomachs that hadn't felt satisfied for days. It was only after Alexa had scraped the very last of the sauce off her plate and drained her glass of water that she felt ready for further exploration. Lirzhan was still eating, as he seemed more inclined to savor each mouthful rather than inhale them the way she had. Maybe not her most elegant moment, but she wasn't going to worry about that right now.

"I'll check the cupboards," she said, and pushed out her chair. There was a small sanitizer on the right side of the sink, just large enough to accommodate half a dozen plates and glasses, with accompanying flatware. She put her used items in it, then opened the cupboard that held the remaining dishware to see if the beacon had been secreted up there. Generally, the beacons were small square devices that could fit in the palm of your hand, and so it would be easy enough to stash one anywhere. However, she didn't find it in the dish cupboard, nor in the one that served as a makeshift pantry.

"Must be in back," she told Lirzhan.

He nodded, even as he rose from his seat and brought his own used plate and glass over to the sanitizer. "Do you want me to help you look?"

"No, that's all right." They'd have to figure out the sleeping arrangements sooner or later, but for right now she thought it would help if she could poke around in the other rooms first and get the lay of the land before she had to cross that particular hurdle.

No reply, although he did step out of the way so she could pass him and go on down the short corridor on the other side of the room. As she'd thought, there was a small, extremely utilitarian bathroom with a toilet, sink, and cramped shower enclosure. Luxury bathing was definitely not in the offing here, but a shower of any sort would be heavenly, cramped or no.

She supposed it would have been too much to expect for there to be two bedrooms here. No, she found only the one, small and spare and with two sets of bunk beds, each of them on opposite sides of the room, with a closet on the empty wall facing the door. The beds had all been neatly made up, gray blankets smoothed flat, pillows in place. It seemed the last team to be stationed here had strictly followed protocol; this wasn't always the case, as she'd read that some teams left the stations in some disarray as they moved on to their next assignment.

Glad that the place looked more or less serviceable, despite there being only one bedroom, she went immediately to the closet and opened the sliding metal door. Inside were five or six empty hangers and—wonder of wonders—two pairs of black coveralls hanging at the very back. Coveralls might not be the height of fashion, but at least they were clean, and one of them appeared to be smaller than the other, clearly intended for a woman.

On the shelf above the clothes rack were spare blankets and pillows. Alexa went up on her tiptoes and felt between the blankets. Sure enough, her fingers closed around a square metal object, and she pulled it out in some triumph.

It was a small gray cube with a data port on one side, intended to be hooked up to an external device such as a tablet or computer. Clutching it in one hand, she took it out to the front room and set it down on the table.

"Ah, so that is the device," Lirzhan said, looking at it with some curiosity but not picking it up. "I can see why it would be easy to conceal. So what now?"

"We hook it up to this," she replied, and pulled her tablet out of the emergency kit. A push on the side, and a thin cord with a data connector extended from the interior. She attached it to the beacon. Immediately her tablet lit up, showing an unfamiliar screen, one that the beacon itself must be generating.

Every member of the Consortium's government, whether in the military, the Exploration Commission, or the Diplomatic Corps, had been taught the code to send out a general SOS. Alexa knew she wouldn't have to provide their coordinates, since the beacon would automatically embed those in the outgoing message. But as she settled her fingertips on the screen to begin typing in the first sequence of letters, Lirzhan's voice stopped her.

"Perhaps we should consider where we are sending that before we go any further."

Puzzled, she shot a wary glance up at him, although she did stop typing. "What do you mean?"

His expression was almost studiously neutral. "I mean that we do not know who it was that shot down our shuttle, or who attempted to pursue and neutralize us here. By no means am I saying it was anyone from the Consortium…but I know for a fact that it could not have been any of my own people."

"Oh, really?" she inquired in acid tones. "And how can you be so very sure?"

"Because my people do not murder, Alexa. I will allow that perhaps—*perhaps*—the shuttle being pulled from subspace was some sort of mistake. But being fired upon immediately afterward was certainly no accident, and neither was being shot at by whoever was piloting that skimmer. These are not the actions of my people."

She wanted to retort that they weren't the actions of her people, either, but she knew that would be a bald-faced lie. Humans had been murdering one another for millennia before they emerged into the wider galaxy and began killing members of other races as well.

"So what do you want me to do?" she asked. "This thing is hard-coded to send its messages to the GEC HQ on Gaia. I don't know how to reprogram it. Do you?"

This last question was flung at him as a challenge. She halfway expected him to say that yes, of course he could, just as he'd been able to handle every single obstacle they'd faced so far without even batting an eye.

But he shook his head, saying, "No, I don't have that sort of training. But please, let us consider this for a while. The last thing we want is to draw unwanted attention."

She couldn't argue with that, much as she would have liked to. Yes, getting off Mandala was a priority... but so was staying alive. "All right," she said, after a long pause. "Let's sleep on it. First, though, I'm getting that shower."

And she got up and went past him, heading back into the bedroom so she could check the one small chest of drawers to see if it contained anything of use. Glory of glories, there were two undershirts, and a package of unopened underwear. Yes, it was men's underwear, but she wasn't going to quibble at this point. At least it was clean.

After that it was just hot water and soap and the miracle of scrubbing away the last of Mandala's dirt and grime, feeling some of her worry and exhaustion rinse away with the soap and shampoo. They weren't out of the woods yet, but it was a lot easier to be hopeful when you weren't caked with several days' worth of grime and sweat.

She got out of the shower and dried herself off with a folded towel from the shelf above the toilet. The undershirt and briefs were next, and she almost had to laugh at the sight of herself in the oversized clothing. To keep the briefs from slipping down too far, she rolled the waistband several times. There was a clothing sanitizer mounted on the wall on the other side of the shower stall, and she shoved her own much-abused underwear and skirt and jacket into it. No, it wouldn't be quite the same as having them properly cleaned, but at least she'd be able to wear them again without feeling disgusted at the prospect.

As she exited the bathroom, she almost bumped into Lirzhan, who apparently was heading back from the bedroom. No doubt he'd been inspecting the sleeping arrangements.

Although he kept his gaze steady on her face, she couldn't help blushing a little at the amount of leg she was currently showing. All right, she'd flashed her entire bare back at him when she was getting out of her wet camisole and into her jacket after their dip in the lake, but that wasn't really the same thing.

"It's all yours," she said steadily, refusing to show any more of her discomfiture than she already had.

His eyes widened slightly. "I beg your pardon?"

She jerked her chin in the direction of the bathroom. "The shower? And there was some clean underwear in the bedroom. I took one pair, but—"

In response he lifted his left hand, showing a wad of gray fabric. "I did locate those, and the other shirts, which I assume are some sort of undergarment." At last his gaze did stray from her face somewhat lower, but since the neckband of the undershirt came up past her collarbone, it wasn't as if she was showing much there.

"Okay, good," she said hastily. Those green eyes seemed a little too clear, too searching. "Well, enjoy your shower. The hot water was still going strong, so it should be good to go."

No one could have accused him of being imperceptive, and he took the dismissal for what it was, inclining his head and moving past her into the bathroom. Alexa hurried down into the bedroom, noted that he'd draped his robes across the foot of one of the bottom bunk beds, and took the other one, sinking down onto the hard mattress with a sigh of relief. At the moment it felt just as good as the most advanced body-conforming heat-activated foam bed ever invented.

She pulled back the covers and slid between them, then pulled the blankets up to her chin. The pillow was memory foam and comfortable enough, so she wasn't too worried about the mattress. It was still worlds better than the floor of a cave.

Although she hadn't expected to fall asleep so quickly, had thought she'd be able to stay awake until Lirzhan returned, weariness won out. Almost as soon as her eyes shut, she was gone, slipping away into the dark, leaving her worries for the following day.

NINE

HER QUIET, REGULAR BREATHING told him she was sleep. Moving quietly, he went to the switch and turned down the lights until they were just barely there, just enough that he could see if he needed to get up in the middle of the night and move about the room.

He could not fault Alexa for falling asleep so quickly. They had walked a great many kilometers today, and that, coupled with the first full meal she'd had in days, was certainly more than enough to send her deeply into slumber. Even so, he wished they could have spoken more, made some plan for the next morning. It was good that she'd agreed to delay activating the beacon until they could do it in a safe manner, but they would have to do something soon.

And there had been that flash of red in her cheeks as she realized he was looking at her, even though he'd tried not to stare. No woman of his people would have ever shown so much of her legs, of course, and he supposed the sight had startled him somewhat. He knew on some worlds the women wore even less than what she currently had on, but he had never visited any of those planets.

Her legs were very lovely.

A heat that had nothing to do with the hot shower he'd just taken moved over him, and he sucked in a deep breath, pushing his thoughts away from the sight of her legs…the memory of the smooth, pale skin of her back as she'd hurriedly slipped out of her wet clothes and into her jacket.

This would never do.

He lay down then and pulled the meager covers over him, making himself breathe steadily, letting his thoughts grow calm. Yes, Alexa Craig was very distracting, but she was not the only one who needed a good night's sleep. They had reached a haven here, it seemed, and he should make use of it.

His breathing deepened, and he began the slow slide into darkness that prefaced the true sleep, the place where dreams lived. Just as he began to approach oblivion, he heard odd little muffled whimpers coming from the bunk where Alexa lay, and at once Lirzhan's eyes snapped open again.

She was huddled into a ball, the covers pulled up almost to her chin. Even in the dimly lit room he could see the way her eyelids were twitching, how her body made terrified little jerks, as if she were fighting off some unseen assailant.

For a second or two he hesitated, wondering if he should let it alone. Perhaps the nightmare would pass soon. But the distress was rolling off her in waves, and he had to hope that she'd rather be woken up than left to suffer whatever visions were currently roiling her subconscious mind.

Moving quietly, he slipped out from under the covers and crossed the room to her bedside, then knelt on the floor next to her. With a gentle hand he reached out and touched her shoulder. "Alexa."

She shuddered but did not wake. He made both his grip and his tone a little firmer. "*Alexa.*"

This time her eyes shot open, and she reached out and smacked his hand away. "What?"

"You were having a bad dream."

She blinked, and the wide, staring look she'd had when she awakened disappeared. One hand went to her head. "Yes, I was. Sorry. Did I wake you?"

"I hadn't really fallen asleep yet," he replied, keeping his voice low, reassuring. "Are you all right?"

"Of course I am," she told him, her tone just a little too hearty. "It was just a dream. Strange bed, I guess."

He could have pointed out that she had suffered no such bad dreams the past few nights when they had slept leaning against a cave wall. Or mentioned that she'd slept well enough when she was snuggled up next to him. Either remark probably would not meet with a positive reception, however, and so he nodded and simply said, "Perhaps."

The logical thing to do next would be to get back on his feet and return to his own bed—and hope he would not be awakened in such a manner a second time. For some reason he seemed unable to move, though, and continued to kneel there and watch her, and note how some of her damp hair had pulled itself out of the braid she'd used to contain it, or the way her deep blue eyes appeared so very dark in the subdued overhead lighting.

"What?" she asked, her tone somehow curious rather than irritated, which was the reaction he had expected, what with him remaining there like a fool instead of going sensibly back to sleep.

He knew then that if he did not take the first step, she would never allow the fragile connection between them to develop any further. From time to time he'd seen it in her eyes, seen the interest, the attraction, but she would not acknowledge it for some reason, wanted to pretend it did not exist. And perhaps he would suffer the consequences, would anger her so greatly that she would not permit any further contact between the two of them. Then again, how much risk was there, when he knew if he let it alone, matters would remain at an impasse?

So he leaned in, and pressed his mouth against hers.

This couldn't be happening. This couldn't be Lirzhan—proper, reserved, *alien* Lirzhan—kissing her.

But it was. *He* was.

And...oh, God. Nothing had ever prepared her for the wave of heat that washed over her the second his lips touched hers, the sudden sense that no one else's lips could match hers like this, that no one else's mouth and tongue could taste so sweet. She reached out and pulled him toward her, felt his long, slick hair brush over her bare arms, sensed the strength of the body pressed against hers.

She wanted more then, wanted all of him, as insane as that sounded. It wasn't even that she could call herself deprived—after all, Trin had given her a pretty decent send-off, and that hadn't even been a full standard week ago. But this wave of need, of lust, was as alien to her as the Zhore himself was.

With a gasp she pulled herself away and stared into his face. His green eyes met hers without pretense, without looking away. She saw in them the same desire that pulsed within her, like a planet with a fiery molten core buried beneath a layer of ice.

"I didn't—" she began, then broke off, shaking her head. "I don't—what the hell was *that?*"

"*Sayara,*" he said simply.

She'd never heard the word before and assumed it had to be a Zhore term. "What is *sayara*?" *Besides red-hot scorching lust, that is...*

"It is the feeling two people share when they are compatible on every level of their souls. It is at the center of our culture, our world. And...you and I share it."

The words were Galactic Standard, but they didn't make much sense. "I don't understand," she said slowly, struggling to sit up. "How can we share a compatibility like that when we're not even the same race?"

Seeming to understand her need for a little distance, Lirzhan moved a few inches away. His gaze, however, remained locked on hers. "My people don't have an answer for that yet. It was only very recently that we discovered the *sayara* bond could be shared with a human. It has not occurred between the Zhore and any of the other humanoid races, so we are not sure if it is specifically a Zhore/human phenomenon or not."

Mind reeling, Alexa latched on to the only thing that seemed to make sense of any of this. "So, what...are you saying you were on board that shuttle because you knew we shared this connection?"

At once he shook his head. "No, not at all. I had never met you before then, or even been in close proximity to you, so I would not have felt it earlier." He actually smiled, and although she felt that she should be angry with him, even if she wasn't exactly sure why, it was difficult to be too upset when looking at that smile...or feeling the pulse of need for him deep within her core. "Believe me, Alexa, I was as surprised then as you are right now."

"You sure didn't show it."

"Those hoods do have their uses."

Despite herself, she chuckled. "All right, you have a point." So many questions were running through her brain, she wasn't sure which one to ask first. But since she had to say something, she remarked, "You've felt it during the past few days…and said nothing to me."

"What could I have said? Your reputation preceded you, Alexa. I was very certain of our *sayara* connection, but announcing such a thing to 'the Ice Queen' upon first acquaintance seemed unlikely to provoke a positive response."

If anyone else had used that epithet to her face, she would have told them to go to hell. Lirzhan, however, wore such a rueful expression that once again she couldn't be angry. Much.

"I will admit that sometimes I can be a little… unapproachable."

"Just a little," he said, and reached out to touch her hand.

The feel of those thousands of tiny scales on his fingers, rather than repulsing her, sent a shiver down her spine. They were so marvelously tactile. The heat returned as she wondered if he had those scales every-where…and what they might feel like against her.

Inside her.

God, I really have lost my mind. She shook her head, trying to free it of those completely out-of-character thoughts. Even so, she didn't pull her hand away from his. His fingers felt too good clasping hers. "So what now?"

"Whatever you want," he said simply. "I will not push you, Alexa, or do anything that makes you feel uncomfortable. This must be somewhat strange for you—although I have to say I was encouraged when I heard you mention that your previous relationship was with an Eridani. At least that proved you have an open mind when it comes to such things."

Well, there was open, and then there was *open*. Lots of Gaians dated Eridanis, married Eridanis, had children with Eridanis. There was a long and glorious tradition of the two races intermingling. But the Zhore? Most of the galaxy wasn't even sure whether they were humanoid or not.

"I don't…." The words trailed off, and she shook her head. "I'm not going to deny that I'm attracted to you, that there's something…but I don't know where to go from here." All right, part of her did—directly to pulling him into the bunk with her and putting out the fire he'd kindled. But that would only complicate things further. At the moment all they'd shared was a kiss. If they slept together—*oh, don't be coy, Alexa*—if they had sex, that would be opening a whole new can of worms. A really big can of worms.

Lirzhan appeared to sense her turmoil, for he squeezed her fingers gently before withdrawing his hand. "Right now, we don't have to go anywhere. We are both tired, and we should try to get some rest. I am willing to wait as long as necessary."

That's very noble of you. I just hope I can do the same. She only nodded, though, and said, "That's probably a good idea. I'll try not to wake you up with any more nightmares."

And what that nightmare had been, she couldn't even remember. Something about running through the dark, something chasing her, but nothing more concrete than that remained. Just as well, she supposed.

To her surprise, he leaned down and kissed her again, this time on the cheek, softly and quickly. Then he rose and went back to his own bunk.

Since when could a simple kiss on the cheek make her insides melt? But his did. She reached up and touched her fingertips to her cheekbone, as if she could still feel the warmth of his lips there.

You, Alexa, are in very big trouble....

No doubt. But she knew she'd be in even worse trouble if she didn't get some sleep tonight, so she rolled over on her side again and tried to pretend that she couldn't hear the creaking of the bunk across the room as Lirzhan settled himself on the mattress, or see the gleam of his eyes in the darkness.

And eventually she pretended enough that she convinced herself to fall asleep.

Some hours passed. Exactly how many, he didn't know, as he was not attuned to this world's rhythms the way he was to his beloved Zhoraan. He had slept, that much he knew, slept and dreamed of holding Alexa in his arms. That she was so near and yet so far troubled him, but he knew he should be glad that she had responded the way she did. The taste of her lips was sweeter than anything he could have imagined, and she had kissed him back, hadn't pulled away or protested. She was troubled by the situation, of course, but he could not fault her for that. In time he knew that he would not be sleeping alone.

Something had awakened him, though, some prickling of unease. No, his people were not precisely psychic, but they were sensitive...and he could feel the edges of negative emotions or intentions or whatever one wanted to call them intruding against his consciousness.

He sat up in bed, glad that he had put his trousers on over the strange Gaian underwear. His tunic and robes remained where he had left them, draped over the foot of the bunk. Moving quietly, as much to avoid disturbing Alexa as to keep from alerting anyone or anything that might be lurking outside, he reached into the bundle of clothing and drew out the pulse pistol. It was a weapon of last resort, but he knew he would not hesitate to use it to protect Alexa and himself. The Gaians sneered at the Zhore behind their backs, calling them pacifists, as if that word were an insult, but Lirzhan did not take it as such. A peaceful solution was always best, but if one did not present itself, then so be it.

A few soft, cat-like paces, and he was out the door and down the corridor. As a precaution, Alexa had locked the door to the station and closed the storm shutters, so Lirzhan guessed it would be almost impossible for any wild creatures to gain entry. The so-called "civi-lized" kind of creature, however....

Pulses of negative energy beat against him as soon as he entered the front room. They had shut off the lights in here before retiring for the night, and so the glow-ing cherry-red circle of metal around the lock told him something was very, very wrong.

He dropped into a crouch at once, using the table where they had eaten their evening meal as cover. Peering between its legs, he saw a flare of sudden light, then heard a clank as the lock came free from the door and fell to the floor. Almost at the same time the door itself swung inward, and human males dressed in dark clothing entered the room, weapons drawn. Although he could not read their thoughts directly, he still felt the malice radiating from them, the intention to kill who-ever they found.

Irzhaan, forgive me for the lives I must take.

The first pulse bolt hit the lead man in the head, and he fell at once. His companions swore, and began to fire back in Lirzhan's direction. Luckily, though, the table took the brunt of the damage, and he shot through its legs, aiming upward, hitting another of the men in the stomach. The intruder dropped to his knees, cursing and shrieking in pain, while the lone man still standing continued to fire at Lirzhan. Bits and pieces of the table and its surrounding chairs began to explode outward under the assault, and he knew he wouldn't be able to hide there much longer.

"Hey—were you looking for me?" Alexa called out, and the man immediately turned to fire in her direction. She dropped to the floor, and Lirzhan took advantage of her attacker's brief distraction to shoot him again twice—first in the knee so he stumbled and lost his balance, and then right through the neck. He slumped to the floor and lay there, unmoving.

"You all right?" she asked Lirzhan, although she did not come to check on him. Instead, she went directly to the man with the stomach wound.

"He's still—"

Lirzhan had meant to say "armed" but didn't have enough time, as she apparently spotted the man's dropped pulse pistol and kicked it away from his desperately straining fingers, then bent over and picked it up herself. She pointed it at the man's head. "Talk."

"Go fuck yourself," he said, clutching his stomach and groaning.

"Well, that's not very professional," she said, then looked over at Lirzhan. "Check the other ones—see if they're carrying any identification."

He pushed himself up from the wreckage of the table and chairs, and went over to the last man he'd shot, as he was closest. Pulse wounds tended to self-cauterize, so there wasn't a great deal of blood. Even so, Lirzhan was not exactly comfortable being so close to the aftermath of that brief round of violence.

But as he did not wish to appear squeamish in front of Alexa, he squatted down next to the dead man and began going through his pockets. All of them were empty, although he did have a second pistol still in its holster and several spare battery packs attached to his belt.

"We're—not—amateurs," the gut-shot man mumbled, his eyes turning glassy. Going into shock, perhaps?

"Well, I'm not so sure about that, considering a couple of diplomats just got the drop on you," Alexa replied coolly. One would have thought she was facing him across a negotiating table while wearing her most tailored suit, instead of standing there in men's underwear and a T-shirt that almost covered up the briefs, the shirt was so long on her.

"Blow me."

Lirzhan reflected on the curiosities of human invective while going over to the first man he'd shot and performing a similar inspection. Nothing there, either.

Despite his deteriorating state, the wounded man couldn't seem to stop staring at Lirzhan as he went about these tasks. "So that's what you look like under those robes. Freaky."

While he himself really didn't care what the mercenary—or whatever he was—thought of his appearance, apparently Alexa did not share those sentiments.

"He's a darn sight better-looking than you," she said coldly. Then she knelt down next to him and placed the muzzle of the pulse pistol against his temple. "You might want to start talking."

"Don't have anything to say."

"I find that highly unlikely," Lirzhan said, as he had completed his search of the second man and found nothing. "Who sent you?"

"Santa Claus."

The words had no meaning for him, and Lirzhan shot a puzzled glance at Alexa. She scowled, saying, "Kids' stories. He's just messing with us."

The man grinned, although his breath was beginning to rattle in his throat. It was clear enough that he required immediate medical attention. The station probably had a first aid kit of some kind, more extensive than the rudimentary supplies included with the emergency bag, but Lirzhan doubted that would be enough to save their attacker. No, he needed surgery and a real medical team…both of which were in short supply on Mandala.

Then Alexa got down on her knees and began rifling through the man's pockets with her left hand while keeping the pulse pistol pointed at his temple. Lirzhan could feel the pulse of animosity before the fallen mercenary even moved. The man reached up, trying to grab Alexa's wrist. She started and pulled the trigger, sending a bright green flash of energy directly into his temple at close range. His head fell back against the laminate floor with a sharp *crack*.

"Dammit," she said softly, and got to her feet.

Despite her studiously casual expression, Lirzhan could tell she was shaken. "Are you all right?"

She appeared to ponder the question for a few seconds, as if she were not entirely sure what he meant.

Then she replied, "Well, I just shot a man in the head. It's not really something I've done before, so I suppose I'm trying to process what it means."

At once Lirzhan went to her and took her in his arms. For the briefest of seconds she remained stiff, not allowing herself to relax into his embrace. But then she buried her head against his chest and took a deep breath.

"I probably shouldn't have shot him."

"You did the right thing," Lirzhan said, and reached up to stroke her hair down to its tangled braid. "He was trying to take the gun from you so he could shoot you. You were only protecting yourself."

She lifted her head and stared into his eyes. Her own looked strained, the pupils dark, dilated, but he did not see anything worse than that in her gaze. "I thought the Zhore were pacifists."

"We are, up to a point. There is nothing wrong with defending oneself."

"You continue to surprise me every day, Lirzhan." Very gently she pulled away from him and surveyed the room, taking in the bodies of their three downed assailants. "I doubted they walked here. So let's see what they've left for us, since they didn't oblige us by carrying any ID or anything else to help us figure out who they are."

"Would you rather not wait until morning?"

"No," she said shortly, going to the ruin of the door. Well, the door itself was more or less intact, but with a hole where the combination lock/latch had been located,

it wasn't going to do much good in keeping anything...
or anyone...out. She pushed it open an inch and peered
outside, clearly making sure the men hadn't left a companion outside before she moved out of the station.

He followed her out the door. The air was cool
and damp, and although it was still very dark beyond
the pool of light provided by the security light next to
the door, he could feel the hush around the world that
seemed to suggest dawn was not far off.

"Jackpot," Alexa said, hurrying over to the skimmer
parked a few yards off among the trees.

It looked identical to the one that had been shooting at them several days earlier, and he guessed the men
they had dispatched were those same unknown assailants. He could see that it was a small open-cockpit craft
intended for low-level atmospheric flight, with wheels
and heavy tires for transport over rough terrain and a
retractable roof. Most likely the tires and wheels tucked
up into the undercarriage when the vehicle was in the
air.

"This would have come in handy a few days ago,"
Lirzhan remarked, as she opened the door and climbed
inside. "But as it certainly won't get us off-planet, I am
not sure how much good it is going to do us now."

She glanced over at him, and even in the gloom he
could see the lift of her eyebrows. "No, of course it won't
get us off-planet, but it'll get us back to wherever they
came from. They've got to have a base of operations
somewhere. I'll just pull up the trip log and backtrack us

to where they came from. They'll have left a larger ship capable of interstellar flight there."

"And do you know how to pilot such a ship?" he asked gently, not wishing to quash her enthusiasm too badly.

"No." She pushed a lock of wayward hair off her forehead, and seemed to be thinking furiously. "But any ship designed to travel between star systems will have a subspace comm system, one that's not programmed to call home directly to GEC HQ the way our emergency beacon is. So we'll use that to contact someone to come get us. You can even get in touch with your superiors on Zhoraan if it makes you more comfortable."

For her to make such a concession told him how much her attitude toward him had changed, even if she were not yet prepared to admit such a thing openly. And he had to confess that her plan seemed sound enough.

"What if there are more mercenaries—or whatever they were—back at this ship you're convinced is there?"

She actually smiled, her teeth flashing in the darkness. "Well, we didn't do too bad a job of handling these three, so it might not be that big a problem. Or they might not have left anyone there at all. Why bother to mount a guard when you've landed on an uninhabited planet?"

"Perhaps. And we will have their guns as well. But I would suggest changing into more appropriate attire before we leave."

A quick glance down at herself, and she smiled and shook her head. "You're right, of course. Well, let's get changed and packed and out of here as quickly as we can, just in case those men did leave a companion behind, someone who might be expecting a check-in call from them at any moment."

"Good point. Very well—let us get what we can, and start moving."

She let herself out of the skimmer and came back to the station, striding past him and inside, then heading on to the bedroom. Once there, she pulled a set of coveralls out of the closet and drew them on over the undershirt and underpants she already wore.

"I figured this would be a little more practical than a skirt and jacket," she explained, tucking the legs of the coveralls into her boots before strapping her belt around her waist. The coveralls were somewhat big for her, and puffed out slightly both above and below the belt.

Lirzhan smothered a smile. "You're probably right." He gathered up his robes and put them on, although he did not draw the hood over his head. Not yet, anyway.

If Alexa was bothered by his wearing the robes once more, she didn't show it. A quick nod, and she went on into the bathroom, taking the spare towels and some soap—"just in case"—before she headed out to the front room and gathered up several days' worth of SRPs.

"I don't want to strip the place bare, just in case another research team gets sent here," she explained as she shoved her loot into the now over-extended emergency bag. "But I also don't know what we're going to find at that ship, so I figured we'd better play it safe."

He couldn't really argue with that. Perhaps he would have raised some protest if she'd attempted to take any more than she had, but as it was....

"Are we going to do anything about them?" he asked, looking down at the bodies of the three dead men, still sprawled on the floor.

"Well, since we don't really have the equipment to bury them or burn them, what do you suggest we do?"

"Drag them outside. If there are any predators or scavengers in these woods, they should take care of them for us."

Her eyes widened. "That is...remarkably realistic of you."

"Is it?" He had not thought of the matter that way. Even predators and scavengers had their place in the natural order of things, and in this situation they would be providing a necessary service. "No worse than leaving them in here to rot. Besides, at least that way some animals may be fed, and since these men are long past worrying about such things, it seems the simplest way to handle the problem."

A reluctant nod. "Okay." She went over to the man she'd shot in the head, as he was closest to the door. "Give me a hand with this?"

TEN

IT HAD BEEN, AS ONE OF HER FOSTER MOTHERS liked to say, a hell of a day. And the sun wasn't even up yet.

Alexa sat in the pilot's seat of the skimmer, as Lirzhan said he had no idea how to operate the vehicle. She wasn't sure whether knowing how to drive a ground transport made her that much more qualified, but she hadn't bothered to argue. If she kept them just above the trees and didn't try anything fancy, she figured they should be okay.

It had only taken a few minutes to figure out the onboard log and program it to retrace its trip to the science station. Judging by the maps scrolling across the screen on the dashboard, their destination was some hundred and fifty kilometers away, which meant a journey of a little less than an hour in a vehicle of this type. An old boyfriend had owned one that was similar, if an older model, and so she had a basic idea of their speed rating. Behind them the horizon began to glow, which meant they were traveling due west.

Lirzhan pulled out a breakfast bar from the rations she had taken and handed it to her. "I don't really see how these are different from the protein bars," he said, opening one for himself and sniffing at it dubiously.

"They are. They're made with fruit and grains—you'll be fine."

He took a cautious bite, and then smiled. "Yes, this is much better."

"Told you."

If someone had told her she'd ever be this at ease with him, especially after sharing a kiss that redefined what a kiss should feel like, she'd have told that hypothetical person they were crazy. And let's not forget the shoot-'em-up with the mercs and dragging the bodies out of the station one by one and leaving them for the Mandala equivalent of wolves or vultures or whatever.

But now....

She sneaked a quick peek at Lirzhan and watched for a few seconds as he munched quietly away on his breakfast bar, his gaze seeming to study the landscape as it passed by roughly forty meters beneath them. The cool morning breeze caught the loose strands of long black hair around his face and whipped them to and fro, but he didn't seem to mind.

What exactly they were heading toward, she didn't know for sure. Maybe the mercs had only been dropped off here rather than flying their own ship. But she and

Lirzhan had brought the beacon with them, so they could always use it wherever they ended up, rather than back at the science station. And the skimmer had provided them with some much-needed mobility.

No need to worry about fuel, as the cell on board would last through more than a thousand trips such as this. Right now it just felt good to be up in the wind and the sun, watching the blue-green forests pass by below them, broken here and there by the shimmer of a stream, and once by an enormous calm lake surrounded by rocky shores.

Lirzhan was right; it was beautiful here.

The instrument panel pinged, signaling that they were closing in on their destination. Below them, the ground had grown rocky again, the trees thinning out as they climbed into yet another unknown range.

"I'm going to bring us down a little bit at a time, in case the men who came after us left anyone behind," she told Lirzhan, and he nodded, then said,

"Luckily, at first they shouldn't notice anything wrong…until we get close enough for them to actually see who's in the skimmer."

"Well, aside from the fact that they were probably expecting their missing friends to have checked in by now. But that can't be helped."

She dropped lower so they were barely skimming the ground, not quite a meter and a half in the air. The rocky terrain slipped past. Getting closer now…

…and she let out a surprised yelp and banked hard

left to avoid coming up on an enormous edifice, all steel girders and flat metal plate, covering at least an acre. Past it she could see heavy earth-moving equipment, but no people.

Without thinking she turned them around, speeding back the way they had come. Beside her, Lirzhan sat up very straight, asking, "What was *that?*"

"I don't know," she said, practically biting out the words to keep her voice from shaking. "It looked like some sort of mining operation."

"Mining operation?" he repeated, casting one last look over his shoulder, even though they'd dipped below the ridge line and the facility was effectively hidden. "I thought you said this planet had been designated as 'containing no exploitable resources.'"

"That's what the write-up said!" she snapped, the jangle of adrenaline along her nerve endings making the words come out far more abruptly than she'd intended. "Look, is anyone following us?"

He unfastened the safety harness he wore and stood up, black hair whipping like crazed snakes around his head. After turning around and surveying the horizon in all directions, he said, "I don't see anyone."

"Well, that's something." Probably they hadn't gotten close enough for anyone on the ground to get a good look at who was really piloting the skimmer. The vehicle itself wouldn't raise any eyebrows, since it had clearly come from the base itself. "We're coming back up on some trees—I'm going to land us there so we can figure out what to do next."

Slowing down, she brought the vehicle lower until it glided between the first few outlying trees. They settled with a soft *thump* on a patch of pale olive-colored grass, and Alexa relaxed her death grip on the controls.

Lirzhan remained standing. He gazed down at her for a few seconds, then extended a hand. She took it and followed him out of the skimmer. How he knew she needed to stand on firm ground to gather her thoughts, she had no idea, but she was grateful for his perceptivity.

"So…" he said at last.

"So," she said heavily, and reached up to push some loose hair off her forehead. She really had done a crap job with that braid this morning. "I have no idea what's going on here, but I'm pretty sure it's nothing good."

"Surely it's only an illegal mining operation," Lirzhan replied. "Of course these things should not be encouraged because of the damage they do to the environment, but…."

"I don't think that's all it is." Alexa couldn't even say why exactly, but something about this really didn't smell right. "That facility looked far too big for anything unregulated. There are outfits that drop small refining stations on out-of-the-way worlds, hoping to get a bunch of whatever ore's hot on the market before someone notices what they're doing and they have to pull up stakes and move on. But this wasn't one of those. It's big enough you could probably see it from orbit. Not exactly the sort of thing you can hide easily, so it can't be something set up by a small fly-by-night operation."

"So what do you think is going on?" He was frowning now, as if he were starting to put two and two together as well.

"I have no idea. But small-time ore thieves aren't going to waste their time sending a team of mercs to take out two crash-landed diplomats. Hell, they might try to rescue us in case there was a reward or something, because those types are always looking for a quick unit, but using mercenaries to kill us?" She shook her head. "No way. Especially since our original crash site has to be a few hundred kilometers from here. We would never have stumbled across this place by accident. The chances of discovery were almost nil."

Lirzhan's expression had grown progressively grimmer during this speech. "Perhaps this is connected somehow to the destruction of our ship in the first place."

Frowning, she crossed her arms and asked, "How so? That is, I'm guessing that once we crashed here, whoever's running that facility decided we were a threat and sent a team to take care of the problem, as it were. But I'm not sure how to connect the actual attack on our ship to that."

His mouth thinned. "I cannot say for certain. It is just…a feeling."

A feeling. Then again, he did seem to have an almost preternatural awareness about their environment that continued to confound her. She decided to go for broke.

The worst he could do was ask her to mind her own business. "Lirzhan, are you psychic?"

A short laugh, although it had little humor in it. "No. That is, not precisely. My people are empathic… we sense emotions, intentions. It is the reason we wear the robes. They are woven with a fiber derived from a certain plant on our home world, one that helps to block the empathic vibrations. Otherwise, it would be difficult to function normally with those outside our closest circles of family and friends. Our empathic faculties are the reason for *sayara*." He blinked, as if bringing himself back to the matter at hand. "At any rate, it is not as if I read the thoughts of the men we killed back at the science station, or picked up anything from our brief fly-by at that facility. It is just…my intuition tells me they must be related somehow."

She wouldn't presume to argue with him. Nothing in her experience had prepared her for being able to fully comprehend the ramifications of being empathic in the way that he had just described. Even so, his revelation merely reinforced in her the belief that they needed to find out more, needed to discover exactly what was going on at that facility…and who precisely knew about it.

"All right," she said. "Then I know what I have to do."

"And what is that?"

His expression told her he'd already begun to guess what she had in mind, but she went ahead and told him anyway.

"I need to get inside and see what they're really doing in there."

Lirzhan didn't know why he should be so surprised. Her boldness continued to startle him. "You can't be serious."

"And why not?" She stared up at him, hands planted on her hips.

Because I have only just found you, and I cannot lose you.

Such arguments would probably not find much of a reception with her, though, and so he only said, "You are a very capable woman, Alexa, but you are not a spy. You have not been trained for such a task."

"Have you?" she retorted, the challenge clear in her voice.

"No," he said seriously. "As you, I have been trained in diplomacy, in working with those not of my race, in languages and statecraft. I am not suggesting that I go in your place—I am suggesting that neither of us do such a foolhardy thing."

Her mouth tightened a little at the word "foolhardy," but she replied mildly enough, "I don't think it's that foolhardy. After all, look at me." She gestured toward the baggy borrowed coveralls she was wearing. "I can take off the belt, and untuck the pants from my boots, and if that facility is anything like most other mining outfits, I'll look more or less like a worker at the facility. No one should pay any attention to me."

Lirzhan wasn't so sure about that, because even in her current less-than-flattering attire and with her hair admittedly a mess, her beauty shone forth, bright and obvious as the sun in the sky. She did not look like a miner...or at least not one that he'd ever heard of. He opened his mouth to say as much, but she forestalled him by reaching down and getting some dirt on her fingertips, then smudging it on her chin and the tip of her nose.

"See? Completely incognito."

At first he could not recall what that particular word meant, and he frowned a little as he dug into the lesser-used portions of his Galactic Standard vocabulary. "Ah," he said, and despite everything, he couldn't help smiling at her pleasure in that minor subterfuge. "I am not sure if that is as good a disguise as you think it is."

"It will be fine." To his shock and infinite joy, she went up on her tiptoes and pressed her lips to his cheek. Warmth seemed to radiate outward from the place where her mouth rested, and then she sank back down on the soles of her feet and sent him a beseeching look. "Besides, you're not going to deprive me of my chance to finally play Nancy Drew, are you?"

The reference was completely unfamiliar to him. "What is a Nancy Drew?"

Alexa shot him a rueful yet somehow amused glance. "I suppose it would be too much to expect you to recognize that obscure twentieth-century reference. Anyway, Nancy Drew is a character in a series of books written hundreds of years ago. I came across them while scouring the public domain archives for books to read. Anyway, she's an adolescent girl who goes around and solves mysteries."

"And her parents have no problem with this?"

"In the books her mother is dead, and her father doesn't seem to have a lot of input." Impatiently, Alexa undid her belt and tossed it back into the skimmer, then pulled the legs of her coveralls out of her expensive-looking boots and pushed them down to her ankles. After completing this procedure, she smoothed her hands over the heavy fabric to get out some of the worst of the wrinkles caused by her belt.

He must have looked rather sour during this whole process, because she glanced back up at him and shook her head.

"It's really not that bad, Lirzhan. I doubt anyone's going to look twice at me. But to make you feel better, we can fly back and come in from the other side, do some reconnoitering, before you drop me off."

"And if it looks too dangerous, you will give up this plan?"

Surprisingly, she nodded at once. "Of course. I don't have a death wish. But we're going to have to do something, because otherwise I don't know how we're going to get off Mandala."

"There is still the beacon—"

"That we don't know how to reprogram."

"We haven't tried," he pointed out. While he certainly was not a programmer, he thought it infinitely more practical to find a quiet place to work on the beacon rather than attempting to infiltrate what was clearly a secret installation.

"Okay, that's true enough. Let's just play it by ear and see what happens, all right?"

Puzzled, he reached up to touch his ear. Galactic Standard idiom could be tricky, and although he was very fluent, some of its nuances still eluded him.

She actually laughed at that. "It's an expression. It just means that we'll go ahead and adjust our reactions based on what we observe. Got it?"

"Got it," he replied. Perhaps he should allow himself to be cautiously optimistic. After all, he had gotten her to agree to wait and do an actual reconnaissance of the facility before running in there completely unprepared. While he understood her desire to discover what was going on in those mysterious buildings, and who was running the facility, caution would serve them better in the long run.

They both climbed back into the skimmer, and Alexa once again took her position in the pilot's seat. This time she kept the craft disguised amongst the trees, following the edge of the forest as the terrain sloped gradually upward. After a few minutes the greenery began to thin out, but she remained hidden within it as long as possible before moving them out into open ground and dropping low. Obviously she hoped that by hovering only a yard or so above the ground, they would be more difficult to spot.

Coming in at this angle, it was easier to see the general layout of the facility. At their first approach they had crested the hill and come upon the back of what appeared to be a large refining facility of some sort. Directly in front of it was a wide road blasted into the hillside, a road that narrowed as it entered a gaping black hole in the side of the mountain. Although he and Alexa were probably still a kilometer away, it was easy enough to spot the large automated haulers coming out of the mountain and heading for the refining facility. On the other side of the road were a series of low, ugly buildings, probably barracks of some sort, and beyond that a landing pad, on which was parked a blocky personnel carrier, with a sleek-looking spacecraft appearing small and fragile next to it.

"I'll be damned," Alexa said.

"What is it?"

"The smaller ship. That's a Sirocco-class personal transport."

"Gaian, I presume."

"Yes, it's Gaian. And pricey. And rare. Not something I would have expected to see on an 'undeveloped' planet like Mandala."

She was frowning, and Lirzhan could feel the uncertainty and puzzlement practically radiating off her in waves. "What do you think it means?" he asked.

"I don't know. But I'm not getting a good feeling about it."

A slight turn of her hand on the wheel, and she had them heading away, sloping downward as they flew to the south. Relief swept over him. Perhaps she had given up on her reckless plan to go snooping around the facility.

"Where are we going now?" he inquired, his tone neutral. He didn't want to reveal how happy he was that they were heading away from the mining plant and not toward it.

"Back into the woods for the moment." She shifted in her seat, and sent him a very sly smile. "Oh, you needn't look so pleased. I'm not giving up. But that place is so exposed it's obvious I can't just slip in. Also, I figured it couldn't hurt to try monitoring some of their comm traffic, see if we can piece together what's going on there." A tap of her forefinger against the unit built into the dashboard of the skimmer, and she continued, "I suppose I should've thought of it sooner, but I really thought we were just dealing with three mercs and possibly one left back at their ship, not a whole clandestine operation."

"I agree that it would be wise to learn more of what they're doing before you go in there." Even to him his voice sounded stiff.

"Your concern is appreciated, Lirzhan, but believe me, I know how to take care of myself."

That much is certain, he thought. Oh, she was certainly not experienced in the wilderness, that much he could tell, but she'd been cool enough when managing that one mercenary back at the science station—and she hadn't shown any real regret over shooting the man in the head, either, once she got past the initial shock of the moment. Not that she'd had much choice, but still....

The trees began to slip past again, and she slowed down as the woods grew thicker. A few minutes later they came to a small clearing, and she eased the skimmer to a stop, then settled the vehicle on the thick grass. From far above some avian creature cackled at them, clearly displeased at having its residence disturbed by the alien contraption.

Alexa shot a brief glance upward, then returned her attention to the skimmer's comm unit. "All right, let's see what you people are up to...."

Really, she was kicking herself for not tuning into that comm in the first place. But done was done, and they seemed safe enough here for now. Lirzhan watched her expectantly but remained silent.

She hadn't operated one of these comm units for a while, not since her college boyfriend had taken her out joyriding in the smaller, less sophisticated version of a skimmer that he'd owned. But the principle should be the same: There were numerous bands available, depending on the strength of the signals from the towers in the area. Etiquette generally required that you find your own channel, one that no one else was using but was still powerful enough to reach the other skimmers in the area if you needed to open a comm channel with them. She hadn't noticed any towers near the mining facility, but then again, she hadn't been looking, either.

Letting her finger rest on the touch pad, she let it seek through the bands, searching for the one carrying other voice traffic. A few crackled in and out, but she could tell that was just background noise. Then:

"…heard anything from the team?" The voice was male, and definitely Gaian. She thought she even detected a Midwest twang to it.

"Not a peep. Should've been back hours ago, but maybe it's taking 'em longer to dig a couple of graves than they thought." The second voice was also male and Gaian, but she didn't recognize the accent for sure. She supposed it really didn't matter. Gaian was Gaian.

She glanced up at Lirzhan, and his cool green eyes met hers. It didn't take a theoretical physicist to figure out whose graves the two strangers were talking about.

"Are you going to send anyone out to look for them?"

"Hell, no. We're shorthanded enough as it is. They were hired because they're professionals—I'm not going to babysit them. Besides, Ono will have my ass in a sling if we're behind on our quota this week."

"Got it. I'm heading back in. I'll check again in a half-hour."

"Roger that."

The transmission ended, and Alexa sat there for a minute, processing what she'd just heard. Too bad the two strangers hadn't referred to one another by name, but you couldn't have everything.

"It looks like you were right," she told Lirzhan. "Whoever's running that base sent those mercenaries specifically to kill us. Loose ends, I suppose, since we weren't obliging enough to get blown up with the shuttle or burn up on reentry."

"I am not all that happy about being right," he replied grimly. "But that doesn't explain what *is* here that they're willing to commit murder to protect. Yes, it is clearly some sort of mining facility, but one wouldn't think such a thing would be that sensitive."

"I supposed it depends on what they're mining." She reached up under her messy braid to rub the back of her neck, which was feeling more than a little tight. Not enough sleep and too much hunching over the steering wheel of the skimmer, she supposed. "We saw a lot of minerals when we were going through the caves to the south of here. Maybe some of them are more valuable than I thought. I'll admit to not being an expert."

"Neither am I," he said. "Especially since, although there are some minerals and ores that seem to be replicated on many planets throughout the galaxy, there are others specific to the worlds on which they form. I suppose if something with specific properties was discovered here on Mandala—"

"—then the GEC would want to hush it up so it could come in and exploit it in peace," she finished bitterly.

Lirzhan shot her a curious glance. "You do seem to have a rather low opinion of the GEC."

"They're not exactly known for their squeaky-clean standards and practices." She and Lirzhan had already hashed this out, more or less, so Alexa really didn't see the need to go over it again. Just because she worked for the government, and indeed had a duty to advance the Consortium's interests, didn't mean she was wearing rose-tinted ocular implants.

"Including murder?" His tone was mild enough, but somehow she could hear the condemnation in it.

"If whatever they're pulling out of the ground here is valuable enough, then…yes." She hated to admit such a thing to him, but she wouldn't lie. Not to Lirzhan.

Besides, wouldn't he see a lie for what it was?

For a second or two he didn't say anything. He only watched her, and she felt some of her resolve begin to crumble. Because she might not be empathic the way he was, but she could see how worried he was for her… for them. Here in the sunlight the elusive rainbow flash of his finely scaled skin was even more obvious, and she wondered again at how his people could hide so much beauty from the rest of the galaxy.

Maybe it's because the rest of the galaxy doesn't deserve it, she thought. *Or at least we Gaians don't. Not most of the time, anyway.*

For all she knew, that was part of the reason why she'd gone with Trin, an alien, instead of another Gaian. Oh, sure, workplace romances were frowned on, but they happened all the time, especially when a group of people was assigned to one post for a lengthy period. At the time she'd told herself it was because she didn't want to be with anyone who knew anything of her origins, of where she'd come from. Those files were supposed to be confidential, but word got around...maybe from a leak in the payroll office, where they'd have to set up the automatic deductions from her salary to begin the reimbursement for her education, all the years she'd spent in foster care. Yes, she'd gotten grants and scholarships, too, but they were never enough. And she had a sneaking suspicion the system was purposely set up that way.

"We will get out of this, Alexa," Lirzhan said, bringing her back to the present, and laid his hand on hers.

Damn right they would. What would happen then, she had no idea, but she wasn't about to let the money-grubbers win this round.

ELEVEN

LIRZHAN HAD HOPED THAT once Alexa had more or less confirmed that the people running the mining facility were behind the murder attempt, she would abandon her notion of trying to get inside and find out more. However, the confirmation only seemed to have strengthened her resolve.

"I can do this," she argued while she rooted through the cargo compartment in the back of the skimmer, unearthing such useful objects as a flare gun, a length of high-tensile rope, a tool kit, and a photo ID with "Mandala Mining Group" printed on it. True, Alexa looked nothing like the low-browed individual pictured on the piece of plastic, but he guessed she was hoping that from a distance it might pass. "Perfect," she added, clipping it to the pocket flap of the coveralls she wore.

"I wouldn't exactly say that," Lirzhan remarked. He knew better than to try to keep her from her current task, so he attempted to redirect her focus. "It is clear that what is going on here is illegal. I still believe the best thing to do is go someplace safe and attempt to reprogram the beacon. If we sent a signal to Zhore—"

"The cavalry would swoop in and rescue us?"

He had to stop and process the word "cavalry" for a second, as there was no analogue on his home world. His people had domesticated animals, true, but they had not used them for transportation. "In a manner of speaking, yes. We already have enough evidence to bring this matter to the Council, so why risk yourself with this so-called 'Nancy Drew' enterprise?"

"Because you don't *know* that you'll be able to reprogram the beacon, while I know for certain that they've got subspace comm equipment in that facility. No base this remote would be built without having a way to call home."

On the surface that sounded logical enough, but the risks involved were far too great. "What will you do if you're caught?"

"I won't get caught."

"You cannot know that for certain." He went to her then, took her hands in his. At first he worried that she would pull away immediately, but she did not, although her full mouth and fine chin were set, indicating she was in no mood to hear any more arguments. "I do not want anything bad to happen to you."

Something in her softened somewhat, and her fingers tightened around his. "I don't want anything bad to happen to me, either. Look, what if I try that transport ship out on the pad first? I didn't see anyone guarding it, and of course it'll have a subspace comm unit as well. I'll transmit the code to contact Targus Station and be out of there in less than five minutes."

That plan did sound marginally better. "You have the code for Council headquarters?"

"Yes." She smiled up at him. "I always make sure to memorize the codes of where I'm going and where I've been, just in case. And of course the home office on Gaia, but in this case I don't think that's going to help us too much."

"Well…" He dragged the word out. It also had no true Zhore equivalent, but he'd found it quite handy for the times when he needed an extra moment to gather his thoughts. He hated that he could not come along with her, but at least she would, as a Gaian, more or less blend in. There was no way he could hide his alien features. "All right. Try the transport first. But if you see any signs of anyone, get out as quickly as you can. And give me the code before you go," he added, thinking it was in their best interests for him to have it as well. Just in case.

"Of course I will." She gazed up into his face, and something in her own features shifted. When he'd first seen her, he thought her beautiful but brittle. There was something much softer about her mouth now…or perhaps that was only because he knew what it tasted like. "I don't know what's happening between us, precisely, but I do know I don't want to lose it."

The only correct response to that was to pull her close and kiss her, feel the charge of the connection between them like a great rush of heat through his whole body. Her mouth opened beneath his, and he savored the taste of her, the warmth and softness and strength all combined into an elixir that was uniquely her.

"I don't want to lose it, either," he said huskily after they pulled apart.

"You won't. I promise." She pulled away, but gently, as if she didn't want him to think of it as a rejection. "Let's head back."

He nodded, but with reluctance, and took the passenger seat again as she resumed her position behind the wheel. She retraced their previous route, but slowly, and settled the skimmer well within the trees, meaning she'd have to hike a few hundred yards in the open to get to the landing pad. Yes, there were some large boulders scattered in that area, as if they'd been pushed there to get them out of the way of the construction of the facility, but he didn't know if they would truly provide adequate cover. He supposed it depended on how good the surveillance at the base actually was. Perhaps they had skimped on it, thinking they had the whole planet to themselves.

One could hope, anyway.

She shut down the engine and turned to him. "This shouldn't take me more than twenty minutes...unless I can't get access to the ship. Then I'll have to get inside the facility somehow."

"Or you could come back here," he suggested, earning himself a very sour look.

"I'll decide when I'm there. If something feels wrong, then I'll run like the wind, okay?"

"Okay." He didn't bother to keep the reluctance from his tone. Alexa knew very well how he felt about the situation.

A kiss on the cheek and a brush from one of the loose strands of hair hanging around her face, and she was gone. He wished she had found some handheld comms in the cargo box, but apparently those could give too much away, and so the mercenaries had not carried any with them.

No, he would have to sit here and wait, and pray that nothing untoward occurred.

The landing pad had seemed much closer when viewed from her vantage point in the skimmer than it did once she was actually on the ground, but there wasn't much she could do about that now. She dodged from boulder to boulder, stopping occasionally to listen, to strain for any sound that might indicate someone had spotted her. Nothing except the faint whistle of the wind, and a rhythmic clanging sound that must be coming from the refinery. It would have been easier, perhaps, to fly the skimmer here directly—except she would have had to transmit the correct code to get permission to land, and of course she didn't have that.

She really didn't want to try to figure out where this sudden burst of boldness had come from. It wasn't that much like her, to take such unnecessary risk. All right, it wasn't precisely unnecessary. Lirzhan kept protesting that he could reprogram the beacon, but she didn't see how that was going to work, since he'd admitted he didn't have any particular technical expertise.

What she was feeling right now was almost as foreign as the sensations she'd experienced when Lirzhan kissed her. Those, however, although unusual, were welcome, appealing. But what spurred her to action now was quite different. The only phrase for it was "righteous indignation." No, scratch that. "Indignation" sounded too polite. It was anger, a fury burning through her with an intensity that surprised even her. They'd tried to kill her, kill Lirzhan. And all to cover up some dirty mining operation, some bureaucrat's or politician's latest scheme to line their pockets.

Screw that.

Almost to the edge of the landing pad now. Alexa paused, scanning the area as best she could from the cover of the last boulder before there was only empty concrete between her and the transport ship. She saw a pair of men walk the perimeter of the pad, then head back inside the building.

Damn. Maybe Lirzhan was right—this plan was crazy, and she should just go back and help him try to figure out the beacon.

Don't be an idiot, she told herself. *You're here now, and they're gone, so suck it up and do what you came here to do.*

Still she waited a minute more, watching to see if they would re-emerge. The pad remained empty, however.

Now or never.

Taking a deep breath, she straightened, then came out from the shelter of the boulder and walked across the landing pad as if she had every right to be there. From her left hand swung the toolkit she'd found in the cargo container of the skimmer. She'd figured it would provide some sort of protective camouflage; if anyone asked her what she was doing out there, she could always try to lie her way out and say she'd been sent to do some maintenance on the transport. Of course, such a subterfuge was predicated on there being enough personnel stationed here that they wouldn't be able to tell at a glance that she wasn't an actual member of the facility's staff.

First things first. She headed for the hatch in the center of the ship, which luckily faced out toward the open space around the pad, and not back toward the barracks on the other side. As she'd hoped, there was a flip-up compartment where the controls to open the hatch and extend the steps were located. She pushed the button, and with a metallic whine the door retracted into the ship at the same time a set of folding stairs lowered to the concrete.

The noise seemed excruciatingly loud to her, but a quick glance around told her that no one seemed to have noticed. All remained empty and still. Probably all the residents of the barracks were down in the mines or elsewhere in the facility, since this would be the middle of their working day, and the guards had not yet returned while making their rounds.

No more time for speculation. She hurried through what was obviously the passenger section of the ship, with rows of uncomfortable-looking seats. Most likely a decommissioned military ship converted to civilian use…or at least made to look that way. She still didn't know who or what exactly was behind this entire outfit.

But the cockpit seemed fairly standard, and there was the comm unit in the center of the console, situated exactly halfway between the pilot's and the copilot's chairs. She wasn't going to bother with either one of those, however—this wouldn't take that long.

Although of course she didn't know how to fly a starship, she'd ridden in enough of them, big and small, to know how the comm worked. Actually, she'd been able to watch it up close and personal, since Trin had owned a small intra-system craft that he'd used to fly her from Eridani's surface to the base on one of its moons and back. Low-gravity sex was definitely an experience, one they'd indulged in during an extended weekend on the Eridani moon base.

She couldn't think about that now, though, and didn't want to, because that would only lead her to thinking about what such activities might be like with Lirzhan… and she didn't know precisely how to react to that. Not now, anyway.

Shaking her head, she reached out and pushed the button to activate the comm unit. The display flashed to life. *Enter comm code.*

She hesitated for a few seconds. Should she contact her superiors back on Eridani, who must now surely think her dead...or should she abandon that idea and send word directly to Targus Station? To do the latter would signal more than anything what a break she had made with her previous existence, because she would be reaching out to the Council then, and not her own government.

Her government, which just might have sent people to kill her.

Mouth twisting, she punched in the code for Targus Station. A few seconds later, a cool female voice, with the soft, rounded tones of an Eridani, came over the speaker.

"Targus Station. Please identify yourself."

"Ambassador Alexa Craig. I—"

"Ambassador Craig!" The unknown woman's voice wasn't sounding quite so cool now. "We were informed that your ship was lost with all passengers and crew. Where are you?"

"A planet called Mandala, system designation GSC 2897. Our shuttle was pulled from subspace and fired upon."

"Pulled from—" The woman broke off. "And Ambassador Lirzhan?"

"He's fine. We need an immediate evacuation, but be warned that there are hostile interests working here on the planet's surface."

"Understood." A brief silence, as apparently the comms officer at Targus Station worked out Mandala's coordinates. "We can have a ship there in approximately six hours."

Relief washed over Alexa. Six hours. That was nothing. She and Lirzhan could just hunker down in the skimmer, eat a picnic, bird watch, or what-have-you, and by the end of the day, this whole nightmare would be over.

A harsh male voice barked, "You there! Stay where you are!"

A wave of cold fear hit her right in the gut. She froze...leaving the comm channel open. That way the officer on the other end at Targus Station could hear exactly what was going on, and get some idea of what sort of situation the rescue party would face. But at least help was already on the way, and would be here in approximately six standard hours.

Assuming she lasted that long, of course.

A flinty-eyed Gaian in a black coverall not unlike the one she wore approached, his pulse pistol pointed right at her heart. Mouth thinning, he leaned past her and shut down the comm channel.

"Out," he said, and indicated with the pistol that she should go back down the narrow aisle between the seats and exit the ship.

Resistance probably wasn't a very good idea, so she nodded meekly, hands held in the air, and walked past him and out of the ship. On the ground at the foot of the stairs stood an elegant Gaian woman wearing a suit so modish it put anything in Alexa's own wardrobe to shame. Beside her was a man in a black uniform with no distinguishing insignia, dark glasses covering his eyes.

The woman looked Alexa up and down, and smirked—at her grubby attire, most likely. But all she said was, "Well, Ambassador Craig, what do you have to say for yourself?"

He didn't like this. He didn't like it at all. All his nerve endings seemed to be thrumming with unease. At this distance he couldn't sense Alexa, but that didn't prevent him from worrying. Actually, it made the situation worse.

Normally, waiting was not something he found difficult. All Zhore knew how to meditate, to go within and find the calm at one's center. That, however, was not so easy to do when the woman he loved was marching straight into danger. She could downplay the risk all she wanted, but he knew better. Anyone who would pull a ship from subspace and destroy it, then attempt to hide all trace of the incident by killing the survivors, was no one to trifle with.

To occupy himself, he pulled out the beacon and Alexa's tablet, and set them on top of the cargo compartment, as that was the only flat surface the skimmer afforded. He activated the beacon, and watched as the screen on the tablet resolved itself into the field where he was supposed to enter what Alexa had called the "SOS" code, along with a brief message. But if he did that, the beacon would transmit directly to GEC HQ…and that, he was fairly certain, would do him no good at all.

Instead, he stared down at the device for a moment, then typed in "help." The screen pulsed, and resolved itself once more into the field awaiting input. He should have known it wouldn't be quite that easy. All right. It was set up to accept data from the tablet, and so perhaps a regular command would be enough to bring him to some sort of setup screen. Perhaps he should try that.

But typing in "setup" did nothing, either. Nor did "configure," or "change coordinates." Obviously the little device was not that literal. It would not help to think of the moments ticking by, of what might be happening to Alexa as he sat here and fiddled with the beacon.

All right, time to try a different approach. Perhaps he needed to reset it somehow. He was not entirely familiar with Alexa's tablet, as it was set up to Gaian specifications, but some things were universal…like that little key at the top right of the virtual keyboard with "Esc" stamped on it in the letters of Galactic Standard.

He pushed that button, and the original input screen disappeared, to be replaced by the words "configure setup now?", followed by "Y" and "N." Hardly daring to breathe, Lirzhan touched his fingertip to the "Y," and watched as the screen changed again, this time to one with several fields to be filled in, some pertaining to encoding and other things he didn't quite understand. What he did understand was the field labeled "destination coordinates."

Thank Irzhaan.

She had used the notepad function of the tablet to write down Targus Station's coordinate code, and so he pulled that up, then copied and pasted it into the field as requested and pressed "enter." Once again the screen changed, this time going back to the original one. The field only accepted up to one hundred characters, so he would have to be brief. *Alexa Craig & Lirzhan shot down Mandala GSC 2897. Hostiles on planet. Pickup requested ASAP*, he typed, then pressed "send." A small blue light on the beacon began to pulse, apparently signaling that it was now transmitting the message.

It made him feel a little better, but not much. He glanced at the chronometer at the top left of the tablet's screen. She had been gone not quite a standard half hour. Not so very much time, and certainly well within what they had expected would be the time required for the operation, but....

Now that he had gotten the beacon to work, he truly had nothing to occupy himself, except his own worried thoughts. The shuttle had been shot down a little more than six hours into a twelve-hour flight, and so that meant help might be here as soon as six hours from now—if all went well. Would those receiving the message even believe it? No reason not to, of course, not when sent via a beacon like that. Or so he tried to reassure himself.

All the same, he knew he'd feel much better once Alexa returned. And if she didn't…

…Well, he'd just have to go find her himself.

The room they'd brought her to was small and gray and absolutely featureless. No windows. Industrial-looking light bars to provide illumination, and a long gray table surrounded by hard gray chairs. No, it wasn't a holding cell, but there also wasn't much here to provide any reassurance.

They'd sat Alexa down on one of the chairs. She wasn't bound, and she supposed she should be glad for that. Then again, where would she run? The hard-faced officer and the well-dressed woman stood facing her, and two men in black coveralls guarded the door outside. Even if she had the sort of training that would allow her to disable the two people standing in front of her—which she didn't—the guards in the corridor would either disable her or kill her outright the second she went through the door.

"Ambassador Craig," said the woman. "Do you want to tell us what you were doing on our ship?"

Alexa lifted her shoulders. "What's the point? I'm sure you had your people in there accessing the comm log as soon as I was gone."

The woman's perfect brows creased. A certain taut-ness about her forehead seemed to indicate that she wasn't as young as she looked, that she'd had more than a few cosmetic procedures to ensure she maintained that mask of plastic perfection. "Very well, then. Do you want to explain why you, as a representative of the Consortium, were sending messages to the Council facility in the Targus system rather than back to your superiors at the embassy on Eridani, or indeed directly to the consulate offices on Gaia itself?"

Lies, truth, or something somewhere in between? None of them seemed all that appealing. The most Alexa could hope for was to stall, to keep them talking to her, questioning her, until the rescue team from Targus could get here. She shrugged again. "It seemed the logical thing to do, as my next posting is to the Gaian consular office on Targus Station. Why would I backtrack to Eridani or Gaia?"

The woman clearly didn't like that answer. Her mouth pinched, and she leaned over and whispered something to the man who stood beside her. He shook his head infinitesimally.

Alexa knew it was probably best not to volunteer any more information, to play dumb as much as possible. While she wanted to demand that they tell her what the hell was going on here, to ask why those men had been sent to kill her and Lirzhan, that would only be tipping her hand, and might provoke them into a very unwelcome response.

Straightening, the strange woman crossed her arms and gazed down at Alexa the way she might have stared at an insect that had had the temerity to crawl across her boot. "It didn't do you any good anyway," she said. "We immediately followed up with a message saying that the previous communication had been garbled, that we had been intending to send an update to HQ on Gaia, and to ignore it."

Goddammit. Maybe the people at Targus Station had believed the lie...which was arguably flimsy...and maybe they hadn't. Alexa couldn't know for sure. And she wouldn't know until some five and a half hours from now, when the rescue team from Targus Station might or might not show up.

"Well, I guess we'll just have to see what happens, won't we?" she said coolly.

"We're not going to do anything of the sort," the flinty-eyed man said, speaking for the first time. His clipped accent clearly betrayed his origins—the United Kingdom, Alexa thought, something northern, like Manchester or Edinburgh. "But you are going to tell us where Ambassador Lirzhan is."

Oh, so you can kill us both at the same time? Like hell.

"I have no idea," she replied, making sure to keep her tone even. After all, she'd had a lot of practice in such things. Only a few months ago she'd stood her ground while a heavy-browed Stacian diplomat practically screamed in her face when she was part of the team attempting to clear up the aftermath of that mess in the Chlorae system. "He dropped me off and went back into the woods somewhere. I said I'd signal him when I was done."

"Signal him with what?" the woman demanded. "We found nothing on you."

No, they hadn't, but it wasn't for lack of trying. The pat-down had been more than a little rough, and she'd endured it while staring straight ahead, ignoring the way the two soldiers or mercs or whatever they were handled her a little too familiarly. But all she'd brought with her was the toolkit from the skimmer, so there wasn't much to find.

"I must have dropped it," Alexa said. "That was some rough territory, coming over here."

The woman made an exasperated sound, although something about the sideways flicker of her eyes told Alexa her interrogator wasn't all that convinced. "How unfortunate." She tilted her head to one side. "So how is your companion going to retrieve you?"

"He isn't," Alexa replied. "I told him that if I didn't signal him, then it meant I'd been discovered and he'd need to stay far away."

The woman appeared to digest that comment for a moment. Then she arranged a sticky-sweet smile on her perfectly glossed lips and asked, "But why stay away in the first place? I would have thought that, once you located this facility, you would have attempted to make contact to get assistance. You are a representative of the Consortium, and this is clearly a Consortium facility."

"Is it?" Alexa inquired in return. "Because I don't see any insignia on that man's uniform, and you have yet to identify yourselves. Forgive me if I was being unduly cautious." Oh, how she wanted to tell them that of course she wasn't going to walk up and knock on the door of the people who'd just spent the last four days trying to kill her and Lirzhan. But that would be revealing far too much. It was clear that this woman still couldn't tell for sure whether Alexa suspected the people at the facility of being the ones behind the assassination attempts, or whether another group was responsible. And as long as that uncertainty existed, Alexa would be sure to cultivate it.

"Forgive me," the woman said, still wearing that plastic smile. "I am Melinda Ono, and this is Captain Marquand. I'm the administrator here."

"And what exactly are you administrating?"

The smile tightened. "I'm afraid that's classified, Ambassador Craig."

Alexa sent her an equally false smile in return. "Yes, but I'm cleared up to level seventeen." Not that that would get her anywhere, but it would be fun to see this woman, who clearly was an executive from some corporate interest or another, scramble to explain why a level-seventeen clearance wasn't sufficient to access the information on this facility.

"And I'm sure in most cases that would be enough, but not here, I'm afraid." Melinda Ono gave an apologetic little shrug that wasn't convincing in the least. "I will assure you that we have all the necessary clearances and licenses to be operating this facility. But perhaps you can explain that to your superiors once you've returned to Gaia."

Some part of Alexa was relieved by these words, as they seemed to indicate that Ono & Company had abandoned the idea of murdering her outright. Then again, Gaia was the last place she wanted to go. Lord knows what story this woman would cook up to explain Alexa's presence here, and no doubt her superiors in the diplomatic corps would swallow the whole thing. Money talked, and Alexa was only one woman, with not a great deal of clout. Yes, on the surface her career had looked promising, but she wasn't naive enough to believe that a junior ambassador had the kind of sway to override input from one of Gaia's mega-corps.

And what about Lirzhan? She had no idea where he was right now. For all she knew, they had parties out searching for him, and he'd been captured as well. What if they tried to take his robes away from him? He'd been wearing them, but with the hood down. She couldn't begin to imagine what kind of a violation that would be for a Zhore.

"Sending me to Gaia would be a waste of resources," Alexa said calmly, refusing to allow any of her inner turmoil to bubble its way to the surface. "My next posting is Targus Station, and if you're going to send me off-planet—which I understand is fully within your rights, as this is a secure facility—then that is the most logical place to send me."

"We'll send you where we decide to, and that's the end of it," Marquand put in, clearly wearying of the back and forth between the two women. "You can cool your heels in here for a while, Ambassador—Ms. Ono and I have a few things to discuss."

Melinda Ono looked briefly displeased by this, but then she nodded and said, "We'll follow up soon, Ambassador Craig," before following Captain Marquand out of the room. The door shut behind them, and Alexa heard the faint tinny *beep* of the electronic lock being engaged.

She didn't even bother to get up and test the door. The sound was final enough, and told her she was stuck in here until they came back and...did what? Shot her outright? Called in a transport to haul her back to Gaia, where her story would mesh so badly with whatever lies Ms. Ono and her cohorts could concoct that she'd be discredited before she even got started?

And then there was the question of Lirzhan. She could only pray that he'd had the sense to lie low, that he wasn't going to play his world's equivalent of the knight in shining armor, coming to rescue the princess. Because the story that never got told, but probably happened more often than not, was of the knight ending up in the dungeon, right next to the princess.

TWELVE

FORTY-FIVE STANDARD MINUTES, and now he knew she must be in trouble. She'd told him not to come looking for her if anything happened, but he knew he could no more do that than stop breathing. Although they'd seen no obvious surveillance during their quick fly-by, it was clear it existed, and it had caught her.

She must be alive, though. Surely he would have felt it if they had killed her, even at this distance. Far more likely that they would be questioning her, probably to locate him so the final loose end could be wrapped up once and for all.

But he wouldn't make it easy for them.

Coming in from the landing pad was clearly not the answer. Too exposed, too close to the barracks. He had no idea of the schedule at the facility, and so didn't know when the people who worked the mines might be coming and going. But there was still the first approach, from behind the ridge. In the shadows of the rocks there he could slip in by the refining factory, and follow its pipes to the main building. From there he would have to improvise, but he thought it might be done.

He glanced at the chronometer on the tablet. Five hours until rescue at the very earliest. A great deal could happen between now and then. It was entirely possible that the rescuers might have no one to rescue by the time they got here.

No. He would not allow himself to think that way, for then he would be admitting defeat before he'd even begun. The universe could not be so cruel as to have brought Alexa to him, only to have them torn apart before they had barely even begun to explore a relationship.

After disconnecting the beacon from the tablet, he tucked the larger device into an inner pocket in his robes, and placed the beacon in the emergency bag, now resting on the floor of the skimmer. The beacon had either done its job or it hadn't, but it was of no further use at the moment.

This would be the first time he had driven their borrowed vehicle, but he had watched Alexa, and the procedure did not seem terribly difficult. Push that button to engage the engine, and the other to set off the thrusters and tuck the wheels into the undercarriage. From there it was a simple matter of steering between the trees, and using the lever off to the left to adjust his altitude.

Even so, he felt the small craft dip a little as he pulled back on the lever, and hastily pushed forward instead, bringing the skimmer up to approximately two meters above the forest floor. That was high enough to avoid any underbrush and boulders, but not so high that he could be easily spotted.

Keeping his forward speed low, he maneuvered around the trees, retracing their first route, the one that would take him back to the ridge line, so he might dip below it and come up from behind the facility. A shadow passed over the sun, and he glanced up, seeing clouds begin to move in. The breeze somehow felt colder, as if the chilly air currents were bringing with them a shift in the weather.

He hoped not, for up until now they had been lucky enough to enjoy a prolonged dry spell. The skimmer was an open vehicle; perhaps it had some sort of retractable cover, but if it did, he could not find the controls to work it, and he didn't have any time to waste.

Slowing to a crawl, the craft emerged from the trees, hanging below the ridge so the skimmer could not be seen by direct line of sight. If they had scanning equipment at the facility, then it would most likely pick up the vehicle's heat signature, but he would have to take that chance.

A slight whine from the engines as he engaged the thrusters again, and settled the skimmer on the rocky ground between several boulders, where he hoped it would be more or less hidden. From there it was a climb of some twenty meters to get over the ridge and down behind the refining plant. With the day growing rapidly darker as the cloud cover thickened, he hoped that he, in his black robes, would appear to be just another shadow.

Pulse pistols tucked into his belt, and the emergency bag slung over one shoulder, he climbed out of the skimmer and hastened up the hillside. The wind caught at the edges of his cloak, whipping the heavy fabric. Grimly, he pulled the cowled hood over his head, glad of the weighted edges, which would keep the fabric from blowing back away from his face.

The ground underfoot was treacherous, loose rock breaking away under his heavy boots. More than once he had to stop and regain his balance, find a surer footing in the scree. But eventually he gained the ridge line, and took the briefest of pauses to scan the area and see if anything looked particularly out of place.

As far as he could tell, it did not, but he had only a scant second or two for that inspection, enough to tell him there were only a few guards about, and not the sort of expanded security presence that might indicate they were actively on the hunt for any intruders. For a second he wondered if he had made a foolish mistake, if he had left prematurely and abandoned Alexa to make her own way back to the rendezvous point.

But then he felt it—a pulse of worry and fear that could only have come from Alexa. There, in that tall gray building, which must be some kind of administrative offices. So they had caught her.

Although he wished nothing more than to go pounding down the hillside to her rescue, such a foolish gesture would only result in his being captured as well. He would have to go about this methodically. At least now he knew she was alive. Almost as important, he also knew where they were keeping her.

The refining plant hugged the hillside, casting a deep shadow behind it. Lirzhan used that shadow, working his way downward until he was at its base and could feel the very ground beneath his feet vibrating as it processed—well, whatever it was that they were mining here.

Now at last he could hear the voices of both men and women, and he held himself still, using a huge metal support column as cover as a group of miners walked down a ramp and toward one of the paths that cut through the installation. Two of them were arguing over whether their bonuses were going to be ten percent or fifteen percent, and another one expressed a hope that it wouldn't be vindiloo —whatever that might be—again for lunch today. And then they were gone, disappearing into the very building where Alexa was being held.

He guessed they had no idea that a Consortium ambassador was being detained in that building. No, they had all sounded like regular working people. They must have some sort of clearance to be working here at all, although he assumed a great deal of the facility's importance had been shielded from them.

Perhaps he was not exactly relieved, but it did gladden him a little to know that not everyone here was a cold-eyed mercenary too ready to commit murder to hide their secrets. Those barracks had not looked large enough to hold more than a hundred people at most, and if the majority of those here worked in the mines, that meant the actual security force might not be that large after all. It made sense in a way—if your facility was so secret that no one even knew it existed, most likely you would not have to expend too much effort defending it.

Well, besides pulling ships out of subspace that got too close. Somehow he knew that was the heart of the puzzle, although he did not have the time now to work at it. All of his focus must be kept on Alexa, on retrieving her from wherever she was being held. He wished now that his people truly were telepathic instead of empathic, for then perhaps he could have sent her a mental message telling her to keep heart, and to expect rescue at any moment. But since he did not possess such skills, all he could do was try to get to her as quickly as possible…and hope there weren't too many people standing in the way.

He ghosted to another pillar and then paused, surveying the scene before him once again. It was clearly time for the noonday meal; more workers were emerging from the mines and heading to that same building, which must house the commissary. Unfortunate that he was so distinctive in appearance. There was no way he could blend in with them. He wondered then exactly how they'd caught Alexa, because she was right—her own disguise of black coveralls and messy hair and smudged face would have made her indistinguishable from the grubby men and women he glimpsed from his hiding place.

Not that it really mattered now. The worry and fear
he'd sensed told him somehow she'd been found out.
Obviously her disguise had not been enough to protect
her. Had she revealed who she was, or did they already
know? Most likely they knew she was one of the shuttle
crash survivors right away; after all, every single worker
here had to be accounted for, and they would have seen
she was not one of them, even if they didn't immediately
recognize her face.

He had reached the last of the pillars supporting the
refining structure, and after this he would have to venture out into the open. It was probably good that the
day had turned gray and dark, a fine drizzle beginning
to descend from the lowering clouds. His black robes
would not stand out as much in this sort of weather as
they would on a blazing-bright sunny day.

The area seemed more or less deserted, the last of
the workers having disappeared inside the building in
search of their noonday meal. Lirzhan scanned the area,
paying particular attention to the eaves of the buildings,
as they were natural mounting points for surveillance
cameras, but he saw nothing. That didn't mean much,
as most types of security equipment were designed to
be small and discreet, difficult to see with the naked eye.
For all he knew, they were watching him now as he hung
back in the shadow of the refining plant, deciding on his
next course of action.

Then he saw an automated cart trundling away from
the plant, heading toward a low building connected to

the tall one where he believed Alexa was being held. The cart was covered with a flat sheet of plastic, most likely to protect it from the elements.

Figuring this was his best chance to get inside without being detected, Lirzhan slipped in behind the cart, crouching low so that it would provide some cover. Then he unfastened the pressure tape holding it down on one end, lifted it, and heaved himself over the side.

He landed in some sort of glinting bluish powdery substance. Frowning, he gathered up a handful of it. The substance felt like very fine sand, but he could not understand what it could possibly be, or why the Gaians would think it so very valuable. Something about the color seemed oddly familiar, though, as if he had seen it before.

Dark rock walls rising around them, with the lanterns picking out a sudden glitter of blue crystals on all sides....

That was it. The crystals he and Alexa had seen in the caves on their journey here. This powder must be those crystals after being pulverized in the refinery he was now leaving behind. But what the Gaians were doing with that material, he couldn't begin to imagine.

The cart rode over a bump, and through the loose flap of the protective plastic he could see that it had passed inside the facility, was now moving through a large open area with bins on either side. A man's voice called out, "Another load just came in."

"We haven't finished processing the last batch. How fast do they think we can work?"

"Not fast enough, I guess. What should I do with it?"

"Just leave it up against that wall for now. We'll come back for it after we're done performing the last crystallization tests."

A thud, and Lirzhan felt the cart being steered off to one side, followed by a final thump as it was apparently pushed up against a wall. He held his breath for a moment, wondering if either of the two men who had been speaking would come to look inside, but they seemed to have more important things on their minds, for he heard nothing further from them. After another moment, Lirzhan pushed the plastic up and risked a quick look around.

He appeared to be in some sort of holding area; in addition to the bins he'd spotted earlier, there was another cart similar to the one in which he now hid pushed up against the opposite wall. To his left was a metal door, and it was from that direction he thought the men's voices had come.

The door suddenly opened, and two Gaians wearing white knee-length coats over their coveralls emerged. At once Lirzhan ducked back down into the cart and dropped the plastic.

The first man said, "Break for lunch? This stuff isn't going anywhere."

"Good idea. I can't work on an empty stomach anyway."

Their footsteps echoed on the concrete floor and eventually disappeared. After waiting another minute,

Lirzhan once again pushed up the plastic and peered out. The holding area appeared to be deserted, so he judged this the best time to get away.

After sliding out of the cart, he paused for a moment to brush as much of the crystalline blue sand out of his robes as he could, then glanced around. No one seemed to have come to replace the two men, so it appeared that perhaps they were the only ones assigned to this part of the facility. They had gone out the way he had come in, which meant he should go through the door, which clearly led deeper into the building. It seemed the best way to get to Alexa.

Besides, he had to confess a certain amount of curiosity about what they were using all that blue sand for.

He pushed the button to open the door, thankful that it did not have a biometric lock or some other security device. On the other side was a long corridor with closed doors on either side. Not much helpful there. And these doors did all have card locks on them, which meant there was no way he could get inside.

Very well, then he would just have to continue deeper into the facility, and hope that everyone else had gone to lunch as well.

"You! What the hell—"

Lirzhan didn't even stop to think. He pulled the pulse pistol from his belt, wishing the weapon was the type with a paralyze setting. Apparently the mercenaries hadn't bothered with such niceties, and so all he could do was aim for the man's leg. A pale green bolt flew down the corridor and hit the man in the knee. He crumpled to the floor, dropping the cup of hot liquid he'd been carrying. Some of that acrid drink the Gaians called "coffee"; Lirzhan could smell it as it splashed over the gray laminate floor.

Moving quickly, Lirzhan ran to the stranger, clapping a gloved hand over his mouth before he could let out anything more than a startled howl. A strip torn from the hem of man's white coat served well enough to gag him, keeping him from making any more noise, and two more strips secured his hands and then his feet. Pain pulsed from him, but the wound was not life-threatening.

Luckily, the man had been alone. Violence was not the answer, or so he had been taught, but Lirzhan reflected, as he more or less set the squirming man in a more comfortable position with his back up against one wall and neatly plucked the identification card from his pocket, that every once in a while it did come in rather handy.

But which of the doors to check first? He decided that the one the man had come through seemed the safest, as there was a chance he had been alone, and so the room he had just exited had a greater chance of being empty. Lirzhan swiped the card and the door opened, revealing a laboratory of some sort. He could not identify all the equipment contained therein, but he did see a sheet of what looked like pale glimmering blue glass with thin leads attached to it.

So they are using the sand to make some sort of crystalline sheet. But to what end?

A heads-up display was located just off to the right of the blue glass or crystal. He was not a scientist, and so Lirzhan could not make much sense of the diagram shown there, or the complex equations set off to one side. But on the tabletop directly below the display was a tablet, with what looked like notes written in Galactic Standard.

There is still notable instability in the field, which will not hold for more than ten standard seconds. This may be due to residual impurities in the matrix. However, the results are promising enough that tests at greater distances and with larger vessels are indicated. With a large enough sheet and better refining methods, it may be possible to reach out and disrupt ships passing several systems away. If—

Lirzhan stopped reading there, his stomach tightening. So this was what they were trying to hide. Somehow the crystals native to this planet possessed a quality that allowed them to reach through the very fabric of space and time to disrupt a ship's subspace passage. And the Gaians were doing everything they could to exploit that quality.

No wonder they did not want Alexa or him alive. They could leave no witnesses who weren't complicit in the cover-up going on here. For if the other powers in the galaxy—the Eridani Hegemony, the Zhore Alliance, the Stacian Federation—ever learned of what the Gaians were up to, it would surely lead to war. No one could allow the Consortium to wield such power.

He had lingered here too long. Yes, this information was valuable, and he must do whatever he could to get it back to his people, or to the members of the Council. But first he must find Alexa. He had felt no more waves of worry or fear from her, so he guessed she must be safe for now, but he could not count on that to continue for much longer.

After opening the door, he glanced out into the corridor. It still seemed empty, although the man he had bound and gagged was moaning loudly. He seemed so far unable to free himself, but that didn't mean someone else might not come along and discover him. As soon as that happened, Lirzhan knew they would sound the alarm. No time to waste.

From his inspection of the facility, it seemed clear enough that this smaller research building was connected to the taller structure that must house administrative and security offices—and apparently the commissary as well. He could only hope that this hallway would lead him there, and that the other scientists and technicians were either safely holed up in their laboratories, or off getting something to eat. The chances of that seemed exceedingly slim, but then again, the chances of his and Alexa surviving the crash had not been all that good, either, and yet they had, and had also lived through the often treacherous trek across Mandala's surface…and below it. He refused to believe that they could negotiate all those hazards, only to be killed by a group of unscrupulous Gaian operatives.

Since there was nowhere to hide here, all he could do was run down the corridor, hoping that if he were spotted by whatever hidden surveillance they had here, he would be gone before they could catch up to him. Surely they wouldn't believe him mad enough to keep burrowing deeper into the complex rather than seeking a way out.

At the end of the corridor was a set of double doors. He swiped the card, and they opened. Good. At least they hadn't yet realized he had access to as many sections of the facility as the scientist whose card he'd stolen. As soon as they realized that, he would be trapped, but with any luck he would have located Alexa before that happened.

He pounded down this new hallway, intent on the set of lifts he'd spotted as soon as the double doors opened. That pulse of fear he'd felt had told him Alexa wasn't on the ground floor, was being kept higher up in the building.

But it was here that his luck ran out, for as soon as the doors to the lift opened, he found himself staring down the muzzles of two pulse pistols held by stony-faced men wearing plain, unadorned black uniforms. He wondered if those particular pistols were set on "paralyze."

"Going somewhere?" one of the men sneered, as the other raised his pistol and shot him point-blank in the chest.

Blackness, black as his robes, enveloped him.

Alexa didn't know how long they were going to keep her cooling her heels in this room, but she guessed no one was going to drop by to tell her. For all she knew, Marquand and Ono were in the hallway outside, arguing over whether to put a pulse bolt through her forehead and finish the job they'd started with the attack on the shuttle.

Waiting and wondering when her fate would be determined wasn't particularly appealing, so Alexa instead stared down at the chronometer on her wrist, watching as the interminable minutes ticked by. Now there were only two and a half hours until the earliest a team from Targus could arrive. If they'd even seen through Melinda Ono's lies and had actually sent a ship to Mandala. Alexa knew she shouldn't be counting on that, but it was the only hope she had to cling to. She was caught, and she didn't know where Lirzhan was, and if the look in that Captain Marquand's eyes was any indication, he would be all too happy to kill them both and throw their bodies down a mine shaft.

Honestly, she wasn't altogether sure why they hadn't done that already, unless they still thought they could use her to capture Lirzhan. And maybe Ms. Ono was finding cold-blooded murder a little more difficult when she had to look her victims in the eyes. Either way, Alexa figured it was a pretty tenuous thread holding her to life at the moment.

The door opened, and two black-clad mercs dumped a wad of black fabric on the floor—a wad that she realized a few seconds later was Lirzhan. She was kneeling down next to him so quickly she didn't even remember getting up off her chair. Neither of the mercenaries said anything; having delivered their bundle, they went back out the door and closed it behind them.

Not that Alexa was paying much attention. *Oh, God, they've killed him....*

She didn't want to think of that. She *couldn't* think of that. Until now she hadn't wanted to think of what he'd become to her, how he'd somehow found a way past the armor she'd worn on her heart for too many years. Four days with him, and now she didn't know how she could go on if he were dead.

Hand shaking, she put her fingers to his throat, praying his anatomy was similar enough to a human's that she'd find a pulse there. And she did, although she had to press down a little harder than she normally would. But yes, there it was—strong and slow. So they'd only stunned him.

Relief turned to anger. Hadn't she told him not to come in after her, no matter what? She'd been right. Here was the knight locked up in the dungeon right next to his princess.

His eyes opened, lashes heavy and thick as his sooty hair revealing pools of deep green. "Alexa."

"You just had to play hero, didn't you?" she demanded. "Now we're both trapped in here, and they're probably going to come in at any moment and shoot us both, and if you'd just *stayed*—"

"Alexa." He blinked, and to her astonishment, he smiled. "I am happy to see you, too."

Since any answer she made probably would have involved swearing, instead she bent down and kissed him. And even though they were locked up in this little room, awaiting a quite possible death, that kiss still set every nerve ending tingling, made her glad that even though she might be dead soon, at least she now knew what it felt like to be alive.

Lirzhan's arms went around her and he pulled her to him, holding her close. "Oh, Alexa," he breathed. "I could not have simply left you here in their hands."

For some reason it was a lot more difficult to be angry with him when she was cradled in his arms. "No, I guess you couldn't. But I'm not sure what you plan to do next. They know I contacted Targus Station, and immediately messaged them back, saying it was a garbled transmission and to ignore it."

He only smiled. "Perhaps that would worry me... except that I was able to reprogram the beacon and therefore got a separate message off to Targus as well. They might have dismissed the transmission from you, but I somehow doubt they will ignore the beacon message, especially coming so quickly on the heels of your own contact."

"You got a message off? Lirzhan, I could just kiss you."

"I would like that very much, actually."

Their lips met again, and she found herself once more reveling in the feel and the taste of him, the silken brush of those fine scales against her skin. But she also realized they were lying entwined on the floor, his hood pushed back, and although those mercs hadn't shown any sign of returning soon, that didn't mean Ono and Marquand might not decide to drop in.

"We should probably get off the floor," she said, and pushed herself to her knees, then offered Lirzhan a hand. He seemed well enough, but she'd heard that people were generally shaky after being hit with a stun bolt.

He let her pull him upright, and then sat, rather heavily, in one of the chairs, after reaching up to pull the hood low over his face once more. "Thank you. It's true—we probably would not want to be discovered like that."

The unwelcome thought crossed her mind that the room was probably under surveillance, in which case whoever was watching had already seen the whole thing. Well, she couldn't do anything about that now, and maybe since they'd been on the floor and partially blocked by the table and chairs, those unseen watchers hadn't gotten too much of an eyeful.

She could hope, anyway.

"How did they catch you?" she asked. "Did you come in the same way I did?"

"No. I thought it better to enter the base by going past the refinery." He lowered his voice, so much so that she could barely catch his next words. "Alexa, I think I have discovered what they're doing here."

Despite their current predicament, she couldn't help but feel a flare of excitement. "You have? What?"

A shake of the hood, as if to indicate he didn't think it was safe to speak of it now. "I will tell you when I can. But believe me when I say that it is vitally important we survive this. What they are hiding here—"

She damned his reticence at the same time she understood it. A quick glance at her chronometer told her that they still had two hours until help could arrive. Would Melinda Ono and Captain Marquand allow them to live that long?

The door opened, and both she and Lirzhan pushed back in their seats, wanting to make sure they revealed as few signs of intimacy as possible. Captain Marquand entered, alone. Alexa had a feeling that was not a very good sign.

"Get up," he said. "We're going to take a walk."

An even worse sign. She scowled up at him and said, "Ambassador Lirzhan is still recovering from a stun bolt. I don't think he's in any shape to be walking anywhere."

A corner of Marquand's lip turned up in what could have been a smirk, or a leer. "That true? I would've said he looked lively enough from the way you two were wrestling around on the floor a few minutes ago."

Goddamn surveillance. You couldn't get away from it anywhere. Even though she knew she should probably keep her mouth shut, Alexa replied coldly, "I was attempting to perform CPR. The ambassador did not appear to be breathing."

Marquand only shook his head. "Call it what you want. Frankly, I don't care if that's what gets you off. It won't matter soon enough anyway."

She didn't like the sound of that. No, not at all.

Lirzhan stood. His robes made him look taller, although he was of a height with the captain. "Where are we going?"

"You'll find out. Go."

A quick glance at Lirzhan, and he nodded, just the slightest dip of the hood. All right, so she wouldn't make a stand here. But she didn't feel very good about calmly marching to what was probably going to be her own death.

Marquand opened the door. Outside were four armed guards—or mercenaries, or whatever they were calling themselves. They stepped aside as Alexa and Lirzhan exited the room, then fell in around them. Obviously Marquand wasn't taking any chances, although she had to wonder what he thought a couple of diplomats could do against five armed men.

"To the lifts," he said, and the company moved silently down the corridor to a bank of elevators. Another guard waited there, holding the door open.

Alexa didn't have much choice but to step inside, Lirzhan following. The guards surrounded them once more, with Marquand coming in last and working the controls to send them to the ground floor. As the elevator descended, she could feel her stomach sinking with it. Was this how everything was going to end? What, was Marquand going to execute them by firing squad?

She knew that asking questions wouldn't get her anywhere, so she clenched her icy hands at her side and tried to take some comfort from Lirzhan's presence beside her. Surely he wouldn't let them go out like this. Perhaps he had a plan.

Maybe she should have been thinking up one herself, but her thoughts seemed to skitter this way and that, as if they didn't dare focus on any one thing for too long, or the reality of what was about to happen would hit too hard. The lift doors opened on yet another gray corridor, and they were marched down it to an exit that led them outside.

It had clearly rained during the last hour; the ground still gleamed wet, and water dripped off the eaves of the building onto her head as she passed beneath them and out into the open. The wind was colder, too, sending chills all through her. Or maybe that was simply because she was cold with fear.

They were heading toward a skimmer sitting on the landing pad near the transport ship. The elegant Sirocco-class ship was gone. Alexa guessed that had been Melinda Ono's ship, and that she'd departed the scene of the crime, leaving Marquand to do her dirty work. Well, that was a typical executive for you.

"If you'd stayed in the woods, you might have made it," Marquand said. "We just don't have the manpower to look for two people in all that forest. But since you had to come snooping around...." He trailed off eloquently, and gave them a mocking little smile. Alexa had seen more warmth in a shark's expression, and just as much humanity. "So we're going to take you back to the woods, and we're going to make sure you disappear there permanently. No hard feelings. Just business."

"Business," Alexa repeated bitterly. "That's a handy excuse, isn't it?"

Beside her, Larzhin stirred, as if he were about to say something, but then one of the guards pointed up at the sky and called out, "Captain! Incoming!"

Everyone looked up, and Alexa did as well, her gaze fastening on the shape of a dark, sleek ship descending through the low clouds, moisture steaming off its sides. An Eridani Vector-class, from the look of it. Fast. Very fast. Maybe not quite as fast as Ms. Ono's Sirocco, but certainly much faster than the poky shuttle that had carried Alexa and Lirzhan here.

Of course. It would've taken the shuttle or a vessel with a similar rating six hours to get here—but not a Vector.

It appeared the cavalry had arrived after all.

THIRTEEN

LIRZHAN WATCHED CAPTAIN MARQUAND bark at his men, and immediately they scattered, disappearing into the barracks. Sensible, Lirzhan supposed, as at least now he and Alexa didn't have an armed escort with them, but only one man. The situation looked far more innocuous that way.

The Vector-class transport settled on the landing pad some ten meters away. A minute or so later, the gangplank descended, and a short time after that a mixed group of Eridanis, Gaians, and even a fellow Zhore walked down it, and approached Lirzhan, Alexa, and Captain Marquand.

"Good day," the captain said in guarded tones. "We tracked your arrival and so made sure the ambassadors would be ready and waiting for you."

"Too kind," said the Eridani man in the lead. The words were innocuous, but Lirzhan could see the way his dark violet eyes narrowed. Half-buried in his thick purple hair, the Eridani's antennae twitched slightly, as if indicating his skepticism. Then he turned toward Lirzhan and Alexa, and bowed. "Ambassadors, I hope you are not too worse the wear for your ordeal here on Mandala."

"No, we're fine," Alexa said quickly, moving toward their rescuers, as if she were worried that Marquand might call in more troops at any moment and capture them all.

Lirzhan did not think that was much of a possibility, but he understood her eagerness to be gone from this place as soon as possible. "We have been very well taken care of, but of course we are ready to move on to Targus and begin our new assignments."

"Of course," said the Eridani. His gaze shifted to Marquand. "Thank you for keeping them safe until we got here. Your kindness will not be forgotten."

As with all his people, the Eridani was being the soul of politeness. However, Lirzhan heard the implicit threat in those last words, and apparently Marquand was not so imperceptive that he did not notice it as well. His jaw tensed, but he said only, "It was nothing."

"Then, ambassadors." The Eridani spread his hand toward the Vector, and Alexa hurried over to the gang-plank, Lirzhan following only a pace behind her. He was just as eager as she to get away from this planet—away from Marquand and the secrets he'd been keeping.

Lirzhan had a feeling those secrets wouldn't be a secret for much longer.

The Vector was larger than the shuttle he and Alexa had traveled in previously, with room for everyone in the Targus delegation and their new passengers, and still with several seats left empty.

"If you will," the Eridani said, indicating two seats in one of the middle rows. "We would like to take off as soon as possible."

"No arguments here," Alexa replied, and dropped into the seat next to the window.

Lirzhan settled in beside her. How he wished he could rest his hand on top of hers as she gripped the armrest, but he knew such a public display would not be wise. He had to settle for taking a quick, reassuring glance at her clean profile outlined by the gray skies beyond the window, knowing they were safe now.

The atmospheric engines kicked in, the ship vibrating ever so slightly beneath him. And then they were lifting straight up from the landing pad, the gray buildings of the facility shrinking to tiny specks almost at once, clouds enveloping the ship until it broke free into the blue-white light of Mandala's sun. The ship angled away from the planet, the black of space surrounding them on all sides, until a minute or so later that black streaked into the ever-shifting colors of subspace, and he knew they were away.

Or were they? For he now knew that the scientists and technicians down on Mandala had the ability to tear a ship from subspace, to leave it stranded where it could be fired upon by an enemy vessel. But as the seconds and then minutes ticked past, he let out a small sigh of relief. It would have brought too much scrutiny upon that system, for two ships to be wrecked so close to it...never mind the very real possibility of a diplomatic incident arising from the destruction of a vessel carrying one of the Council's peacekeeping groups.

Besides, Marquand's security forces had captured him in a corridor that connected some of their laboratories, but they didn't know for sure precisely what he had seen. No doubt they were hoping that he hadn't found anything incriminating at all, that he and Alexa might complain of rough treatment, but with no evidence to back up their claims....

"You're quiet," she murmured, and although she did not precisely reach out to touch his hand, he could see her fingers twitch a little on the armrest, as if she had begun to and realized others were watching.

"I have much to think about," he replied in an undertone. "We will talk, once we reach Targus—"

"—and once we've been debriefed."

"Yes." He wished he could tell her what he had seen back on the base, but he somehow doubted he would be allowed any time alone with her before being asked to make his report. "But then...I will find some way for us to be together."

So much more meaning in those words than simply seeking a chance to speak in private. Alexa's gaze slid toward him for a second, and then her head tilted ever so slightly, as if she'd understood what he was trying to tell her.

How precisely he would accomplish such a thing, when they were both assigned to Targus Station as representatives of two governments which, if not at war, were no more than coldly neutral toward one another, he had no idea. That, he supposed, was a matter for another day. For now it was enough to know they were safe, and that Alexa was here next to him, and that they had a shared destination.

It was enough of a miracle that they were alive at all.

Alexa remained quiet through the voyage, accepting water and a snack of some dried fruit from the Eridani. What she wanted more than anything else was to talk with Lirzhan, but that wasn't going to happen for some time yet. So she watched the odd ribbons of light streak by outside the window, and told herself to relax, and waited for the next few hours to pass.

Which they did soon enough, until the ship dropped into realspace in the Targus system. The station itself orbited one of the four gas giants there, offering jaw-dropping views of the ringed planet below, although she only gave the huge windows a passing glance as she stepped out of the ship. She was acutely aware of Lirzhan behind her. However, she knew she couldn't turn back to look at him, couldn't treat him as anything besides her accidental travel companion of the past few days.

The Gaian ambassador, Alessandro Castillo, was waiting for her in the reception area, flanked by two women who Alexa guessed were his assistant and the junior ambassador she had been sent to Targus to replace. They were both polished and very smartly dressed, making her all too aware of her disheveled hair and the crumpled, oversized coveralls she was wearing. And Castillo himself looked even more proper in his high-collared dark suit, his gray-streaked black hair brushed straight back from his high, aristocratic forehead.

Oh, well...I doubt any of them would be faring much better if they'd just gone through the ordeal I have.

Summoning a smile, she stepped forward. "Ambassador Castillo, it's an honor—"

"Time enough for that later," he cut in, lifting a hand. "Ms. Amadi here is my assistant and will take you to your quarters. If perhaps you would be available to see me in my office in an hour?"

"Of course, Ambassador," Alexa said at once. Arguing with her new supervisor the second she got off the ship was not exactly a good idea. At the same time, she couldn't help wondering what exactly she was going to change into. All her luggage had been lost when the shuttle was destroyed.

The other woman, who was perhaps a few years younger than Alexa, stepped forward and addressed her in a pretty West African accent. "I'll show you the way— when we learned of your situation, we sent up to the PX for some changes of clothing for you. They are perhaps not the most fashionable, but they will do until we can have a new wardrobe sent to you from Gaia."

And deducted from my first month's salary, no doubt, Alexa thought. But the Consortium's policies certainly weren't Ms. Amadi's fault, so Alexa smiled and thanked her, then nodded at Ambassador Castillo and his companion—belatedly, she remembered the woman's name was Mia Nguyen—and then followed Ms. Amadi out of the reception area and down a short hallway to a bank of elevators.

Just as they left the reception chamber, Alexa caught a swirl of black robes out of the corner of her eye and realized that the Zhore delegation had come to collect Lirzhan. It took a good deal of willpower not to look back, not to see where he was going, but she forced herself to keep her gaze forward, to smile as Ms. Amadi exclaimed over what an adventure she must have had, and how fortunate she was to have survived in one piece.

"Yes, very fortunate," Alexa murmured as they stepped into the elevator. She was relieved to see that the Consortium hadn't taken the upper hand in the decor of the station; institutional gray had never been her favorite. But the walls and floors in the Targus facility were soft, soothing shades of sand and blue, and the lighting designed to be gentle as well. She thought she might be comfortable here…depending, of course, on how things worked out between her and Lirzhan.

…and whether her superiors were willing to hear the truth of what had happened to the two of them.

"Here we are," said Ms. Amadi, running a card through the pad next to a door on one of the upper levels of the station. The door opened, revealing a small but comfortable apartment decorated in more shades of sand and blue, with deep copper colors for accents. One wall showed a window with a glittering star field in it, and the others had abstract light sculptures hanging on them. "Living room, kitchenette, bathroom, bedroom, office. Not large, but we hope you will find it comfortable here."

"It's lovely," Alexa replied truthfully. Her apartment on Eridani had been quite nice, but she hadn't been expecting to have this much room on a space station. "Thank you, Ms. Amadi."

"Chima," the other woman said at once. "Since we are going to be working together, after all. Do you mind if I call you Alexa?"

"Not at all."

"Excellent. Well, Alexa, I'll leave you to get settled in. Here is a new tablet for you." She set the device, smaller and sleeker than the one Alexa had lost on Mandala, on the kitchenette's faux-travertine counter. "You'll find a schematic of the station on there, so you should be able to find Ambassador Castillo's office without any problem. It is on Deck Five. I'll let him know that you'll be down to see him in an hour."

"Thank you, Chima," Alexa replied, and hoped she would be able to get herself presentable in just an hour. At the moment she felt as if she wanted to spend at least a day scrubbing the last vestiges of Mandala from her hair and skin. Since she knew she didn't have that luxury, she only added, "I'll be there."

Chima smiled and let herself out, and Alexa locked the door behind her. For a second she stood in the middle of the small, luxurious apartment, looking around, trying to get used to the trappings of civilization after spending days tramping through the woods of an alien planet. Then she took a deep breath, shook her head, and went to the bathroom. She didn't have a day, but twenty minutes was better than nothing.

All right, half an hour.

Lirzhan sat directly across from Ambassador Trazhar in her elegant office decorated in the blue and green shades his people so loved. Her gloved hands knotted on top of the desk of polished pale wood. "You are certain? This woman, this human, is *sayara?*"

"Yes, Ambassador." The disapproval emanating from her was palpable, and he made sure his tone was neutral as he replied, "It is not without precedent."

"The barest precedent," she replied. Then she sighed. "But if you have felt it, then it is true, and we must do what we can to work with the situation. This Alexa Craig—have you told her of it?"

"I have." *More than told her—kissed her, tasted her lips, knew then that she was the missing half of my soul.*

Ambassador Trazhar leaned back in her chair. "And how did she react?"

"At first she was dubious, but—"

"But?"

"I convinced her of the truth, Ambassador."

Of course he could not see the Zhore woman's face, as they were not connected closely enough to interact without wearing their hoods, but he sensed that she smiled somewhere within those heavy black folds. "It seems you did. Well, then, Lirzhan, you may proceed however you think wise, but do be…discreet. This station is not so large that much passes without someone noticing."

"I will be very careful." He hesitated. "But then there is the matter of Mandala itself."

"Yes. Tell me more of how this accident occurred."

"It was no accident," he said flatly.

She sat up a little straighter at those words. The hood tilted to one side. "Explain."

"The shuttle was deliberately pulled from subspace and fired upon. Once we were on the planet's surface and made our way to the science station, we were again attacked. It was only after we discovered the mining facility that I realized what the Gaians were up to."

"Mining facility? I was led to believe that Mandala was an uninhabited and unimproved world."

"That is precisely what the Gaians *want* us to believe, Ambassador. But it appears that they have established a mine and a research facility there. I have no idea how precisely it works, but it seems that a certain mineral unique to the planet has a peculiar quality that, when refined and attached to some sort of targeting equipment, is capable of pulling a ship from subspace."

For a long moment Ambassador Trazhar said nothing. Lirzhan could sense the sudden roil of her emotions, even cloaked and hooded as she was. Outrage first, then worry...then fear.

"This would change things greatly, if the Gaians were able to continue developing this technology. And not for the good."

"My thoughts as well."

"And Ambassador Craig? Is she aware of what her people are doing on Mandala?"

"Not yet, Ambassador. We were separated, and it was while attempting to recover her from the mining facility where she was being held captive that I discovered what the Gaians were doing. Afterward, I did not have an opportunity to speak to her in private."

"Good. Then please do not say anything of this to her."

He leaned forward. "And why not? Surely she has the right to know exactly why an attempt was made on her life—not once, but several times."

"Normally I would agree with you, but as she is an agent of the Gaian government, and it is clear that the Gaians have been hiding even more from us than we previously suspected they were, then I think it far better for her to remain ignorant of the subject, at least until I have sent word on to the Assembly back on Zhoraan. It is for them to decide what should be done with this information, but as it violates every treaty currently in existence in regard to safe shipping lanes and the right to uninterrupted commerce, I am sure our government will lodge a formal complaint." Her voice hardened. "So until that time, you will hold your tongue, Ambassador Lirzhan, whether this woman is *sayara* or no. Do you understand?"

So many arguments bubbled to his lips, but he knew none of them would do any good. On one level, he did understand Ambassador Trazhar's position.

That didn't mean he had to like it.

"As you wish, Ambassador. If I may go now? I have had a wearying several days, and wish to rest and meditate before I take up my new duties tomorrow." That was all he would allow himself to say. He knew that she would be picking up the resentment and worry churning within him, so there was no need to use any words to express it.

"Go, Lirzhan. You have your liberty for the next twelve standard hours. After that I will expect you to be in your office, beginning your work here."

It was not as much as he wanted, but better than nothing. He inclined his head, and left the chamber.

It was good to feel human again. Hair washed, face and body clean, makeup carefully applied—Chima Amadi had been very thorough, and so there had been cosmetics and hair products in the small, well-appointed bathroom, in addition to three new suits and assorted underclothing, along with a new pair of boots and another pair of flat-heeled shoes for when the boots were not appropriate. Everything fit, more or less, and seemed stylish enough to Alexa, who had never worried too much about fashion, as long as her outfits were sleek and plain and not likely to go out of style anytime soon.

She sat now in Ambassador Castillo's office, which wore darker tones than most of the spaces, both public and private, that she'd seen so far on the space station. Here were wine and deep brown and smooth cocoa tones, and real plants drooped graceful green leaves from stands in several places around the room.

"Here you are," the ambassador said, setting a cup of what smelled like real coffee in front her.

The heavenly aroma reached her nostrils, and Alexa inhaled deeply. When was the last time she'd had a real cup of coffee? There had been none on Eridani, as the senior ambassador didn't care for it and so preferred to avoid the expense of providing it for his support staff. Obviously that was not going to be an issue here on Targus Station.

"Now, then," Castillo said, and although his manner seemed kindly enough, something about the almost undetectable narrowing of his dark eyes told her that she would have to watch her step, "tell me about this adventure of yours on Mandala."

"Ambassador," she began, then paused. It was so difficult to decide what the best approach was here. She'd known from the beginning that she could mention nothing of her relationship with Lirzhan. Even so, how much should she say about the attempts on their lives? What if Castillo knew something of the operations on Mandala?

No, she could not believe the conspiracy was quite that far-reaching...for the simple fact that the more people knew about something, the greater the chance that someone would slip up and reveal sensitive information. Besides, if Castillo were in on the plot, he would have done whatever he could to prevent the rescue party from going to the planet to rescue her and Lirzhan.

She took a breath, and continued. "I am not certain exactly what is happening on Mandala. It is clear that someone—most likely Gaian, but perhaps some other interests are involved—has established a secret facility on the planet. They are mining something. I did not have the opportunity to see what precisely it was. What I do know is that the attack on the shuttle was no accident, and neither were the subsequent attacks on Ambassador Lirzhan and myself."

Throughout this speech Castillo's heavy black brows were lowering, so much so that by the time he was done, his eyes were partially obscured. "Attacks? What others were there, besides the initial assault on the shuttle?"

"Armed men in a skimmer shot at us the day after we landed in the escape capsule, and again at the science station several days later. I can't say for certain whether it was the same team or not. Mercenaries, it looked like, but definitely human. And then of course I was detained at the mining facility itself, although I was not mistreated." Well, that was only a partial lie. She hadn't been hurt. True, it had seemed clear enough to her that Marquand intended to execute her and Lirzhan, but the rescue team had gotten there first, and so…technically…she wasn't poorly treated.

The ambassador's frown did not lessen. "This is… troubling. I will need you to make a full report so that I can send it on to both the Defense Force and the GEC. It sounds as if someone is operating an illegal facility on the planet's surface, and the authorities will need to know about it."

Oh, I'm pretty sure they already know all about it. She didn't bother to say such a thing out loud, though. She could already tell that Castillo knew nothing about what was really going on down on Mandala…or he was one of the galaxy's best actors. Too bad she didn't have Lirzhan's gift of empathy so she could sense whether the ambassador was nervous, whether he was deliberately lying to her.

"Of course, sir," she said automatically. It would be a carefully edited report, but she'd known all along that she would have to give some account of what had happened to her on the planet's surface. "Do you need anything else?"

"I'll have Chima show you your office, get you set up. Ms. Nguyen has already removed all her effects, as she's leaving on the outbound shuttle tomorrow. Once you're settled, you can begin with the report. Luckily, the representatives from Miris and Bathsheva won't be here until the day after that, so you'll have plenty of time to go over the agreements in question and get ready to sit down at the table with them." He stood, and extended a hand. "Welcome on board, Alexa. The Consortium would have lost a great asset if you hadn't survived Mandala."

"Thank you, Ambassador." Empty words, but necessary ones. She summoned a smile and left Castillo's office, only to be greeted by Chima, who rose from her desk, dark eyes warm.

"Let me show you where everything is, Alexa. The office has been cleaned and prepared for you, and the computer set up for your use. The files for the upcoming talks are already there for you as well."

And so she chattered and smiled, and made Alexa feel far more welcome than she thought she had any right to be. She wondered what Chima would think of her if she'd heard some of the traitorous things Alexa had uttered to Lirzhan back on Mandala. Not so much the good little Consortium drone there. Oh, no.

But she forced those thoughts from her mind and made what she hoped were the appropriate responses, and eventually Chima went back to her own desk and left Alexa alone to make her report. For a long moment she could only stare at the micro-thin screen before her, fingers resting on the virtual keyboard projected on the gleaming desktop. Then, finally,

I was en route to my new assignment on Targus Station when the shuttle I was traveling in was abruptly pulled from subspace and suffered heavy fire. Lirzhan, the Zhore ambassador, and I were able to flee the ship in an escape pod....

FOURTEEN

Two days passed before Lirzhan had a plausible reason for seeing Alexa. The separation pained him in every fiber of his body and soul, but if he were too importunate in his pursuit of her, someone would be certain to notice. He knew she had participated in the talks with the representatives from Miris and Bathsheva, but as the Zhore were not directly involved in that shipping dispute between the two Gaian-controlled planets, he had no reason to be present.

But then the Eridani ambassador suggested a formal reception to welcome the two new ambassadors to the station, and since the support staff at Targus Station loved nothing more than a party —anything to break up the monotonous routine of their days—the idea went from suggestion to reality quite quickly. The arrangements were made, the invitations issued on the station-wide 'net, and the very next evening a group of some hundred or so beings of various races had gathered in the large chamber used for everything from holiday gatherings to motivational inter-delegation team-building events.

The group from the Gaian delegation came in a little later than the Zhore, and so Lirzhan was already there when he saw Alexa enter, flanked by a tall dark-haired man he knew was Ambassador Castillo, as well as a pretty young woman with skin almost as ebony as Lirzhan's own. But once he saw Alexa, he barely noticed anything else.

Instead of the severe dark suit that seemed to be the unofficial uniform for Gaian women who held important positions, she wore a fitted long tunic over straight narrow pants, all in a gleaming blue-green fabric with embroidery of a darker teal around the open neckline. For once her dark gold hair was loose on her shoulders. The only ornament she wore was a pair of thin gold hoop earrings.

He had always thought her beautiful, but seeing her now, like this, she took his breath away. In fact, he was so occupied with staring at her that he didn't even hear the question that Arizhal, Ambassador Trazhar's assistant, had asked him.

"I beg your pardon?" he said at once, and somehow managed to shift his attention back to the hooded young man who stood next to him.

"I was asking whether this sort of thing was usual protocol," said Arizhal, who had arrived at Targus

Station only a standard week before Lirzhan and Alexa had.

Lirzhan lifted his shoulders. "I am not certain. Targus Station is rather unique in having so many different delegations under one roof, as it were. But I do not think it is that unusual to have some sort of ceremony to welcome new ambassadors. Besides, I have heard that the Eridanis in particular are always looking for an excuse to throw some sort of get-together."

"Curious. They do seem to be rather pleasure-loving, but even so they are a highly effective race."

Under the hood, Lirzhan's mouth twitched. He could not quite decide whether Arizhal were really this pompous, or whether he was just trying to impress one of his superiors. "Yes, they have certainly made a number of very important contributions to the galaxy as a whole. But if you will excuse me—I would like to speak with Ambassador Craig, as we have not had much of a chance to talk with one another after arriving here." He could only hope he was keeping his anticipation in check, for he did not want his fellow Zhore to know how much he desired to go to Alexa, to be with her, even if it only meant standing a careful distance from each other and engaging in the sort of empty discourse usually required at these sorts of events.

"Oh, yes, Ambassador Craig. You two shared something of an ordeal, after all. She seems to have survived it quite well."

That might have been a flicker of curiosity at the edge of his words there, as if the younger man would have liked to know exactly what had passed between Lirzhan and Alexa on Mandala. But Lirzhan had said nothing to anyone, save what he had told Ambassador Trazhar during his initial debriefing, and he certainly wasn't going to start now.

He bowed slightly and made his way across the room to Alexa. She had just picked up a plastic goblet of the pale golden liquid humans referred to as "champagne" when she turned and saw him. The blue eyes lit up—but only for a second. Then her face was a mask of cool politeness as she extended a hand.

"Ambassador Lirzhan."

"Ambassador Craig." Even through the thin leathery fabric of his gloves he could feel the warmth of her fingertips, the heat scorching through him all the way down to his loins. In that moment he was very glad of the concealing robes he wore. "You seem to be fully recovered from your ordeal."

She glanced down at herself. "Too much? Chima insisted that I should be festive."

"It's perfect," he said, barely above a murmur, for these were words he did not want anyone else to hear. "*You* are perfect. Besides," he added in more normal tones, "it seems that many of the women here did dress up for the occasion."

"That's true. I suppose any excuse to get rid of the business suit will do." A tilt upward of her head, as a strand of burnished hair touched her cheek before she pushed it out of the way. "Do you Zhore ever get tired of wearing the same thing day in and day out?"

"I hadn't thought of it," he admitted. "It is just how it has always been for us."

"I suppose it does make getting ready in the morning that much easier."

He could tell now that she was teasing him, but he found he didn't mind very much. It was so good simply to be near her, to smell the intoxicating sweet scent emanating from her hair, to see the light in those lovely blue eyes of hers. "And how have you been?" he asked in an undertone. "Any questions you have found... uncomfortable?"

"No," she replied, in an equally low voice. "I made my report as requested, but no one has followed up on it. I don't know whether to be worried or relieved."

"Perhaps some of both." Truly, he was not sure what to make of the situation. He had thought the interests controlling the facility on Mandala would be more proactive in ensuring that word of the operations there did not get out, but perhaps because he had only reported to his own superior, and Alexa had done the same thing, the powers behind the Mandala facility were willing to wait and see what happened next. After all, if their operatives did anything too obvious, they would only be tipping their hand.

After taking a sip of her own champagne, she asked, "Your own people have done nothing?"

"Ambassador Trazhar has passed the information on to the Assembly on Zhoraan. At this point I can only wait to see what their reaction will be."

"Ah, and I thought you two would have had enough of each other on Mandala," said Ambassador Castillo as he approached them, a champagne glass clutched in his left hand.

"We just wanted to see how we both were doing," Alexa said smoothly. "I haven't had much opportunity for the past few days."

"True, I have been keeping her busy," Castillo remarked.

"Which is as it should be," Lirzhan said, making sure his voice was formal and polite. Something about the man seemed to set him on edge, but perhaps that was merely resentment for his interruption. He turned toward Alexa. "Ambassador Craig, I am glad to see you well." A bow then as he took her hand, and slipped the tiny data bead he held into her palm.

Her fingers closed around it at once, and she said, as if nothing untoward had occurred, "And you, too, Ambassador Lirzhan." She turned toward Castillo. "I suppose I need to make the rounds."

"It would be the hospitable thing. Here, let me introduce you to Ambassador Delas, from Eridani."

They wandered off, Alexa smiling and nodding at the various persons of importance to whom she was introduced. But because he was watching her closely, Lirzhan saw her slip the data bead into the side pocket of her tunic before she extended her hand to the Eridani ambassador.

It would have to do.

All though the reception Alexa wished she could excuse herself so she could go back to her rooms and crack open the data bead Lirzhan had given her. She knew that was impossible, however, so she put on her public face and greeted everyone with equal courtesy, even the scowling fierce-browed members of the Stacian delegation. Here they were supposed to be on neutral ground, but she could tell they were having a difficult time pretending to act even barely social.

Well, she wasn't going to worry about the Stacians now. She had no reason at the moment to be interacting with them directly, so they could be as rude as they liked. After all, she'd experienced far worse than rudeness over the past week.

What worried her more was that she'd heard no whisper of reprisals, no sense that Melinda Ono and her cohorts were going to retaliate for the violation of their facility and its secrets. Alexa tried to convince herself that there was no real need to—after all, she still didn't even know what they were hiding. Lirzhan obviously did, but he'd had no chance to speak to her in private. And when they would gain that privacy, she had no idea. Targus Station was a large facility, with diplomatic personnel numbering around one hundred and three times that many support and operations staff, but even so it was a very confined space, one with little opportunity for solitude.

Eventually, though, the evening ended, and she walked with Chima back to her apartment, since Chima's own rooms were just down the corridor. Alexa reflected that maybe she shouldn't have had that second glass of champagne, as she was now...well, not even tipsy, really, but...elevated. Feeling just barely surreal. Perhaps it was the slightly higher oxygen content of the air on the station, combined with the alcohol.

"I think the Ambassador will be all right with you coming in at 0900 tomorrow instead of eight," Chima said with a wink.

"Oh, no, I'll be fine—"

"See you at nine, then." She grinned and headed off down the corridor, the silk of her long side-slit gown swishing slightly. No, Alexa had definitely not been the only one to dress up for the reception.

She let herself into the apartment, poured herself a cold glass of water, and then fished the data bead—which was really shaped more like a capsule—out of her pocket. The beads were designed as one-use items for transmission of sensitive information, and she didn't want to wait any longer to see why Lirzhan had given it to her.

After taking a sip of water, she set down her glass and grasped both ends of the bead, twisting them in opposite directions from one another. Immediately a tiny holographic projection appeared a few inches from her face, showing a schematic of...what? A series of lines that zigged this way and that. She blinked, regretting that second glass of champagne more than ever.

As she squinted at it, she realized what he had sent her was a map—a map that showed a circuitous route through the service corridors of the station and ended up...well, she wasn't sure where it ended up, but clearly it must be someplace where they could meet in private. And that was good enough for her.

She dropped the two pieces of the bead in the trash compactor, then went to her wardrobe and grabbed the dark gray drape that Chima had included with the rest of the new clothes. The drape served well enough to cover most of the gleaming dark turquoise tunic and pants Alexa wore, and she hoped it would make her less conspicuous.

Then she slipped out of her apartment, going the opposite direction from where Chima had headed, and found a service lift, one probably used by the station's maintenance staff. She pushed the button, glad that this elevator didn't need a key card or a code of some sort to operate it. The map Lirzhan had sent her indicated she should go down three levels, so she selected that floor and waited, hoping the service staff would be all tucked safely in their beds at this hour of the station's standard rotation.

The lift stopped at the designated floor, its doors sliding open. Alexa peered out and looked in either direction, making sure the corridor was empty. Yes, the entire station was under some sort of surveillance, excluding the private rooms of the delegations and the staff, but she thought there was probably at least a fifty-percent chance that whoever was watching the surveillance feeds was really not paying much attention. After all, there hadn't been an incident on Targus Station in the sixty years since it was built.

So she slipped down the corridor, found a doorway into an actual stairwell, and hurried down the steps to the next level. After opening the door there, she went on into another hallway, turned left, and found herself at a dead end with yet another door, this one guarded by a key card reader.

Great, Lirzhan—so what do you expect me to do now?

Feeling slightly foolish, she raised her hand and knocked. The door opened at once, and he pulled her inside, shutting the door just as quickly as he'd opened it.

"What on—" she began, but she didn't get any further than that, as he drew her to him and kissed her, his mouth urgent on hers, as if he needed her kiss in order to breathe.

It had to be the residual effects of the champagne that made her so dizzy. She wasn't sure she wanted to admit how his touch made her head swim, how the entire universe seemed to swirl around the two of them when they embraced.

Finally, though, he moved away from her. She blinked, forcing herself to focus on her surroundings. This was no forgotten storage chamber or access corridor. This had to be his apartment.

The walls were a soft shade halfway between blue and green, the furniture upholstered in similar tones, only deeper. Where Ambassador Castillo's office had a few carefully placed plants, here they seemed to be everywhere, falling from cunning little metal sconce planters on the walls, draping themselves over pedestals, proud and upright on the small round dining table and the lower one that fronted the sofa. In the corner a softly lit fountain burbled away.

"You brought me to your apartment?" she asked at last. "Isn't that…dangerous?"

"We do not allow surveillance in our section here, so once you were past the service corridors, you were safe enough," Lirzhan replied. "I thought it the safest place for us to talk."

Talk? She'd halfway hoped he had better things in mind. She could keep denying it if she wanted to, but after this last kiss it was pretty clear that her body wanted him, even if her brain still had a few reservations.

"All right," she said, not bothering to hide her reluctance. After all, he could probably read it in her emotions, even if she kept her tone as neutral as the one she used at the negotiating table.

In response he pushed back his hood and shot her a wicked smile. "Well, perhaps not only talk. We shall see. But please—sit down."

He indicated the sofa, and she took a seat there. A pitcher of water and two glasses already sat on the polished stone table, so clearly he had been confident in her ability to follow the directions he had given her. He poured some water for her before sitting down himself.

Although they had spent so much time together, had slept in one another's arms and shared a few scorching kisses, there seemed to be something very intimate about sitting next to him like this, of having him less than a foot away, close enough she could feel the warmth of his body, sense how very solid and real he was...so different from the wraith-like appearance he presented while wearing his robes. Incongruously, her current position reminded her of being back in school, of making out on the couch with one of the boys from her advanced composition class, and how she had gotten in so much trouble when her foster mother came home from work early and caught her.

She forced her mind back to the present, and away from such dangerous topics. "All right," she said. "Are you finally going to tell me what you saw on Mandala?"

"Yes." Something around his eyes seemed to tighten. In that marvelously supple scaled skin, she could see no lines, no signs of age, but he did look suddenly older, and tired. She reached out and wrapped her fingers around his, gave them a small squeeze, giving him the encouragement to go on. "Alexa, it was someone on that facility who pulled us out of subspace. They are mining those blue crystals—you know, the ones we saw in the caves."

Somehow she managed to nod. She could see those crystals again in her mind's eye, so delicate, so lovely.

How could something that beautiful be used to do something so dangerous…so terrible?

He continued, elegant planes of his face still and calm, but his jade-colored eyes cloudy and troubled. "I do not know how they are doing it, precisely, but somehow they've learned how to refine the crystals and use them in a device that can disrupt a ship's subspace passage. I don't suppose I need to tell you what the ramifications of such research might be."

No, he didn't need to tell her. Claims over planets might be fought in the real world, or merely around bargaining tables, but space itself—and subspace, that odd non-reality which allowed faster-than-light travel—was sacrosanct. Any planetary authority giving itself such an advantage over all the other worlds and their governments was in effect declaring open season on all such shipping. And by doing so, the Gaian Consortium was only a step or two away from causing an intergalactic conflict so cataclysmic Alexa could barely begin to imagine its effects.

"God damn them!" she burst out, and pushed herself to her feet.

Lirzhan watched her carefully, but did not attempt to rise as well.

Anger coursed through her, destroying the afterglow of the kiss, of the champagne, of the party's pleasantries and laughter. What the hell had they been thinking? Surely those involved in the research had to know where such a thing might lead, once word of it got out. The

Eridani Hegemony, the Stacian Federation, the Zhore Assembly—none of them could allow Gaia to have sole ownership of such technology. They would fight to take it away, even the peaceful Zhore.

They would have no other choice.

"No wonder Melinda Ono and her gang wanted us dead," Alexa said at last.

Finally Lirzhan rose to his feet. "Yes, it is a secret they thought was worth killing for. But I cannot help but notice that there have been no further attempts."

"No, they're biding their time. My report was harmless, because I didn't know what they were up to. And I was damn careful not to say anything too incriminating. But you"—she stared up into his eyes—"you said you told your own people?"

"Of course," he replied. "I had no choice but to tell them the truth of the matter. I have heard nothing since, however. No doubt they are examining the situation from every angle before filing a formal complaint, because of course once they do that, there is no going back. The secret will be out."

"And the rest of the galaxy will be clamoring for Gaia's blood," she finished heavily. "Lirzhan, what should we do?"

"As we have done," he told her, and stepped closer. He paused then, as if attempting to measure whether she would appreciate the overture or not. "We wait, and we see what happens."

Alexa stood very still, sensing that she paused on a knife edge now as never before. Maybe it would be better if she left now, before anything else between them could change. She could feel the tension in his lean body—his worry over what their discovery might mean for the galaxy as a whole. Yes, that was there, but it was more.

They were alone in his apartment. No one had seen her come here. He was waiting to see what she would do, whether she would duck away once more.

Or whether she would do what her heart had been trying to tell her for several days now.

And she was so very, very tired of being logical and practical.

She went to him then, let him wrap his arms around her, felt his lips brush against her hair, then move lower, sliding over her temple and down her cheek, under her jaw, and down the line of her neck, kisses slipping over her collarbone and onto the cool exposed skin of her chest in the low-cut tunic she wore. Heat was building in her, and she knew this was what she wanted, his touch on her, everywhere, just a few minutes or hours of necessary oblivion before the galaxy came crashing in on them once again.

Maybe she said his name. Maybe it didn't matter, because he could tell what she was feeling. He would know what she wanted before she did. Those arms tightened around her, lifting her up and carrying her out of the living room and into his sleeping chamber, where they fell onto the bed, mouths meeting in a desperate flare of heat, her hands pulling the heavy robes away from his body, pushing them onto the floor, then finding the little tabs that held his tunic closed and pulling that away as well. Such a marvelous flicker of those tiny scales all over his muscular torso as they caught the light from yet another fountain trickling away in a corner of the room.

His hands were busy, too, finding the zipper at the back of her tunic and pulling it down, then lifting the garment over her head and tossing it away, perhaps to land on the pile of robes already lying on the floor. Those long, elegant fingers moved over her bare torso, found the clasp to her bra and undid it, then drew it away.

He let out a low, ragged gasp. "Alexa, you are so beautiful…."

She wanted to tell him the same thing, but the words were startled out of her as he lowered his head, mouth closing on her nipple, tongue slowly moving over it. A shocked little cry escaped her lips, and then she buried her hands in his long slick hair, felt it cascade over her skin as she held him against her, letting him suckle on her, even as the heat built between her legs.

This was good, but she wanted more. More from him…more *of* him. She reached down and found the fastener for the trousers he wore and unlatched it, then pushed them down over his hips. His underwear was simply a wrap around his body, covering his privates, and was easy enough to pull away. Tiny shimmering scales there, too, and she let out a moan at the mere thought of him inside her, moving against her flesh.

He must have caught the notion from her, because the next thing she knew he had undone the button and zipper on her own pants, was yanking them down, taking her underwear with them. His hands were on her, moving between her legs, touching, stroking. She was so ready for him. Had she ever been this wet, this aroused? She didn't know, because it seemed as if thinking of anyone else besides Lirzhan was a foolish exercise. In this moment, he was everything.

Although she had been expecting him to push into her, instead he moved lower, his breath hot against her belly, against her mound. And then he was tasting her, tongue sliding over her with insidious grace, the heat within her building to impossible levels. His long, slick hair brushed against the insides of her thighs, and that was enough to drive her over the edge, to have the pulsing need finally explode outward, sending shockwaves along every nerve ending, along every muscle and vein.

She bit back her scream, knowing that there must be other Zhore on either side of Lirzhan's apartment. Or could they sense that rush of ecstasy as it raced away from her like ripples away from a stone thrown into a pool?

"It is all right," he murmured, his breath hot against her flesh. "All our chambers are specially muffled, to avoid having our emotions intrude upon one another."

If only he'd told her that a few seconds earlier. "All right," she said, her voice hoarse, "then I suppose it won't matter if I do this."

And she pushed herself up to a sitting position, then turned so she could grasp him in her hand, feel the tiny delicate scales against her skin as she worked her fingers up and down his shaft. He moaned then, slipping down against the pillows, letting her touch him, fingertips moving their way down to the small patch of sleek black hair at his base, going lower to fondle him, seeing how much he was built like any other man.

But would he taste like one?

She took him into her mouth then, letting her tongue slide over him, tiny scales tickling against her taste buds. His skin had a clean, almost metallic taste, subtle, not musky like the other men she'd been with.

"Alexa." His voice was rough as well, so different from the elegant, smooth tones she'd grown accustomed to. "If you keep doing that—"

Perhaps some other time she'd bring him to a climax this way, would truly taste all of him, but that wasn't what she wanted right now. No, she wanted him in her, just as she'd imagined a few minutes ago. So she lifted her mouth from him, slowly, with one last tantalizing swipe of her tongue across his tip before she got up on her knees and then sank onto him, letting him fill her, letting the exquisite sensations of that delicately scaled shaft inside her tremble their way along every nerve ending.

He groaned, his hands reaching up to her caress her breasts, shimmering ebony against her pale skin, and she moaned as well, beginning to rock with him, his hips thrusting up into her, pushing deeper, taking away every doubt, every worry, every fear, until she could think of nothing else but him, all that alien beauty melding with her, where she could not be sure where one began and the other ended. And then finally the climax shuddered its way through her, heat pulsing along her limbs, just as he exploded within her with more heat, bucking against her, long black lashes sweeping down over his equally dark cheeks. He cried out, then reached up and pulled her against him, their hearts thudding against one another in the aftermath of the shockwave.

For a long moment Alexa was content to lie there, to feel his amazing body pressed against hers, but eventually she knew she needed to get up. She rolled off him as carefully as she could, and was about to push herself up from the bed when his hand went around her wrist.

"Don't go."

"I'm not going far," she replied, smiling. "I just need to get cleaned up a little. I'll be right back."

He nodded, although he was clearly reluctant to let her go. She gave his hand a squeeze and then pulled away, going to the door she hoped led to the bathroom. That was exactly what it turned out to be, the fixtures more or less familiar, although she had to wonder at the extravagance of having an actual steam unit on a space station. Then again, it might be fun to get in there with Lirzhan later....

First things first. She cleaned herself up as best she could, then ran the water and splashed some on her face. Her cosmetics had run, leaving black smudges under her eyes. She looked—well, she looked like a woman who'd just had a spectacular lay.

Grimacing a little, she patted her face dry on one of the towels and went back into the bedroom. Lirzhan still lay in the bed, although he'd pulled the covers up to his waist. The green eyes sought her out immediately as she approached him, and he pulled back the blankets and sheets a little, clearly inviting her back in.

She hesitated at the edge of the bed. As tempting as it might be to climb back under the covers, to let him hold her once again...and try for round two in a few more minutes...she knew that the longer she was away, the greater the chance someone might notice she was not in her chambers.

"I don't know if I should," she said at last.

He sat up immediately, eyes narrowing. "Do you— that is, do you regret what has passed between us?"

"Oh, no." The words came out in a rush, because she had to make sure he didn't think she was rejecting him. "No, Lirzhan, that was—wonderful. It was perfect. So perfect I want nothing more than to crawl back in bed with you and do it all over again." She spoke the simple truth, since he would know if she were lying. No regrets, no matter what happened.

Not that she had to worry about the logical aftermath of such activities, since she'd had her contraceptive shot just three standard months ago, and wouldn't need another booster until three months from now. If humans and Zhore could procreate at all, that is. Yes, Eridanis and humans had been interbreeding for decades now, but the Eridanis were far more similar to Gaians than the Zhore. Either way, it wasn't something that even had to be an issue.

"But..."

"But I'm away from my quarters in the middle of the night. What if there's an emergency and someone tries to contact me? And with me sneaking around like a teenager seeing the boyfriend her parents don't approve of—" She broke off, and lifted her shoulders. "It wouldn't look good. So I think it's better if I go back to my apartment now."

His expression shifted from worried to resigned, and he sat up, then bent down and retrieved that wrapper of a pair of underwear from the floor. Alexa wasn't sure exactly how it worked, except that one moment he was naked, and the next he wasn't.

Her own discarded clothing shimmered against the close-weave beige carpet, and she picked up her panties and bra and drew them on, followed by her tunic and pants. For the first time she noticed it was slightly chilly in the room, as if the Zhore preferred a lower ambient temperature than most Gaians. She supposed it made sense, what with the heavy robes they wore all the time.

In an attempt to take away the sting of her hasty departure, she went to Lirzhan and kissed him—no quick peck on the cheek, but a lingering touch of mouth against mouth as she tried to show that she was leaving because she had to, not because she wanted to.

"I understand," he said simply, once she drew away.

Because he was a Zhore, she knew he did. She reached up with one hand to touch his cheek, marveling again at the silky brush of the scales against her skin, and then hurried out. If she stayed any longer, she knew she'd lose her current battle with her conscience.

Luckily, at this hour in the station's standard rotation, she didn't have to worry about dodging too many people. Of course there were security personnel always on duty, but long ago the Gaians and every other space-faring race had learned that people functioned better on a daily cycle similar to that of their home worlds, and so on Targus Station there was day and night—even if you couldn't tell the difference by looking out the many view panels.

Alexa slipped out of the service elevator and made her way back to her apartment. All was quiet and still, and she let out a sigh of relief as she slipped her key card through the reader and let herself inside.

That relief proved to be short-lived, however, for as she flipped on the lights, she saw Chima Amadi sitting on the couch, watching her with a smile that was far from friendly.

"So, Alexa," she said in her singsong accent. "You want to be telling me where you've been this evening?"

FIFTEEN

ALTHOUGH HE MISSED HER ALREADY, Lirzhan understood Alexa's reasons for leaving. Openly admitting to their relationship now was probably not wise. It was enough that she had come to him, had finally realized what he had known all along, that they were meant to be together. He could still taste her, feel her, hear her voice. The day would come when she would stay with him, once they had decided how to make such a thing possible.

In the meantime, he had slept well, and awakened with a light heart, despite the threat of the Mandala project hanging over all of them. Somehow it was difficult to be worried about the future when he had held Alexa in his arms, had felt their bodies come together in the perfect joining of *sayara*. Surely a universe that contained such beauty could not allow anything truly bad to happen.

Ah, well...even the afterglow of that magical hour with Alexa wasn't quite enough to convince him of that.

But he would admit he was in an extraordinarily good mood that morning.

Until he entered the Zhore delegation's office suite, and sensed the waves of dark energy coming from Ambassador Trazhar's office. Lirzhan paused at Arizhal's desk. That young man was pretending transcribe a dictated report left behind by Lirzhan's predecessor, but he could tell Arizhal was distracted, as his hooded head kept turning toward the ambassador's office, as if he thought he could hear something of what was going on behind the closed door.

"What is it?" Lirzhan asked.

Arizhal pulled the audio bud from his ear and nodded toward Trazhar's office. "Two members of the Assembly showed up early this morning."

"They did?" Lirzhan inquired. Prickles of unease began to run down his spine. He thought he had a fairly good idea as to why they were here. They'd received his report, and processed it…and now they were here to follow up in person.

"Yes. We had no official notice of their arrival, until station operations contacted the ambassador and said their ship would be here in fifteen standard minutes. There was quite the scramble, as you might imagine."

Lirzhan could imagine quite a thing all too well. For a second or two he wondered why he had not been summoned, and then realized that they would wish to meet with the ambassador herself, and that Arizhal had been called in because, as her assistant, it was his duty to be on hand for such meetings. No doubt they would request Lirzhan's presence when they were good and ready, and not before.

He sat down at his desk and pulled up the notes on the latest back-and-forth between Zhoraan and Gaia over the settlements on Lathvin IV. Whether that particular matter would ever be handled to either party's satisfaction, he had no idea, but the Gaians' inability to admit that the Zhore had first rights to the obscure little planet was beginning to wear a little thin.

The door to Ambassador Trazhar's office opened, and she looked out. "Lirzhan. A word, if you please."

He waved a hand, and the heads-up display disappeared into the ether. Although he willed himself to be calm, nevertheless his heart began to beat a little faster. He had known there would be some reaction to the Gaian duplicity from his home world…he just hadn't thought it would come as swiftly as this.

Even so, he made himself be calm, his head up as he entered the ambassador's chambers. Seated in front of her desk were two Zhore, the only sign of their office a thin cord of green draped over their shoulders. As he entered, they rose and bowed, and he did the same. This was simple courtesy. It bore no indication as to what might follow.

"You may sit, Ambassador Lirzhan," Trazhar told him, and so he did, in the only seat left.

The office should have been soothing, with the ubiquitous Zhoraani complement of plants and fountains, and the hangings on the walls in shades of green and blue. But Lirzhan found himself sitting on the edge of his seat, dreading what the two assemblypeople were about to say.

"We have read Ambassador Trazhar's report," said the slighter of the two, female, her voice soft and low, and with the barest huskiness that bespoke some age. "It is troubling. Do you assert that what she has told us is what you experienced on this world called Mandala?"

"Yes, Your Honor," Lirzhan said.

"The Gaians are not aware that you know of their experiments?" asked the other assemblyperson, a man this time, his voice deep and warm, belying the tension which underlaid his words.

Lirzhan lifted his shoulders. "I have no way of knowing for certain."

The female assemblyperson spoke. "And so they are no doubt remaining silent for now because they think that the worst they will suffer is some sort of slap on the wrist for setting up an unlicensed mining facility on a world that was supposed to be unimprovable."

That seemed the most likely explanation for the continuing lack of any sort of reaction from Melinda Ono and her cohorts. "It would seem so, Your Honor."

Ambassador Trazhar folded her gloved hands on her desktop. "What are your wishes, Your Honors?"

"The situation cannot be allowed to stand. We wish to bring a formal complaint to the Galactic Council," said the second assemblyperson, and Lirzhan forced himself not to flinch.

A formal complaint meant that every representative on the Council, whether Gaian, Eridani, Stacian, or Zhore, would know exactly what the Gaians had been attempting to keep concealed on Mandala. And once the representatives knew, their planetary governments would know as well, and the ripples would continue to move out from the splash. What that meant for all of them, Lirzhan didn't know, but he knew it wouldn't be good.

When she spoke, Ambassador Trazhar's voice was serene enough, although Lirzhan could feel the waves of dismay coming from her. They were too strong for her robes to completely muffle. "Because of the gravity of the matter, I will move to bring it to the full Council at our earliest convenience, which I hope will be this afternoon. The talks with the Bathshevans and the representatives from Miris Prime went more quickly than expected, and so we should have time today."

"I thank you for your promptness," the female assemblyperson said. "This is not a matter that we feel can be delayed."

"It won't be." Ambassador Trazhar glanced over at Lirzhan. "You may go, Ambassador, but be ready to give a full report at fourteen hundred."

"I will," he replied, and bowed toward both the assemblypeople before leaving the office. He supposed a human would have reached up at this point and run a hand through his hair or performed some other gesture of relief, but he had no such outlet. Instead, he returned to his desk and brought up the Lathvin IV report again, although his eyes could not focus on the words on the screen.

He wondered what Alexa was doing at this moment, and whether he would have time to speak to her before the two members of the Zhoraani Assembly dropped their bombshell on the Galactic Council.

"I should have known," Ambassador Castillo said in conversational tones, although the scowl he wore was anything but pleasant. "I should have known when I heard about your relationship with that Eridani that you were an alien-lover and couldn't be trusted."

Alexa clenched her icy hands in her lap. Forcing herself to meet Castillo's disdainful stare, she replied coolly, "My loyalty is and always has been to the Consortium. Sir."

He waved a hand. "You have a funny way of showing it, then, Ms. Craig."

At least Chima had allowed her to take a shower and change, do something with her mussed hair. If anything, the Ambassador's assistant had looked almost amused as Alexa reappeared wearing her plainest suit, long locks twisted into a severe bun at the back of her neck.

Assistant, Alexa thought then, and barely repressed a bitter chuckle. *Spy, more like.* Oh, she'd known all the hallways were under surveillance, and had been aware that she was taking her chances sneaking off in such a way. What she hadn't known was that every time she went in and out of her apartment, a text alert popped up on Chima's handheld, letting her know where the new junior ambassador was every hour of the day. Chima had been almost gleeful when divulging this tidbit, as if being Castillo's spy added a little spice to her everyday routine.

It had been stupid and careless to go to Lirzhan's apartment.

But oh, it had felt so good....

Voice still calm, she replied, "There is nothing in the terms of my employment that restricts who I can see in my private life, Ambassador."

The heavy brows drew together. "Not specifically. However, one might say that a personal relationship with a member of an alien species whose affairs do not align with those of the Consortium signals a serious conflict of interest. Or do you not see it that way, Ms. Craig?"

"There was no conflict. I did not discuss politics with Trin Elsen when I was posted to the embassy on Eridani, nor did I do so with Ambassador Lirzhan. Frankly, sir, the ambassador and I were more concerned with staying alive."

"It seems that wasn't the only thing that you were concerned with."

Heat flared along her cheekbones—curse of her fair skin, the one thing she'd never been able to control—but she only said, "It appears, sir, that you are determined to think the worst of me no matter what I might say in my defense. Therefore, I must ask whether I am being formally charged with anything. I will admit that I'm curious what I'd even be charged with, considering that I am technically a civilian and so am not subject to the same fraternization rules as someone in the military or even the GEC."

Castillo glanced over at Chima, and she gave him the barest of nods. "Yes, Ms. Craig, you do have a point there. But I can still write you up for questionable behavior, and that will go in your permanent record. In the meantime, I'd advise you to rethink your relationship with Ambassador Lirzhan." An expression of disgust passed over his aristocratic features. "A Zhore. I never thought I'd see the day."

And you have no idea what you're talking about, she thought, but she didn't bother to correct him, to let him know that under their hoods the Zhore were very beautiful in their own way, certainly not the repulsive monsters that rumor and innuendo had made them out to be. She wouldn't betray Lirzhan's confidence. The Zhore preferred to keep their appearance hidden, and she would respect that.

"Is there anything else, sir?" she asked coldly.

"No. Go back to your office and get to work on the Minari paperwork. Their delegation is coming in first thing tomorrow."

Alexa got up from her seat and exited Ambassador Castillo's chambers, then went to her own office. The cup of coffee she'd poured nearly half an hour ago was almost cold, but she drank it anyway. Chima had not allowed her to sleep, but had instead brought her down her to wait on the ambassador's convenience. He hadn't come in until past 0800, at which time Alexa was already on her third cup of coffee. She knew it was the only thing that would keep her going, since she had had no sleep—and it didn't look as if they were going to allow her to get any today. A subtle form of punishment, but a very real one.

The words on the display in front of her seemed to blur into one another. Maybe another cup of coffee was in order. On the other hand, since she hadn't eaten anything, that might not be such a good idea. Surely they couldn't keep her from running down to the commissary and fetching some toast or a turnover to soak up the stomach acid.

She'd just begun to rise from her seat when she saw Chima come and lean against the door frame, her dark eyes alight with curiosity.

"What is it, Ms. Amadi?"

The other woman's eyes narrowed at the switch back to her surname, but then she shrugged. "A Zhore, hey? And what must that be like? What have they got hiding under those robes?"

If Chima thought Alexa was going to tell her anything about Lirzhan, after the way she'd ratted her out to the ambassador, she must be crazy. Besides, even if they'd been the best of friends instead of the next thing to enemies, Alexa wouldn't have given away any details of Lirzhan's appearance. Not without his express permission, anyway.

"I'm afraid I don't know what you're talking about," she replied, tones chilly enough to give the other woman frostbite.

"Oh, come on, now—I was only doing my job. The ambassador, he wants to know what his staff are up to. Needs to be able to trust them. We're in a sensitive position here, you know."

"I'm well aware of that."

The half-smile Chima had been wearing abruptly disappeared. "Ah, fine. Be that way if you want, but remember, you're the one who screwed up here, not me." And she turned and stalked off back to her desk in the reception area.

Maybe she shouldn't have been so openly antagonistic toward Chima, but it couldn't be helped now. She was just so damn tired. No, this wouldn't be the first time she'd pulled an all-nighter, but she'd had days of inadequate sleep before this, and it all seemed to be piling up on her.

The day before she'd discovered a discarded protein bar in one of her desk drawers, probably left there by Ms. Nguyen. Since going down to the commissary before the lunch hour probably wasn't going to happen, Alexa figured it was the only thing that could help to prevent the unending cups of coffee from eating a hole in her stomach lining.

She'd only eaten a few bites before she heard Ambassador Castillo bellow, "Ms. Craig! In here…*now!*"

Oh, God, what is it this time? She halfway hoped he'd discovered something so heinous about her that he'd fire her. What that would mean, she had no idea, because the thought of being separated from Lirzhan wasn't something she wanted to contemplate. On the other hand, spending the next three standard years with two coworkers who couldn't stand her didn't seem very appealing, either.

With a sigh she rewrapped the half-eaten protein bar and set it down on her desktop, then headed into the ambassador's office. He was reading something on the heads-up display over his desk, but because of the angle she couldn't see precisely what it was.

"What is it, sir?"

"I just received a message summoning me to a special meeting of the Council this afternoon at fourteen hundred—'to discuss the disturbing intelligence uncovered on the world known as Mandala.'" If the frown he'd sent in her direction when berating her for her relationship with Lirzhan had been fierce, this one was truly formidable. "Do you know anything about this, Ms. Craig?"

Somehow she managed to prevent herself from taking a step backward. In that moment she wished Lirzhan had not told her what he'd seen in the mining facility on Mandala, that she was still blissfully ignorant of the GEC's latest subterfuge. Since she didn't wish to lie, she settled for equivocation. "No, Ambassador, I know nothing about a special meeting."

But he hadn't been made special envoy to the Galactic Council for nothing. "That is not what I asked, Ms. Craig."

All right, then she would lie. Unlike the Zhore, she was constitutionally able to do so, even if she didn't like it very much. "No, sir. Perhaps Ambassador Lirzhan saw something that I did not—as I said in my report, we were separated once we reached the facility."

His scowl only deepened. "Very well. I suppose we will find out when we attend the hearing this afternoon."

"'We,' sir?"

"Of course," he snapped. "You're the junior ambassador. You'll be there as well, to hear exactly what this is all about."

Unfortunately, she knew all too well what it was probably about. Since she couldn't say that, she only inclined her head and replied, "At fourteen hundred, sir?"

"Yes." His dark eyes might as well have been lasers for the way they seemed to bore into her. "Don't be late."

No chance to get in contact with Alexa, unfortunately—Lirzhan had attempted to reach her through her handheld, since he knew messaging her directly through her computer was not a good idea, as the security-conscious Gaians no doubt would be able to read every word. But she wasn't responding to calls or texts, and there was no way he could go see her in person before the hearing at fourteen hundred.

This was the first time he'd had a chance to see the Council chambers, and he had to admit they were impressive. The vaulted space took up two levels, with one wall a vast viewscreen that looked out over the ringed gas giant that Targus Station orbited. Behind the dais where the councilmembers sat was a bank of monitors that cycled through a series of images from all the Council worlds—Eridani, Gaia, Stacia, Zhoraan.

All the members of the Council already sat in their high-backed chairs, with a Stacian at one end and the Gaian representative at the other, and the Eridani and Zhore councilmembers sandwiched between them. Safer that way, Lirzhan supposed—they might sit on the Council together and pay lip service to that body's supposed neutrality, but since the two governments were more or less at war, it was better that they be located as far apart as possible.

He followed Ambassador Trazhar to the Zhoraani delegation's assigned seating area, and watched as the various entourages made their way to their own sections. Then he saw Ambassador Castillo enter the chamber, followed by Alexa, and his breath seemed to catch in his throat.

For while he'd enjoyed a restful sleep after she'd gone back to her apartment, it did not seem as if Alexa had done the same. Although her hair was sleek as ever and her face artfully made up, he could see the shadows under her eyes, the taut look to her mouth and jaw, as if she were propelling herself forward through sheer force of will. Waves of exhaustion seemed to emanate from her.

What exactly was the matter? What had happened after she left his apartment?

It required his own force of will to remain in his seat, to have his gaze continue to sweep the room without lingering too long on the junior ambassador from Gaia. What he really wanted was to get up and take her in his arms, hold her close and ask her what was wrong. But of course that would be impossible.

The delegation from Eridani was the last to arrive. In a mirror of the Council's seating arrangements, they took their place next to the Zhore, with the Stacians on their other side. Because this was a closed session, no spectators were allowed beyond the members of the various delegations, and the rest of the seats in the chamber remained empty.

After everyone had more or less settled themselves, the Eridani councilmember stood, addressing the company. This was a role that alternated amongst those on the Council; Lirzhan wondered whether it was happy accident or design that had a neutral party conducting the proceedings today.

"We are here today to hear a complaint brought by the Zhoraani Assembly against the Gaian Consortium. Ambassador Trazhar, do your assemblypeople understand the ramifications of this complaint, that once it is brought it cannot be retracted, and that they must abide by the decision of this Council?"

Ambassador Trazhar rose from her seat. "They do, Your Honor."

The Eridani, a man called Lir Danos, inclined his head. He was older, his purple hair streaked with lavender the way a Gaian's hair might be streaked with gray. "Then proceed."

"Your Honor, it is our wish to present the testimony of Ambassador Lirzhan, a member of our delegation. He witnessed firsthand the conditions that precipitated the Zhoraani Assembly's complaint."

"Step forward, Ambassador Lirzhan," said Lir Danos.

The weight of all those watching eyes seemed to settle upon Lirzhan. As much as he wished to glance in Alexa's direction, he knew he did not dare do such a thing. So he got to his feet and went to stand in the empty space in front of the dais, then inclined his head.

"Good members of the Council, I assert that what I am about to say is the complete truth as I know it, and as I experienced it." Formal words, the ones he was expected to use as a preface to his statement.

"We hear this assertion," they echoed in unison.

Now that custom was satisfied, he knew he could do nothing else but continue. He recounted their escape and crash landing on Mandala, the journey through the forest, the attack by the mercenaries in the skimmer, and his and Alexa's subsequent flight underground. He purposely left out any mention of the intimate nature of his relationship with Alexa Craig. The members of the Council did not need to know that she was his heart-mate, the center of his soul. Such information had no bearing on the operations at the mining facility, or the experiments the GEC was performing there.

"…and it was when I went in search of Ambassador Craig, fearing she had been taken prisoner or worse, that I discovered exactly what was being mined on Mandala, and what it was being used for."

"And what was that, Ambassador Lirzhan?" asked Councilor sen Barthran, the Stacian. He was a fearsome-looking individual with heavy brow ridges and an impressive mass of knotted hair, all bound in silver and gold, hanging down his back.

Lirzhan guessed that the Stacian's interest was not wholly academic. Anything that made the Gaians look bad was a welcome gift to the Stacians, even though members of the Council were supposed to be above the squabbles of their individual home worlds.

This was the moment he dreaded, when all would be laid bare before the Council and the watching delegations, but he had no choice but to continue. "Your Honors, they were mining a crystal that I believe is unique to Mandala, that has a peculiar property which allows it to be refined and used to pull a ship out of subspace. How they have managed this, I do not know, as I am not a scientist. I—"

He got no further than that, because as soon as that bombshell escaped his lips, all the members of the various delegations began murmuring amongst themselves, and even the Eridani councilmember looked shocked. Sen Barthran pushed himself up out of his chair, exclaiming, "You see how the Gaians once more attempt to take the upper hand over all of us? Will you once again allow this sort of behavior to stand?"

"Councilor sen Barthran, I must ask you to take your seat. We are here to listen and observe, not hurl insults and accusations. You do your position no justice."

Scowling, the Stacian reclaimed his chair, but not before he shot a look of such ire at the Gaian councilmember that the man couldn't help shrinking back in his own seat. He did look quite relieved that the Eridani and Zhore representatives sat between him and Councilor sen Barthran.

Impartial observers? Obviously not.

The Eridani moderator stared down at Lirzhan, clearly perturbed by both the secrets he had revealed and the observers' reactions to them. He hesitated, then asked, "And did you see anything else?"

What else was he supposed to have seen? Lirzhan shook his head. "No, Your Honor. I saw the facility, and I saw the refined crystals being brought to the laboratory, as well as the final product being used in some sort of experiment. I thought that was enough."

For a long second Lir Danos stared down at him, as if by doing so he could somehow see into Lirzhan's thoughts. But he knew that was not a gift the Eridanis possessed, even though they were certainly skilled in many other areas.

"Thank you, Ambassador Lirzhan."

He bowed, then took his seat next to Ambassador Trazhar, glad that his part in these proceedings was now over. Risking a quick glance toward the Gaian delegation, Lirzhan saw that Alexa sat very still and calm, her face betraying no reaction he could see, although even from this distance he felt the pulses of worry and fatigue coming from her direction. In the seat next to her, Ambassador Castillo was practically throbbing with anger, although his expression was equally impassive.

The ambassador stood then, saying, "Permission to address the Council?"

A nod from Lir Danos. "Of course, Ambassador Castillo."

"With no disrespect intended toward the junior ambassador from Zhoraan, I must protest that his accusations of intent are baseless. Yes, we admit that there is an unregulated mine located on Mandala, but its purpose is entirely benign, as the crystals mined there are simple quartz, used in millions of applications throughout the galaxy. The ambassador himself has admitted that he is not a scientist. How, then, is he able to be so certain as to the purpose of what he saw, or thinks he saw, in that facility? It is unfortunate that his shuttle malfunctioned, and I assure this body that an investigation is being made into the cause of that malfunction. But to assign such malignant intentions to the Gaian Consortium on the base of such flimsy evidence is not something we would have expected from the Zhore."

The ambassador settled heavily back into his chair. Lirzhan wished he could be surprised by such bald-faced falsehoods, but he knew the Gaians had used such tactics before, and it was perhaps logical that they should use them again. Especially now, with so much at stake.

Lir Danos turned and appeared to confer with his colleagues, then addressed the assembly. "We will take the matter under advisement. In the meantime, it should go without saying that nothing discussed here should leave this chamber. Also, we ask that all parties involved be available for further questioning, should the need arise. That is all."

Since the dismissal was clear, all the delegates rose and began to exit the chamber as they murmured amongst themselves. Lirzhan followed Ambassador Trazhar out into the corridor, although he wanted nothing more than to stay behind, to exchange even a few whispered words with Alexa. But he knew that was impossible. She must stay with her delegation. Indeed, it would look highly suspicious for them to speak at all at this point.

So he ignored the whispers and the curious gazes that followed him as he and the ambassador and her assistant made their way to the lifts. Thank Irzhaan that his robes blocked most of the bombardment of suspicion and wariness and downright hostility which followed him as he made his escape. Enough seeped through, however, that it effectively drowned out whatever emotions might be coming from Alexa Craig.

He wished he knew what she was thinking.

SIXTEEN

ALEXA SUPPOSED SHE SHOULD HAVE expected that counter-attack from Castillo. After all, the claims that Lirzhan had made were not exactly the type that the Consortium would take lying down. On the surface, Castillo's arguments even made some sense.

Except she knew better. Lirzhan would never lie, and although he wasn't a scientist, he was certainly very intelligent. He knew what he had seen.

Mind churning, she was glad to retreat to their offices. Neither the ambassador nor Chima said anything to her as she resumed her seat after pushing the door to her office almost but not all the way closed. Alexa was doubly glad the Council had not required her testimony. Yes, they'd said they might call in any of the parties involved for additional questioning, but perhaps they wouldn't wish to speak with her at all. She hadn't been the one to see those labs, so any input she could provide would be limited at best.

That was a specious argument, though, and felt a little too much like throwing Lirzhan under the aircar. She should be defending him, not looking for a way to stay out of the whole mess.

At the moment she was so tired she could barely put one foot in front of the other, so it was no wonder her thoughts weren't making any sense. At least she'd been allowed to eat a decent lunch, so she thought if she just tipped another cup of coffee or five down her throat, she might be able to last until the end of her shift. And then—

Well, then she'd go to her apartment and sleep for about twelve hours straight. Not a chance of sneaking off to see Lirzhan, that was for sure. As much as part of her craved him now, wanted his touch, wanted to feel his arms around her, she knew that even if she did somehow manage to give the bloodhounds the slip, she'd only end up passing out the second her head hit his shoulder. There wouldn't be a repeat of last night's activities, that was for sure.

Castillo had disappeared into his office, and Chima had taken up her place at the reception desk. On the surface, everything in the Gaian delegation's offices looked more or less normal. Alexa knew better, though. She could practically feel the tension simmering in the air around her, and thought then that maybe the Zhore had the right idea with those hooded robes that could somehow block other people's emotions so they wouldn't intrude.

But since draping herself in Zhoraani robes didn't seem too likely at the moment, she pulled up the documents on the Lathvin IV dispute once again and pretended to be studying them, even though she could feel her eyelids beginning to droop despite that fresh cup of coffee she'd poured for herself. She took an extra-large swallow, telling herself, *Just a few more hours...just a few more hours....*

Her computer beeped, and a window with Chima's face in it popped up on the screen. "Ambassador Craig, Ambassador Castillo would like you to meet him in the conference room."

Wonderful. Since she couldn't decline the invitation, Alexa said, "I'll be there directly."

"I'll let him know."

The window disappeared, and she tried not to sigh. Conference room? That didn't sound good. If he wanted to speak to her alone, he'd have simply called her into his office. Had the members of the Council decided that they wanted to interview her after all? Maybe, but one would think she'd be called back to their chambers instead of having them come here.

She drained the last of the coffee and hoped it would be enough to keep her alert for whatever was about to come next. Then she got up from her seat, picked up her tablet, and headed for the conference room.

Although she had never been there, Alexa knew the conference room was the largest space in the delegation's suite, and was located just past Castillo's office. The door had been shut since she'd come to work here a few days earlier, as they'd had no need to use it before this.

But now that door stood partway open, although Alexa couldn't see clearly inside, since the ambassador's tall form blocked most of the opening. He must have heard her approach, for he turned and shot a smile at her that only increased her wariness, then said, "Ah, Ambassador Craig. There's someone here who would like to speak to you."

And he moved out of the way, revealing a dark-haired woman sitting at the shining polished granite conference table.

"Hello, Ambassador Craig," said Melinda Ono.

He had expected to be called in to speak with the members of the Council again. Lirzhan just hadn't thought it would be so soon.

This time they were not in the grand semi-public chambers used for hearings, but in a smaller room located on the same level. One would have thought that the slightly more intimate surroundings would have made for a less intimidating atmosphere, but Lirzhan found it to be the reverse. Being in here with the four Council members, all of them radiating suspicion and worry but attempting to hide it, was far worse than standing out in the main chamber and delivering his report from a relatively safe distance.

Worse still, they had asked to see him alone. That was their prerogative, and of course he was a grown man, used to making his own decisions and choices, but even so, he was new to Targus Station, new to its politics, and having Ambassador Trazhar at his side might have made this a little easier.

"Ambassador Lirzhan," said Lir Danos, "we thought it best to speak to you alone, where we do not have to worry about outbursts from the rest of the chamber." Although his tone and expression were neutral enough, Lirzhan caught the flicker of his violet eyes toward the Gaian councilmember, one Gerhard Stolz, and knew at once that Danos was referring to Ambassador Castillo's derisive comments at the hearing earlier that afternoon.

"I understand, Your Honor," Lirzhan replied. "I am ready to deliver whatever clarifications you might require."

"Excellent," said the Zhoraani councilmember, whose name was Nelazhar. She leaned forward in her seat. "We would like more explanation of precisely how you knew what the crystal being mined was used for, if you did not see it actually being used. For by your own admission you are not a scientist."

"No, Your Honor, I am not." Lirzhan deliberately kept his gaze fixed on the Zhoraani woman, although it was difficult to ignore Gerhard Stolz's cutting blue stare. Unlike Alexa's blue eyes, which were tinged with green and reminded him of the sky and the gentle oceans of his home world, this Gaian's eyes were ice-blue, like the depths of a glacier that would never thaw. "However, when I was in one of the laboratories in the facility on

Mandala, I came across some notes from one of the researchers there. In those notes it was quite clear that the intent of the crystal device was to disrupt a ship's subspace passage and bring it into realspace, so it might be…." He let the words trail off and gave an eloquent lift of his shoulders. "Your Honors, I do not wish to speculate as to the intent of the researchers in terms of returning a ship to realspace at their whim. That was not written down."

"It did not need to be," the Stacian councilmember, sen Barthran, said in his gruff voice. "It is clear enough that the Gaians are attempting to take control of all the shipping lanes. If they have this power, then they can charge whatever tariffs they wish to allow safe passage through subspace. And for those who do not comply…." He stopped then, his copper eyes gleaming fiercely, and shot a narrow glare at Gerhard Stolz before adding, "I should think the implications are clear enough to everyone."

"I protest," Stolz said at once. "We have no evidence save this Zhore's that such notes or devices even exist."

"'This Zhore,'" said Nelazhar, "is of unimpeachable character, Mr. Stolz. If he says he saw something, then he saw it. He would not lie."

"My friends, we are here to judge the matter on its merits, and not how it reflects on our individual home worlds," Lir Danos told them. He shook his head, although whether he did so because of the tension in the room, or the complications of the situation as a whole, Lirzhan was not sure. "I do believe that the matter requires further inquiry."

"As do I," Nelazhar put in.

"Of course you would," Gerhard Stolz snapped, heavy bray brows lowering.

She drew back, obviously affronted, and sen Barthran said, "I think there is an easy enough way to get more evidence. Ambassador Lirzhan here was not the only person marooned on that world. Let us question Ambassador Craig and see what she has to say."

"That does seem reasonable," Lir Danos replied.

It was the logical next step, but for some reason Lirzhan did not find it all that appealing. Taking care to keep his tone mild, he told them, "Ambassador Craig never saw the research section of the facility, and so she would be of limited use in corroborating what I saw there."

"Perhaps," said the Stacian councilmember. "But she was on that flight with you, and so she still can tell us about her experience of being pulled from subspace and attacked, both while on the shuttle and on the planet's surface, can she not?"

No use denying that. "Yes."

"Very well, then." The Eridani looked at his fellow councilmembers and nodded slightly. "We will send for Ambassador Craig to give her side of the story, and then once we have analyzed both accounts, we will decide whether to pursue the matter or whether it should be abandoned due to lack of evidence."

Gerhard Stolz looked less than happy at this prospect, but he did not offer up any protests. The other two councilmembers also indicated their agreement with this plan.

"Thank you, Ambassador Lirzhan," Lir Danos said. "That will be all. We will send for you if we need anything further."

"You are most welcome, Your Honors," he replied, and bowed formally. Since there was nothing else he could say, he left the Council's private chambers, mind churning, and wished more than ever for the opportunity to speak to Alexa. Not that he didn't trust her to tell the truth, but at the very least it would be good to be able to convey to her what they had asked him, let her know about some of the undercurrents he'd sensed among the councilmembers, who, rather than the serene givers of wisdom he'd expected, were just as contentious and arbitrary as the planets they represented.

Unfortunately, there didn't seem to be much he could do at the moment...except wait.

That last cup of coffee churned away uneasily in Alexa's stomach. She'd taken a seat at the table as Ambassador Castillo had invited—or instructed—her before he left the room, and now she sat watching the other woman warily, and wishing she were someplace else. Anyplace else.

Melinda Ono looked as if she didn't have a care in the galaxy. Immaculately coiffed and dressed as before, she sipped at the cup of tea Chima had brought her and looked around the conference room with interest, from the old-style paintings of Gaian scenes on the walls to the startling contrast of the starscape outside the windows.

At last she set down her cup and said in conversational tones, "I've been hearing some interesting things about you, Ms. Craig."

"Indeed?" Alexa doubted it could be anything good.

"Indeed. Oh, Captain Marquand made a few rather... provocative comments, but I thought he must be exaggerating. But when Ambassador Castillo told me about your recent...activities...then I realized Marquand must have been telling me the truth." She smiled, but her dark eyes were cold. "Tell me about your relationship with Ambassador Lirzhan."

Her hands felt like ice. Alexa swallowed, then said calmly, "I don't believe that is any of your business."

"Oh, but it *is* my business, Ms. Craig. You see, your Zhore is in possession of information that could be very damning to the Consortium, and so we must all do our best to make sure that information is contained and, if at all possible, discredited."

Worse and worse. "I'm afraid that will be quite difficult. Ambassador Lirzhan is a very honest person. If he says something, it's because it is true."

Melinda Ono's smile only widened. "Oh, perhaps he does tell the truth...but does he tell the *whole* truth?"

"I don't see what you're getting at." Gone was the weariness of a few minutes ago; now Alexa felt alert, charged, adrenaline surging through her. She had no idea what the other woman was up to, but it couldn't be good, not when she was sitting there and smiling like the proverbial cat that had eaten the canary. And that meant staying sharp, whatever the cost.

"You two were alone together for what, five days?"

"More or less," Alexa replied, her tone guarded.

"And I suppose the ambassador was a perfect gentleman."

"He was more than that. He—" She hesitated, then said, "I would be dead if it weren't for him. He saved my life on more than one occasion."

"How very noble. And so of course you felt drawn to him out of gratitude."

"Again, my feelings for Ambassador Lirzhan are not a topic for discussion."

"I think they are." Melinda opened a leather case lying on the tabletop and drew out a tablet. After bringing the screen to life, she tapped a button or two, then pushed it across the table to Alexa. "You might want to take a look at this."

Puzzled, Alexa picked up the tablet. Displayed on the screen was a pretty young Gaian woman with reddish-brown hair. She looked to be around twenty or twenty-one standard years old. "I don't understand. Who is this?"

"That is a young woman named Annika Jespers. Her family has a homestead on Lathvin IV."

"And?" True, the Gaians and the Zhore had been arguing over the rights to that obscure colony world for some years now, but Alexa couldn't begin to see the connection between Lathvin and her current situation with Lirzhan.

Melinda Ono sipped at her tea again. "Her family's homestead was very close to a property owned by a Zhore named Sarzhin."

"I still don't see the point."

"Then let me spell it out for you." She set down her teacup and folded her hands on the polished granite tabletop. "We have gathered intelligence that not only did this Annika Jespers cohabit with the Zhore Sarzhin, but they also recently had a child together."

Well, that answered one question. Thank God she was up to date on her contraceptive shots. Alexa leaned back slightly in her chair and raised an eyebrow. "I suppose congratulations are in order for the lucky couple, but I still don't understand what this has to do with me."

Melinda Ono's smile returned. This time it had an oily quality that made the hair on the back of Alexa's neck prickle. "Maybe it will be clearer once I tell you that for some time the Zhore have been experiencing a near-catastrophic collapse of their birth rates. They've done their best to keep the situation secret, of course, but there are limits to how much these sorts of things can be concealed. As far as we have been able to determine, the Zhore are now attempting to keep their race from slowly dying out by interbreeding with other races—especially Gaians."

Forcing her expression to stay neutral was one of the more difficult things Alexa had ever done, but she thought she'd managed it. Barely. "That is unfortunate for the Zhore. But if they were simply attempting to find another female to impregnate, surely I'm not a very likely candidate."

"One would think that, on the surface." She pushed her teacup to one side and fixed Alexa with a penetrating stare. "However, the Zhore are patient...and choosy. We do not completely understand the mechanics of the process, but it seems they must have some sort of emotional bond with the mate they choose. What better way to bond with you than through days of hardship and isolation, where Lirzhan could function as a protector and guide, and conveniently 'save' you as necessary?"

"That's—" Alexa broke off. She had been about to say "crazy," because that's what this whole situation was... completely insane. Drawing in a breath, she finished, "That's not very plausible, Ms. Ono. Our ship was pulled from subspace and fired upon. Surely you're not accusing the Zhore of manufacturing that entire situation?"

"I am," Melinda Ono replied without blinking.

Somehow Alexa managed to prevent herself from bursting into laughter. "All so I would be driven into Lirzhan's arms? Please—even if he does believe that he shares some sort of bond with me, how on earth could the Zhore have come up with such a plan at such short notice? We'd never even met before he stepped onto that shuttle!"

"Not that you know of," the other woman said darkly. "After all, how can you *really* tell the difference between two Zhore by just looking at them?"

All right, she had a point there. Alexa had crossed paths with one or two Zhore on Eridani; it was the Eridanis who had given the enigmatic aliens subspace flight, and so you did see them around, although they were not great travelers and generally did not leave their home world. "So…what? You're saying that Lirzhan saw me on Eridani, realized he could bond with me and therefore reproduce with me, and so the Zhore engineered the attack on the shuttle and our crash? Don't you think it would've been easier if he'd just asked me out for a drink?"

She hoped she'd injected the right amount of disbelief into her words without sounding too mocking. Exactly what Melinda Ono's position was, Alexa didn't know for sure, but clearly the woman had power, and influence, or she would not have been managing the facility on Mandala, and certainly wouldn't have been allowed into the Gaian delegation's sanctum here on Targus Station.

"They're aliens," Melinda said, with a lift of the slender shoulders under her expensively tailored suit—a suit that had probably cost the equivalent of a month's salary for Alexa. "We still don't know very much about the Zhore. Their motivations can sometimes be very cloudy. But I'm guessing it would also have been a good test for their subspace disruptor."

"Their—so, what, now *they're* the ones who developed that device? What about the equipment Lirzhan saw on Mandala?"

"The equipment he *claims* he saw. What better way to obfuscate the entire issue than by claiming the Gaians were responsible for your shuttle being pulled from subspace? What Admiral Castillo told the Council earlier today was no more than the truth. What we're mining on Mandala is basic, garden-variety quartz, although it is very high quality and requires less processing than the material we've found on most worlds. It will power your watch and your tablet and your computer, but it certainly doesn't have any mystical quality that allows it to disrupt a ship's subspace passage."

Everything Melinda Ono said sounded plausible enough. That was the problem. Alexa couldn't tell how much was lies and how much was truth mixed with falsehood so you couldn't begin to figure out where one ended and the other began. All this would be difficult enough to process on a decent night's sleep, but now, when she'd been up for more than thirty-six standard hours—

"If that's the case, then why all the secrecy on Mandala? Why the people shooting at us? I can tell you that those mercs Lirzhan and I neutralized at the science station weren't Zhore."

"You think the Zhore are above hiring mercenaries when it suits them?" The woman frowned. "And the heightened security was specifically because we'd had reports of outsiders in the area. That mining facility represents a significant capital investment, and of course we would take steps to ensure that it was protected."

Alexa's head began to throb. There was something fundamentally wrong with what Melinda Ono was saying, but Alexa couldn't put her finger on it. Everything made sense—if you began with the supposition that everything had been maneuvered by the Zhore to make it look as if the Gaians were up to no good. Not that difficult, really, since most of the other races would assume the Consortium was at fault in any given situation.

"This Lirzhan was playing on your sympathies," Melinda Ono said, her tone soft, persuasive. "And your weaknesses. The young woman raised in foster care, who had no true family, who had never been loved? Who better to exploit than someone like that? Given time, I'm sure the ambassador would have convinced you he loved you, that he wanted to give you a better life and sanctuary on Zhoraan. Then he would have been in a position to demand as many offspring as possible from you, once you were safely removed from your current situation."

"I can't—" The words seemed to choke in Alexa's throat. "I can't believe that of him."

"But you would believe instead that your own government would knowingly invent a device that would upset the balance of power in the galaxy?"

"I didn't say that—"

"You didn't have to." Melinda Ono's eyes might have been chips of polished jet, so black and glintingly hard they were in that moment. "You think he had you come to his apartments last night simply for a quick lay? He *wanted* you caught—wanted you discredited so you'd be vulnerable. I'm sure he was hoping Ambassador Castillo would dismiss you outright. Then you'd have no place to go…except back into that Zhore's arms."

No. Alexa refused to believe that. And yet…it had been reckless of him to ask her to come to his quarters last night. She wasn't so vain as to believe he couldn't live another moment without taking her to bed. So he could have done so coldly, hoping their liaison would be discovered…indeed, expecting that it would be. But he hadn't counted on Castillo being more or less forgiving, if grudgingly so. She'd been given another chance. The thing was, what was she going to do with it?

Her jaw tightened, and she lifted her chin and stared squarely at Melinda Ono. "What do you need from me?"

A wide smile, showing off the best teeth that cosmetic dentistry could buy. "Oh, that's simple enough. The Council will call you in to get your side of the story. And when they do, make sure you tell them that the Consortium is an innocent party in this, and that it is the Zhore whom they should be investigating. Do that, and we'll all be willing to overlook your brief lapse in judgment with Ambassador Lirzhan. After all, I doubt you want a promising career sidelined because of one mistake. Am I correct?"

And although something inside her seemed to break as she replied, Alexa forced herself to nod, and smile, and say, "Yes, you're correct. And I'll do whatever I need to in order to fix this."

Miranda Ono's eyes glinted, even as she leaned forward and replied,

"Yes, I know you will."

SEVENTEEN

HE COULDN'T UNDERSTAND WHY Alexa wasn't responding to any of his text messages. Calling her would be too obvious, but surely just a few words to let him know that she was all right weren't too much to ask. Unlike the previous night, when he'd slumbered deeply following the lovemaking he'd shared with her, he hadn't slept well at all the evening after he'd made his statement to the Council, as he found himself brooding over Alexa's silence, and attempting to determine the reason for it.

Now, as he sat at his desk the next morning, a crawling sense of foreboding seemed to overtake him, and he found himself staring out the window, watching as the glittery starscape slowly moved past, giving way to the pale glowing shape of the ringed gas giant below, and then shifting once again to a starscape dotted with the slightly larger circles of the planet's moons. Such a cold, austere view, and one he did not particularly think he would enjoy watching for the next few years. In that moment, his desire for service off-world appeared to him as a peculiar fancy, one he should never have indulged. Now he wished he could be back on Zhoraan, feeling its gentle breezes on his face, smelling the scent of wildflowers and grass and sun-warmed earth.

But he did not expect to see his home world for some years. It was a sacrifice he had made willingly, so to be regretting it now, simply because things around him were in turmoil, struck him as childish. In time this matter with the Gaians would be sorted out, and he would be free to pursue his connection with Alexa. The taste of her seemed to fill his mouth again, and he pulled in a deep breath. Why in all the galaxy's worlds was she ignoring him so completely now?

Perhaps she was discovered, and she is being disciplined somehow. The thought sent another chill over him. He'd believed they were being careful. Would they dismiss her? And if that happened, where would she go?

Back to me...and then to Zhoraan.

He dismissed the thought almost as quickly as it had come. Surely he couldn't expect her to give up everything to go to his home world. And he had his own post here, although he knew his superiors would allow him to return to Zhoraan if it meant a chance at another precious child.

But if she is relieved of her current post...what will she even have to give up?

No. He would not allow himself to think such things. Their relationship was so new, so fragile. One push in the wrong direction, and it could shatter into thousands of pieces. He knew she was the one for him, had known from the beginning, and having her share his bed two nights ago only confirmed that. Most likely she was only busy. Perhaps the Council had called her in to give her side of the story. Yes, that had to be it. And of course if she was in chambers with the Council, then she could not be answering her text messages. He would have to be patient, and wait for her to be available.

In fact, he should be glad that she was getting a chance to provide her own account of what had happened to them on Mandala. It would only corroborate his own report, and show that the Gaians were engaging in highly dubious research, research that should be scrutinized by responsible parties.

And once she was done with her own account, surely she would be back in contact with him.

She'd thought this would be easier after getting— well, not exactly a decent night's sleep, as she'd still tossed and turned even though she was in desperate need of rest—but at least *some* sleep, and a decent breakfast and a hot shower and all those things that were supposed to make it easier to get through the day. However, now that she'd come to the Council's chambers alone, prepared to make the speech Melinda Ono had requested of her, Alexa didn't feel good at all. In fact, she felt terrible.

What Ms. Ono had said to Ambassador Castillo, Alexa had no idea, but he'd been all smiles this morning, clearly relieved that she'd decided to do the right thing and support her home world and her government. And she thought she should be feeling better about it as well, now that she knew what Lirzhan had really been up to, but she didn't. Doubt still nagged at her. Melinda Ono could ascribe whatever motivations she wanted to Lirzhan, but she hadn't been there when he carried her across that underground lake...when he'd kissed her for the first time...when he'd made love to her.

Alexa jerked her thoughts away from those memories. For one thing, she shouldn't even be thinking of such matters while sitting here in the Council's private chambers, decorated in serene shades of blue, and on a much smaller scale than the main audience hall. Besides, she was an idiot if she thought just because Lirzhan had made love to her that his motives were pure. When it came to such things, probably a majority of the time a man's intentions were anything but pure. Why should a Zhore be any different?

"Thank you for coming to see us, Ms. Craig," said Gerhard Stolz, after they'd all formally introduced themselves to her and taken their seats. "Since we did not get to hear your side of things yesterday, and because we are all attempting to determine the best way to move forward on this matter, we thought we should have your input before proceeding any further."

"I understand, Your Honor," Alexa replied. The words hardly sounded as if they were coming out of her mouth. They were cold, clear, clipped. They were not the words of a woman who had spent the night trying to find some justification for what she was about to do, for the betrayal she was about to commit. Or was it even a betrayal? Melinda Ono's plausible truth-twisting statements had confused things so much that Alexa couldn't begin to guess who was in the right anymore.

The Stacian councilmember got up from his seat, looming over her. Since she was sure he had done that for effect, she kept herself from flinching and gazed directly into his hot copper-hued gaze. "Ambassador Craig, the junior ambassador from Zhore has made some fairly sensational claims about what he witnessed on the world known as Mandala. Do your own experiences support these claims?"

Nothing for it. Chin high, she replied, "No, Your Honor, they do not."

The Stacian's eyes widened, even as the Eridani Lir Danos frowned at her and Gerhard Stolz, the Gaian councilmember, seemed to be fighting to keep a grin from his face.

The Zhore councilmember said, voice mild, "Please explain."

"Well, for one thing, we were separated for some hours. It was during that time that he claims to have seen the equipment and devices that supposedly had been used to pull our ship from subspace. Since I did not personally witness any of these things, I can't in good faith say that he saw them, or that they even exist."

The Eridani councilmember cocked his head to one side and appeared to study her for a few seconds. "Ambassador Craig, you spent a good deal of time in Ambassador Lirzhan's company, did you not?"

"Yes," she replied, attempting to force from her mind the memory of the time she had first seen him, the alien beauty of his face...the sound of his voice...the feel of his arms around her.

"Would you say that it was an adequate amount of time to form a good opinion of his character?"

"I'm not quite sure what you mean by 'good,'" she said. "Are you asking whether I formed an accurate opinion, or whether I found his character to be honorable?"

"The first," Lir Danos responded. "For if you do not think your opinion was accurate, then it hardly matters what that opinion was."

"At the time he seemed trustworthy enough. Certainly he was very proactive about ensuring our safety, up to and including killing in self-defense."

Nelazhar, the Zhore councilmember, stirred at that revelation. "So it was Lirzhan who killed the mercenaries who attacked you at the science station?"

"Well, two of them," Alexa admitted. "I—I took care of the third." *There's a roundabout way of confessing to murder.* "At the time, I didn't quite know why Lirzhan would ignore his people's customs and take the life of another, but I didn't think to question it. I was just glad that he'd turned out to be so good at keeping the two of us alive."

"'At the time'?" Gerhard Stolz repeated. "Are you now in possession of new information that clarifies his actions?"

She hesitated. From the way Melinda Ono had spoken, it was not common knowledge that the Zhore population was in decline, and so Alexa was not terribly eager to mention the subject here in front of the members of the Council. What had passed between her and Lirzhan was one thing; dragging the Zhore home world and its problems into it was another matter altogether.

"Not new information precisely," she equivocated. "More that, once I was out of the situation, I had additional time to evaluate our interactions and realize Lirzhan might not have been acting from the purest of motives."

"If Ambassador Lirzhan has been involved in anything dishonorable, I want to know about it," Nelazhar said, quietly enough, but there was a ring of steel to her smooth tones.

"No—not that at all, Your Honor," Alexa replied immediately, and then realized she should have kept her mouth shut. She was here to cast doubts on Lirzhan's account of what had occurred on Mandala, not to defend him. In that moment, however, she found herself unable to do so. Perhaps it was simply that she worried the Zhoraani councilmember would sense any lie she told, and so the sensible thing would be to say as little as possible.

No, it was more than that, even if she didn't want to admit it to herself.

Nelazhar shifted in her seat, hood cocked to one side. Even though Alexa knew the alien woman couldn't precisely read her thoughts, she feared she would detect enough to know something was terribly amiss.

After a long pause, Nelazhar turned to address the three other members of the Council. "Gentlemen, would you mind terribly if I spoke to Ambassador Craig alone for a few minutes?"

"Yes, I do mind!" protested Gerhard Stolz, while Lir Danos interposed,

"If you think it will be valuable."

"I think it will be *very* valuable," Nelazhar replied. She tilted her hood upward in the Stacian councilmember's direction. "Councilor sen Barthran, it is up to you to cast the deciding vote here. Do I have your permission to speak with Ambassador Craig in private?"

"Of course you do," he rumbled.

No huge surprise there. Of course the Stacian councilmember would do the thing that irritated the Gaian representative the most.

"Well, then," the Zhore woman said mildly. "I believe that settles it. I don't think this should take very long."

Lir Danos nodded and rose from his seat, and a few seconds later Gerhard Stolz did the same, although he was clearly displeased at the turn the interview had taken. They exited the room, sen Barthran a pace or two behind them. The door shut, leaving Alexa alone with the Zhoraani councilmember.

"You are very troubled," Nelazhar said, once they were alone.

That was an understatement. Even though she knew it wouldn't do any good, she replied, "No, really, I'm not."

Silence for a few seconds. "I'm surprised Lirzhan did not tell you that it is foolish to lie to a Zhore."

"Are you saying I'm lying?" Alexa replied in desperation. Perhaps if she tried to bare-face her way out of this, she might be able to salvage the situation.

"That is an ugly word, so perhaps we should attempt to avoid it. Rather, you are saying things that you know are not correct, and are conflicted over it. I believe you are saying what you think you should say, rather than what you want to say." Her tone softened. "It must be difficult for you, to try to protect your home world and your reputation and your career, when the things you should actually say and do are so diametrically opposed to those goals."

This was impossible. Alexa wondered what the penalty would be if she just got up and walked out, ran away and didn't look back. But that was the coward's solution, and she refused to believe that was her only option.

"I—"

"Do you believe Lirzhan was telling the truth about what he saw on Mandala?"

Oh, God. Alexa's fingers twined around one another, twisting as they lay in her lap. No way out of this.

Except one. The path she should have followed all along. She could not fight against it anymore.

"Yes," she whispered.

"And you were sent here to try to salvage Gaia's reputation, to cast doubt on Lirzhan's assertions about the Consortium's activities on Mandala, because you were told that to do otherwise would be to jeopardize your career, and indeed the very future of your world."

"Yes." Alexa's head drooped, and she stared down at her pale hands, at the nails she'd broken on that rough world and filed down to almost nothing once she'd gotten back to civilization. Foolish that she'd be thinking about such a thing at a time like this.

"Do not be ashamed," Nelazhar said in her smooth, gentle voice. What was it about the Zhore that gave them such beautiful speaking voices? Was it because their native tongue was so lovely?

"I should be ashamed," Alexa replied at once. "I wouldn't listen to my conscience, even though I knew what I was doing was wrong."

"No, the ones who should be ashamed are the ones who manipulated your trust and coerced you into telling such falsehoods in the first place. True, you were trying to protect yourself, but you were also trying to protect your home world. It is difficult to recognize sometimes that the things we wish to protect might not always be worth saving."

"I'm afraid I can't just write off my home world like that," she said harshly. "No matter what the people who run it might have done."

A small sigh escaped the hood. "Loyalty can be a wonderful thing, but not if it is misplaced. You can love your world, love the beautiful things about it, and still recognize that the motivations of those governing it are far from beautiful."

That was for damn sure. Everything was about getting ahead, about furthering the Consortium's place in the galaxy, without stopping to think whether what was good for the Consortium was good for the planets it annexed or the people it exploited. Put that way....

"I don't want to be a traitor," she said, and raised her head to stare directly into Nelazhar's hood, even though she couldn't see the alien woman's face.

"Another ugly word. And what are you betraying? A government that sees you only for your use, and not for your intrinsic worth as a human being?"

The ugly words spewed from her lips before she could cut them off. "And what of my use to Lirzhan, or to your own world? Lying to me so I can bear the children your own women can't?"

Nelazhar did not flinch. "So they told you that? I cannot lie, Alexa, and so I will tell you yes, fewer and fewer of us are able to conceive, despite our scientists' best efforts to cure this terrible malady. And it has been discovered that we are able to interbreed with humans, just as the Eridanis have been for many years. But it is still a difficult thing, because unless the human in question is *sayara*—did Lirzhan explain this to you?"

All Alexa could manage was a nod.

"Good. Well, then, unless a human is *sayara*, it does not matter whether or not the genes are compatible, because the only way life occurs with us is when that bond is present. So, while I cannot say that Lirzhan did not hope to have children with you one day, the only reason he had that hope in the first place is because you were *sayara*. Because he believes you are the other half to make him whole. There was not—*could* not be—anything cold-hearted or calculating about it, whatever you might have been told."

Oh, how Alexa wished the Zhore were capable of lying, because then she could discount what Nelazhar had just said, could brush it off as simply more convenient words to force her to do what the Zhore wanted. But she knew the alien woman was incapable of such a thing, just as Lirzhan himself was. He loved her, plain and simple, because she was his missing half. Nothing more to it than that…

…and nothing less.

"So what am I supposed to do now?" she whispered.

"As your heart tells you," Nelazhar replied. With one gloved hand she reached out and touched Alexa's fingers lightly, but even in that brush of fingertip against fingertip Alexa felt the other woman's warmth, her sincerity. No unnavigable subtext here, only a desire for Alexa to listen to her instincts this time, instead of the advice of those seeking only to further their own ends.

"Thank you," she said simply, and rose from her chair and left the room. She knew what she had to do.

The other three councilmembers, who had been waiting outside in the main council chambers, turned toward her as soon as she appeared. In response to their questioning looks, she replied, "Your Honors, my apologies for making you wait. Councilor Nelazhar already has heard my statement, but I would also like to tell you that I am retracting my remarks regarding Ambassador Lirzhan's statement on Mandala. Everything he told you is the truth. Do with that as you will."

And she moved away from them, heading toward the exit, even as Gerhard Stolz began spluttering and Lir Danos stared after her in astonishment, and Councilor sen Barthran began to demand an immediate inquiry into the mining facility on Mandala and the research being carried out there.

Melinda Ono, Alexa thought as she headed toward the lifts, *isn't going to like this at all.*

After leaving yet another text for Alexa, Lirzhan went back to his apartment. He'd already lingered in the Zhore delegation's offices for almost an hour past the time he could have left for the day, but there had seemed to be no reason to go anywhere else. Only after Arizhal had closed down his own workstation and gone out, issuing an invitation to join him for dinner in the commissary, an invitation Lirzhan refused, did he finally shut off his computer and exit the suite. The thought of going to his empty apartment was not particularly appealing, but he had no particular wish for company, either.

Well, anyone's company save Alexa's.

He let himself in and went to the small kitchen, where he stared at the boxed salad left over from the previous day before shutting the door to the refrigeration unit and turning away. At some point he would have to eat, he supposed, although his appetite had certainly deserted him for the moment.

With a sigh he shrugged out of his robes and draped them over the back of a chair. Here, in the solitude of his own quarters, he had no need of them, and they suddenly felt confining, heavier than they'd ever been before.

The door chime sounded and he started, reaching instinctively for the heavy dark cloth. No one should be visiting here save another Zhore, but even so he was not on such intimate terms with any of the delegation staff that he could face them without the protection of his hooded cloak. As he pulled it on, he tapped a button on the security unit next to his door so he could access the camera feed and see who was visiting at such an odd hour.

It was Alexa.

Forgetting the hood, he tapped the button to open the door, and she pushed inside at once, her arms going around him, almost knocking him off balance even as he remembered enough of himself to shut the door again and give them some privacy. He barely managed to get out, "Alexa?" before she began to sob into his chest, her entire body heaving from her tortured breaths.

Nothing else he could do but gather her up and carry her over to the sofa, then sit down as carefully as he could, holding her tightly against him. As much as he cared for her, thought he'd begun to know something of her mind and heart, still it shocked him to see her so upset, the steely strength he'd thought a permanent fixture of her character brittle and broken.

Finally he asked, "What is it? What is wrong?"

She lifted her head, her blue eyes reddened, her cosmetics leaving dark smudges on her cheeks. Even so, she was the most beautiful woman he had ever seen. "They wanted me to lie about Mandala—lie about *you*—and I tried, but I couldn't. I couldn't do it. Nelazhar—she knew I was lying. And I had to admit it, admit everything was wrong, and now I feel better, but I also feel terrible." Her dark lashes were tangled with moisture, and she angrily blinked the tears away before continuing. "I don't know where this leaves me, Lirzhan. As soon as they find out—as soon as Ambassador Castillo discovers what I've done, I'll be dismissed at best, and possibly brought up on charges of treason. I didn't know where to go."

"My love, it will be all right." He brushed a damp strand of hair away from her face. It almost broke him as well to see her so tragic, so bereft of hope. "I am glad you came. I will not let anything bad happen to you."

Despite everything, she managed a watery smile. "I love you, Lirzhan, but I'm not sure what you think you can do to hold off the Consortium's lawyers once they get a whiff of this."

It was the first time she'd ever told him that she loved him, and although his heart sang at the words, he knew he could not allow himself to be distracted. Not now, when her very safety depended on some quick and level thinking. "Can I ask you something, Alexa? Something important."

She went still then, her gaze sharpening as she stared up into his face. "Go ahead."

"Your coming here—was it only because this was the most convenient refuge you could think of, or was it because you have made a choice to leave your life with the Consortium behind?" Even as he asked he felt his heart beating more quickly, dreading what her answer might be, but he had to know. They were not playing a game.

Her answer was immediate. "I left it behind the second I decided to tell Councilor Nelazhar the truth. The Consortium doesn't appreciate those who don't play by its rules. And I'm so tired of the games, the convenient lies. I didn't even realize how tired of all of it I was until Nelazhar told me to listen to my heart. When I did that, everything became clear. I want to be with you, Lirzhan. Whether that's here or on your home world or on a colony someplace where no one knows who we are, I don't really care. We can figure that out later."

His heart swelled, and he pulled her closer, kissing her again, trying to let her know by his touch how much her words had moved him, how much the terrible decision she'd had to make tore at his heart. For she would be leaving everything she knew behind to go with him. From this choice, there could be no turning back.

Her mouth opened to his, and she returned his kiss with a feverish intensity, her body pushing against his, and he could sense the need in her, the terrible aching want. He had to take her, and reassure her, and let her know that she had made the right decision.

How light she felt in his arms as he carried her to his bedchamber, and how perfect her body as she tore off the severe suit and threw it on the carpeted floor. In that action he thought he saw more of her denial of her past, of the person the Consortium had wanted her to be. He pulled her close, feeling the silkiness of her flesh against his, lending her his warmth and his strength. In their joining, he wanted her to taste their future, and know it held only joy, not pain.

It was the least he could do for her.

EIGHTEEN

ALEXA OPENED HER EYES and stared up at the unfamiliar ceiling, painted in a soft cloudscape that echoed the serene greens and blues around her. Above the gentle trickle of the fountain in the corner of the room she heard the light, sussurant sound of water flowing behind the wall, and guessed Lirzhan had quietly stolen out of bed so he could take a shower before she awoke.

It should have felt odd to be here, to have fallen asleep in his arms, but it didn't. For the first time in so long she couldn't even remember, she could take a full, deep breath and simply enjoy the moment, the soothing colors around her, the quiet flow of the fountain over its river rocks, the faintest whisper of an herbal scent that might have been coming from the plants or the sheets or simply the air the Zhore had circulating in their section of the space station.

Or maybe she'd never felt this way, had never been able to relax her whole life. She wouldn't bother to reflect on the irony of only being truly relaxed when in alien surroundings, after an alien had made love to her.

No, not an alien. Lirzhan. Because if he was alien, then so were her heart, and her mind, and her very soul.

He came out of the bathroom then, one pale blue towel wrapped around his waist, another in his hand as he used it to blot his long wet hair. Once again she was struck by his beauty, by the fine bones of his face, the long, lean muscles of his arms and legs. And if anyone had ever asked, she would have said that she didn't much care for men with long hair, that it was very unprofessional, but she loved those long black locks of his.

Or maybe she just really loved the way that hair felt as it brushed against the insides of her thighs.

Heat awoke in her core, and she had to keep herself from sitting up and reaching over so she could pull him back into bed beside her. But he'd just gotten out of the shower, and so that wouldn't be quite fair. Besides, she had to get herself ready as well.

Ready for what, she wasn't quite sure. All she did know was that she wouldn't have to face it alone.

"I didn't wake you, did I?" he asked, giving his hair one last squeeze with the towel before he folded the length of pale blue cloth, then draped it over the arm of a chair that was placed up against the wall by the bathroom door.

"No. I did that on my own." She pushed herself upright and held the covers against her bare breasts. Not that she minded if he saw her, of course, but since she'd already made the decision not to initiate that kind of activity, she thought it would be better if she were more or less circumspect. From her new position, she could see her discarded clothing on the floor, and her mouth twisted in distaste. It had felt so good to rid herself of the confining suit jacket and tight skirt. The thought of having to climb back into it after such a night of freedom was more than a little distasteful.

Apparently noting her expression, Lirzhan said, "I can have someone go to your apartment to fetch you some fresh clothing."

And wouldn't that be obvious? She might as well hang a sign that said I *spent the night with Ambassador Lirzhan* around her neck. "No, I should probably just go back and shower and change there."

"And I will come with you."

"You really don't have to—"

His brows lowered. "I wish to. I want to be there, in case—well, in case anyone is waiting for you."

Would they be that obvious? Quite possibly. She hadn't dared to check her handheld to see what sorts of messages it contained. At least no one had come to fetch her here. Well, that she knew of. She was safe in the Zhoraani section of Targus Station, after all. The Gaians could bluster all they wanted, but the Zhore security team would not let anyone in unless given the command, and she guessed that Nelazhar had quietly passed along word that Ambassador Lirzhan was not to be disturbed.

"All right," she conceded. "I'll admit that I'd rather you were there. Just—just in case."

"Good." He went to the wardrobe on the opposite wall and opened it. Inside were multiple identical high-necked black tunics and narrow black pants, as well as three sets of the hooded robes. He drew out one of the tunics and pulled a pair of those oddly wrapped under-pants from the top shelf, then proceeded to get dressed.

As much as she enjoyed watching this process, Alexa knew she had to get her own clothes on as well. Nose wrinkling a little, she pulled on her underwear and bra and camisole, then shrugged into her jacket and slid on the skirt. Her boots were last. Such a waste of time when she was only going to climb back out of all of it when she got to her apartment, but it wasn't as if she could go wandering around the station's corridors naked.

Once they were both dressed, Lirzhan asked, "Are you ready?"

She wanted to say that she wasn't, but she couldn't hide here in Lirzhan's apartment forever. "Sure," she said in casual tones that wouldn't have fooled anyone, let alone an empathic Zhore.

But he only nodded and went out of the bedroom, pulling on his hooded robe as he did so. She ran her fingers through her hair and followed him, forcing herself not to bite her lip as he opened the door to the hallway. What she'd expected to see out there, she wasn't sure—a pair of Consortium security guards waiting to take her to the brig?—but the corridor was empty. It was still a little early; the delegation offices wouldn't have their staff arriving for almost an hour, and that probably explained the distinct lack of activity.

This time they didn't bother with the service lifts but took the main elevators. Whether that was a statement on Lirzhan's part that they didn't need to be hiding anymore, she didn't know, but going the direct route was certainly a lot faster.

Then again, maybe getting there more quickly wasn't as attractive a proposition as she'd thought it was. They rounded the corner to the hall where her apartment was located and saw two guards standing in front of her door. So she hadn't been too far off the mark—they'd simply come here to wait for her instead of attempting to accost her on Zhore territory.

As soon as they saw her, one of the guards spoke into the microphone embedded in his jacket collar. "She's here, sir."

And who had posted the guards? Castillo? Stolz? She supposed it really didn't matter, as their presence was a clear enough signal that she had become *persona non grata* to the Consortium government.

"Stop there," said the other guard, and Lirzhan paused, looking back at her.

She shook her head slightly and stepped forward, staring down the guard. "I would like access to my quarters."

"Sorry, ma'am, but my orders are that you are not to be allowed entry."

"Whose orders?"

"Ambassador Castillo's orders, ma'am. Further, pursuant to Section 57, Paragraph 93, of the Consortium code of conduct, you are hereby put under arrest for treason and conspiring with enemy forces."

"'Enemy forces'?" Lirzhan cut in, his normally smooth voice rough with anger. "Is the Consortium now at war with the Zhoraani Assembly?"

The guard's mouth thinned in distaste. "I was not speaking to you, sir."

Alexa's mind churned. Obviously Castillo and his crony Melinda Ono were playing hardball. She didn't have many options now. Only one desperate card she could still play, and there would be no going back from it.

"Ambassador Lirzhan," she said, turning toward him, her tone deliberately formal.

Being Lirzhan, he picked up on her change in tone at once. "Ambassador Craig."

"I am hereby formally requesting asylum from the Zhoraani government. As a representative of that government's diplomatic arm, you are legally able to provide this asylum. Do I have it?"

"You do," he replied quickly, as the guards appeared to at last understand what she was up to, and surged forward.

"You can't do that—" began the one who had contacted Castillo through his uniform mic.

"Yes, she can," Lirzhan broke in. "And she has. And now that she is formally under the protection of the

Zhoraani government, you have no legal jurisdiction. Any attempt to stop her now would be considered an act of aggression against the Zhore. Do you understand?"

Clearly, they did. After shooting a disgusted look in her direction, they backed up toward the door to her apartment and resumed their positions. "Understood," said the first guard. "But you have no place here now. Go back where you came from, and take that hooded freak with you."

Anger flared in her then, and she opened her mouth to protest, but Lirzhan's gentle touch on her arm told her that to argue with them was useless. She subsided, and followed him back around the corner, retracing their steps.

And that, it appeared, was that.

The anger had not subsided during their walk back to his apartments, nor after she yanked off her crumpled business suit and shoved it into the trash bin in his bedroom. "I'm having a shower," she said, and disappeared into the bathroom.

He understood her anger. What he found far more intriguing was her complete lack of surprise, as if she had more or less expected something like this to happen.

First things first. Since it was clear that they were not going to allow her back into her apartment to fetch any of her personal belongings, he had to procure some new clothing for her, and quickly. It was a simple enough matter to log into the PX's intra-web storefront and choose a few outfits, selecting items like the fitted tunic and pants she had worn to the reception several days ago. A quick look at the tag on the inside of the suit she'd discarded told him her size, as did the bra and underwear she'd dropped on the bedroom floor.

He paid for everything and put a rush on the order so it would be brought directly to his apartment rather than being kept waiting for him down at the PX. No doubt eyebrows would go up at such a request, but the thing was, for all intents and purposes, out in the open now. What Ambassador Trazhar might think of the situation, he had no idea. On the other hand, Nelazhar had more or less given her blessing to his and Alexa's union, so he had to hope that Trazhar would understand as well.

They obviously didn't get many rush orders at the PX, as a young woman in the dark blue uniform of the station's support staff delivered the bundle before Alexa was even out of the shower. Lirzhan thanked the woman—little more than a girl, really, probably no more than twenty standard—and went back into the bedchamber just as Alexa emerged from the bathroom, a towel wrapped around her torso and another one twisted turban-like around her wet hair.

"What's that?" she asked, glancing down at the bundle he'd deposited on the bed.

"A new wardrobe. It seems you were being denied access to yours. I hope you don't mind—"

Apparently she didn't mind at all, for she came to him at once and kissed him thoroughly, so thoroughly that he was of half a mind to pull the towel off her damp body and push her down on the bed. But, pleasant as that notion sounded, he knew now was not the time. Instead, he kissed her back, then pulled away.

"You should get ready," he told her. "I have a feeling—"

"That the shit's really about to hit the fan."

Curious expression, although the resulting mental visual did seem to be an accurate description of the situation they were currently facing. "Yes, something like that. I—" His handheld chimed, and Alexa shot him a rueful glance.

"There's some timing for you." She turned to the parcel on the bed and undid the pressure tabs holding it closed, then began to lift the various garments he'd ordered out of it. Her expression shifted from wary to pleased as she held up a midnight blue tunic and nodded her approval at him.

He could only nod in reply, as he'd already lifted the handheld to his ear. "Ambassador Lirzhan."

Trazhar's strained tones came over the tiny speaker. "Lirzhan, I have Ambassador Castillo and Councilor Stolz here in my office. They are demanding to see you at once—something about diplomatic immunity and obstruction of justice—"

"We'll be there in"—he glanced over at Alexa— "fifteen standard?" He ended on a rising inflection, trying to see if that timeframe met her approval. She nodded and disappeared into the bathroom to finish getting ready.

"'We'?" repeated Ambassador Trazhar. "That is to say—is Ambassador Craig there with you?"

"Yes, she is. We are in this together, and we will both hear what Ambassador Castillo and Councilor Stolz have to say. Did Councilor Nelazhar say nothing to you on this subject?"

"She did, but not in any great detail." A pause. "Lirzhan, are you *sure*?"

"More sure than I have been of anything else in my life."

"Then Irzhaan bless you, and your path. I will see you shortly."

She ended the transmission, and Lirzhan tucked his handheld away in an inner pocket of his tunic. That would be all she said on the subject, he knew, for once a declaration of *sayara* had been made, no one—not family, not friends, not one's superior—could gainsay it. The bond of *sayara* took precedence over all else.

A few minutes later Alexa came out of the bathroom, hair dried and lying loose and shimmering over her shoulders instead of bound in the tight little knot she seemed to prefer for work. The dark blue of the tunic and pants seemed to darken the blue of her eyes, and he thought she had never looked so beautiful.

"If I'd known you were calling down for some clothes, I would have put in an order for some mascara and lipstick while you were at it," she said with a smile.

"But in the meantime I stole some of the lip balm you had in your cupboard."

"What is mine is yours," he said formally.

She paused then and gazed up at him, as if understanding that the words were not merely a casual comment. Finally, "You mean that? I'm afraid it's not a very equitable arrangement, considering I've been cast out with nothing."

"Oh, yes, I mean it." He went to her and kissed her on the cheek, willing her to understand. "The greatest gift you can give me is yourself. I don't care that you have come to me now with only the clothes on your back."

"Not even that, really," she said with a small laugh as she glanced down at the wadded fabric of her suit, shoved into a trash bin that was far too small for it. "Sorry about that. It was rather a childish gesture, I suppose."

"No, it wasn't. You wanted to free yourself. It makes perfect sense to me."

Her smile faded. "Thank you, Lirzhan."

"For what?"

"For...you. For being you." She pulled in a breath and seemed to steel herself. "Let's get this over with."

He was only too glad to comply. For once they had cleared this last hurdle, there would be nothing else standing in their way.

The Zhoraani consular bureau was set up in much the same way as the Consortium's suite, with a large conference room located past the individual ambassadors' offices. Alexa followed Lirzhan into the chamber, past the hooded Zhore who sat in the reception area, and past the open doors of rooms that were usually occupied by Lirzhan and the senior ambassador. This conference room, however, was not sterile and cold, the way the Consortium's chamber was, and instead was faced with polished stone, with plants everywhere and another of the ubiquitous water features sending cascading water down the far wall of the space.

Ambassador Trazhar was already there, as were Councilor Stolz and Ambassador Castillo. Alexa could not see Trazhar's face, of course, and she found herself wishing Stolz's and Castillo's expressions were equally hidden. At the moment the two of them were staring at her with a mixture of outrage and disgust.

As soon as she and Lirzhan entered, Castillo took a step forward. Ambassador Trazhar's calm voice halted him immediately. "Ambassador, please keep in mind that Ms. Craig has asked for diplomatic immunity and that it has been granted to her. She is now under the protection of the Zhoraani Assembly."

"Hiding behind your robes, is that it? Ms. Craig—"

At this Gerhard Stolz laid a hand on Castillo's arm, and the ambassador subsided. Stolz paused for a second or two, staring at Alexa in rather the same way she thought he might stare at a cockroach that had hitched a ride on his pant leg. Then he said, "Ms. Craig, you are aware that your actions have put you in direct violation of Consortium codes of conduct, are you not?"

"I am," she said, her tone clear and firm. "That is, I decided that I would not lie for you—or rather, the corporate operative who's pulling your strings. If telling the truth is against the Consortium's code of conduct, then I'm afraid I want nothing to do with the Consortium."

His eyebrows lifted. "Ms. Craig, are you sure you know what you are saying? I might venture to say that your emotions are clouding your judgment."

Lirzhan shifted beside her, as if forcing himself to remain silent. She wanted to reach out and lay a reassuring hand on his arm, but something told her that to do so would only provoke Councilor Stolz even further. Instead she stood quite still and met Stolz's angry blue gaze. "No, Councilor, I'd venture to say that my emotions have clarified my judgment. I'm seeing for the first time so many things I should have noticed years ago. Or maybe I did notice them, but I pushed that awareness aside, made myself ignore everything that was wrong with my government, with the way it operated. I love Gaia, sir, but it hurts to think of what it could be and isn't, simply because somewhere along the line the people running things forgot that they were supposed to serve their people, instead of having their people serve them."

"You don't know what you're talking about—"

"Oh, I think I do. I almost wish I didn't. Sometimes it's easier to go through life with blinders on." She looked past him to Ambassador Castillo, who was frowning at her as if he'd never seen her before. "If I hadn't crashed on Mandala, maybe I would have gone along being the unquestioning drone you wanted me to be. If I hadn't seen with my own eyes what the Consortium is willing to do to gain an advantage, then maybe I would have believed all the propaganda about Gaian superiority. But I did go there, and I have seen all that. I can't unsee it. I can't turn who I am now into who I was then. I don't think I'd even recognize her anymore."

Stolz made an impatient gesture with one hand, as if trying to wave away everything she had just said. "That sounds very noble, Ms. Craig. So you're willing to go into permanent exile just because you've had your idealistic little bubble burst?"

"Is it exile if you want to go?" At last she did move closer to Lirzhan, and took his gloved hand in hers. "Because I want this, more than I've ever wanted anything in my life. I don't expect you to understand. I certainly don't *need* you to understand." Lirzhan's fingers tightened around her hand, and she smiled then as she shifted her gaze toward Ambassador Trazhar's robed form. "Ambassador, I don't think I need to say anything else. I'll sign whatever paperwork is required to formally resign my commission and my citizenship—"

"Resign!" Ambassador Castillo thundered. "You are dismissed, summarily and with no further discussion! You will be publicly branded a traitor, and your friends and family will have nothing further to do with you!"

"I have no friends," she said clearly, head held high. "And, thanks to the Consortium's policies, I have no family, either. So believe me when I tell you that I care very little for your threats." A deep breath, and she looked up at Lirzhan, thought she saw the glint of his green eyes in the depths of the hood. "I think we're done here, Lirzhan. Shall we go?"

"Of course," he replied. A brief nod in Ambassador Trazhar's direction, and he and Alexa exited the room, hands still grasping one another's.

Alexa did not envy the ambassador the mess they had left behind. But then she felt the warmth of Lirzhan's fingers against hers, felt the comforting strength of him, and realized now, for the first time in her life, she was truly free.

EPILOGUE

It had rained earlier, but now the skies were a serene blue-green once again, the pale white edges of trailing clouds painting the horizon beyond the dark trees that bordered their property. A few meters away a stream burbled, full again after the afternoon's downpour.

Lirzhan came out onto the patio of paved pale gray stone holding two glasses of *zhir*, a mildly alcoholic drink similar to a very light white wine. Since it was only the two of them here, he wore just the usual tunic and pants, his hooded robes hanging in the closet against the time when he might have to leave their quiet little corner of Zhoraan for the greater world.

"Thank you," she said as he handed her the drink before sitting down next to her on the padded bench.

He smiled and leaned over to kiss her gently on the cheek. "What were you thinking about?"

"Nothing," she replied. "And believe me, that is a welcome relief." A relief, indeed, after the years of studying and planning and scraping by, followed by more years of always looking ahead and looking behind, pondering her next step up the ladder while simultaneously looking over her shoulder to see who might be trying to tip her off that precarious rung. Here on Zhoraan, Lirzhan was slowly teaching her how to be, how to breathe in and accept the beauties of the universe for the gift they truly were.

A laugh and a shake of his head. He raised his glass to her, then took a sip. "And perhaps that is the beginning of wisdom."

She regarded his clean profile for a few seconds before turning to look out over the green vista before her once again. The property was large, as were all Zhore homesteads. They needed their buffers of fields and streams and tall, wide-branched trees.

"When I see how beautiful Zhoraan is, I wonder how any of you could ever leave it to go into the diplomatic service. If Gaia were like this, I would never have left."

"I will admit that there are not so many of us who choose to go. I was considered something of an oddity for wanting to go into space, to see other worlds and meet those of other races." He fell silent, gaze fixed on a vista only a slightly darker green than his eyes. "And I am very glad of it, for if I had not wanted to leave Zhoraan, I would never have met you."

Her hand touched his, and a quiet thrill went through her at the feel of those delicate scales against her skin. No need of gloves here, of course, or any other concealment. Although it had rained, the day was mild, and his tunic was open at the throat, showing the strong lines of his neck. A soft, fragrant breeze touched the long strands of his loose black hair.

"I'm glad, too." If someone had told her that she would be happy on an alien world, living a life of quiet retirement, she would have laughed. And yet once she was here, she'd fallen in love with Zhoraan much as she'd fallen in love with Lirzhan, almost without understanding how it had happened. "So what's happening out there? I saw that you had a communiqué from Councilor Nelazhar."

"She sends her best wishes, and hopes that you are settling in well here. As for the rest…." He lifted his shoulders, and a few strands of gleaming blue-black hair slipped forward over the smooth fabric of his tunic. "Councilor sen Barthran has had his way, and the Council is opening a full investigation into the facility on Mandala. Not that they are going to find much, apparently, as it seems your Melinda Ono had the place dismantled as soon as she saw which way the wind was blowing."

"I'm not surprised," Alexa replied, not bothering to keep the rueful annoyance out of her voice. So typical; when things went south, it was standard procedure to remove as much of the evidence as possible, and then lie and obfuscate to cover up the rest. "So they're getting away with it."

"Not precisely, for at least the other governments are now aware of what the Consortium was plotting, and are watching their movements even more closely than before. And as no one wants a war, I believe your government—"

"Former government," she corrected him, and he smiled.

"Yes, I believe your former government will be on its best behavior, if perhaps only for a while. Still, it gives everyone else some breathing space."

Breathing space. That sounded like an excellent idea. She knew that here on Zhoraan, she'd finally found a way to breathe…and so much more. It was time to leave Gaia behind, and make this place truly her home, now and forever.

"And are you still thinking of nothing?" Lirzhan asked softly. "For your eyes have taken on a rather wicked sparkle."

"Have they?" she replied, and helped herself to a largish swallow of *zhir*. "I suppose it's because I was thinking it's been three months, so the last of my contraceptive shots has worn off. And I was thinking of finishing this drink…and going back into the house…and seeing if we can do something about Zhoraan's population problem."

It was hard to say who finished their drink more quickly. Laughing, they ran through the house, hurrying to the bedroom and falling into each other, with no thought of Gaian and Zhore, no thought of anything but one another, and the future they would make together.